Tom and Huck's Final Adventure

J.T. JONES

A THURSTON HOWL PUBLICATIONS BOOK

ISBN 978-1-945247-01-9

TOM AND HUCK'S FINAL ADVENTURE

Edited by Chelsea Dub.
Book design by Arbor W. Barrow.

First Edition, 2016. All rights reserved.

A Thurston Howl Publications Book
Published by Thurston Howl Publications
thurstonhowlpublications.com
Murfreesboro, TN

Mailing address:
439 Lemont Dr
Nashville, TN 37216

jonathan.thurstonhowlpub@gmail.com

Printed in the United States of America
10 9 8 7 6 5 4 3 2 1

INTRODUCTION

I have been asked why I chose to tell this story….why I chose to "finish" Mark Twain's story of Tom and Huck. I have only two defenses. I have always been a huge Mark Twain fan. Not an expert, just a fan. And as I grew up reading and re-reading Tom and Huck, I was always left wondering what happened to them when they grew up. I had to know. So I sat down with Tom and Huck and let them tell me their story. As I put pen to paper, they took over and told me exactly what happened. Sometimes I would try to steer the story in the direction I felt it should go, but they would refuse to go. So, if you disagree with the events described in this "ending", you will have to take it up with Tom and Huck.

No work could be completed without plenty of editing. And I had plenty of "editors". I would like to thank the following for their input and encouragement: Alta Wilson, Angie Brown, Barbara and Kenneth Allen, Bonnie Lilly, Brandy Hixon, Brittany Blair, Dean Smith, Delilah West, Glenda Waddell, Jane Wallin, Janie Killian, Jean Wheeler, the Honorable Joey McCormick, June Wood, Karen Putnam, LaDonna Guttery, Lantz Powell, Laura Castleberry, Linda Jones (my mom), Linda Yanez, Lisa Townsend, Loretta Mullins, Mary Moore, Rhona Westbrook, Rodenna Avans, Roger Killian, Sabrina Tate, Sarah Voiles, Scarlett Hannah, Serena Keel, Shannon Darby, Sharon Stevens, Shirley Barton, Tommy Crider, Vesta Crow, Vickie Brown, and Vonda Cuzzort.

I would like to thank Karen Buffington for painting the cover for my book. I had searched high and low for an artist, and finally found her….attending the same church as I do.

And finally, to my two favorite editors, my daughter Rachel and my wife Libby, without whose support I may have never finished…I dedicate this story.

Dear Mark,

So sorry to hear about your recent illness. Hope this finds you improving. I would have written sooner, unfortunately my frequent travels abroad have kept me occupied.

Recently something happened that reminded me of the stories you told of Tom Sawyer and Huckleberry Finn. On my last voyage from Europe, I had the pleasure of dining on several occasions with the ship's captain, a Mr. Johnny Watson, who, as it turns out, knew Tom and Huck. I, of course, took the liberty of writing down the tale he told, which I am now sending you.

The last time you and I visited, you related to me how Huck had run off, down the Mississippi River, traveling with his friend Jim, a runaway slave. They made it all the way to Pikesville, Arkansas, where Jim managed to get captured by Tom's uncle, the Rev. Silas Phelps. I was fascinated by the coincidence of Tom's unexpected visit and his extravagant escape plan that resulted in him getting shot and Jim being re-captured.

As you can tell from my notes, a lot has happened since you left. The boys grew up. They got educated, "book learning" I believe you call it. But they still had to learn how to handle the big things: love, God, and losing at poker. A lot of men don't survive the final exams in those courses.

They addressed their problems pretty much the same way I suspect you would, which accounts for the way things ended up. I'm sorry if they didn't turn out the way you hoped they would, but I didn't make this stuff up. I just wrote down what actually happened.

You commented once that someday you might consider writing a book about their adventures. Hopefully, some of what I have recounted here will be worthy of inclusion if you ever do attempt such an undertaking.

Well, I guess I better close now. I look forward to spending some time with you reminiscing, depending on how the weather is there.

Your friend,
J.T. Jones

PART ONE
1852

-1-

I ain't never heard of nobody nearly killing themselves trying to free a free nigger."

"You're right, Huck, and I wish I'd done different." The huge smile that took up most of his face gave away the lie. "But it's done and it was a great adventure, even with me getting shot."

Huck pulled a pouch out of his pocket, removed his corncob pipe and began cramming tobacco into the bowl. "You probably planned that too, Tom, just to show off."

"Well if I did, it worked. You sure are jealous."

"Jealous? Over a little sore like that?"

"A little sore? Huck, my leg's been shot clean through."

"I know, but I've seen better."

"Maybe on a dead man."

"On a dead man for sure, but they don't count. I've seen sores that a fellow could be proud of, sores that would last for weeks. I've even had some myself. Now, if this one festers up good, then we'll have something to show the gang back home, if it don't heal up before we get there."

Tom tried to push himself up higher against the headboard. He grabbed his leg and moaned. Jim jumped up and adjusted the pillows under Tom's leg, causing him to moan even louder, this time in earnest.

Jim pulled the quilt up under Tom's chin, and Tom pulled it back down. He had spent two days in bed with the fever and tonight, with the windows open, he was enjoying the cool breeze blowing across his chest.

Tom leaned his head back onto his pillow and took a deep breath. He gently rubbed his thigh with both hands until the spasms stopped.

Huck waited until Tom seemed to be comfortable again before continuing. He took a deep draw on the pipe. "Tom, that was a mean trick you pulled on me and Jim, especially Jim, taking all that time breaking him out of that cabin. And you knowing all along that old Miss Watson done freed him in her will."

Tom grinned. "Yeah, I know." He frowned. "But what about ya'll? Running off, a thousand miles, all the way down here to Arkansas. The whole town thought you were killed, and that Jim had done the killing. Not a word or sign out of either of you. If Jim hadn't got himself caught by Uncle Silas, I'd have never seen either one of you again."

"Well at least we had a reason for what we done," Huck said. "Jim heard Miss Watson talking about selling him down to New Orleans to work on a plantation, so he had to run off."

Tom looked at Jim. "Really?" Jim nodded. "Okay then Huck, but what about you?"

"My old man's after my half of the treasure. And I ain't giving it to him. I knew he'd kill me, sure as living, in one of his drunks, so I lit out."

Jim jerked upright in his chair with a solemn look on his face.

"What?" Tom asked.

Jim said nothing.

"Jim, what's the matter?" Huck said.

Jim just stared over their heads at the wall behind them, refusing to answer. Tom looked at Huck and shrugged.

"Well, Huck, it looks like you got me beat on that one. I can admit to being beat when I see it, and dang if y'all ain't topped me." He turned to Jim and pointed to the chest in the

6

corner of the room. "Jim, will you reach into that drawer, the second one, way in the back there, and get me that red handkerchief?"

Jim pulled on the drawer. It came out crooked and jammed, shaking the chest, almost knocking the globe off the lantern. He pushed it back in and tried again. The handkerchief jingled when he dropped it in Tom's lap.

Jim's eyes grew wide as Tom untied the knot and unfolded the handkerchief. He had never seen as much gold as Tom spread out on the blanket. Tom selected two shiny twenty-dollar pieces and handed them to him.

"Jim, that's for your trouble, for playing such a good prisoner."

Jim rolled the coins over in his hand, staring in disbelief. He'd once had fourteen dollars, but he'd never been this rich. He put one of the coins between his teeth and bit it. "Weren't no trouble at all," he said. "I didn't know I's playing prisoner, so I's okay." He bit the other gold piece, then put both coins in his pocket.

Tom tied the handkerchief back up and slipped it under the covers. "I can't wait till we get back home," he said. "We'll be the envy of the whole town."

"Are you worried about the whole town," Huck said, "or just Becky?" Huck and Jim laughed as Tom's face turned red.

"Huck," Tom said, "you're just jealous about that, too." As Tom and Jim laughed, it was Huck's turn to be red-faced.

"Anyway," Tom said, "I bet there'll be a parade and speeches. They'll even let school out, I just know it."

"But, Tom," Huck said, "it's summer. They ain't having no school now."

Tom frowned at him. "Well, I bet they'll call it into session, just so they can call it off. It ain't every day that something this big happens."

"Tom," Jim said, "can old Jim be in your parade? I ain't never been in no parade and it sure would make me proud."

"Sure. The parade'll be mostly about you anyway. Couldn't have it without you."

"Well," Huck said, "you'll have to have your parade without me. I can't never go back."

"You got to come with us," Tom said. "We'll figure some way to handle your pa—"

There was a tap at the door. Tom's Aunt Sally eased into the room and tiptoed over to his bed. She felt Tom's forehead. "It's time you two let our hero here get some rest. Everybody else is already asleep." She walked around to the other side of the bed and took the pipe out of Huck's mouth. "Not inside, young man. Jim, we've got the cabin all cleaned up for you. You should be real comfortable out there now."

"Yes, ma'am," Jim said. "Thank you kindly, ma'am." He paused in the doorway as he followed her out of the room. "Huck, I didn't want to tell you, but you got to know. Remember that old house that was flooded into the river, and we climbed in and found that dead man, and I wouldn't let you look at him? Well, you can go on back home now and not give no more thought to your old man. That dead man was him."

The two orphans, Tom and Huck, listened as Jim clomped down the stairs, each step creaking under his weight. Aunt Sally shushed him at the bottom of the stairs. Through the open windows they heard the door on the back porch slam. Another shush from Aunt Sally and a muffled apology from Jim.

Huck stared at the door for several minutes after Jim left. Tom stood the silence as long as he could.

"Huck, you okay?" He didn't seem to hear. "Huck?"

"Huh? Oh, sure. I'm fine." He shook his head. "I don't know. I figured he'd get himself killed someday. Drowned in the river drunk, or cut up in a fight. Now he's gone and I don't even know how he died. Didn't get to bury him or say nothing over him. I know he was a sorry excuse for a pa . . ."

"But he was still your pa."

"Yeah. I didn't ever miss him before, when he wasn't around. He was always beating on me, and cussing me. I don't reckon we ever had any good times together, least I don't recollect any. But now . . . I don't know . . ."

"I know how you feel," said Tom.

8

Huck looked away, his eyes misty. "How can you know? I got no kin. Ain't nobody back in Missouri waiting on me." A tear ran down his cheek. "Least you got your Aunt Polly, and Sid and Mary—"

"So do you, Huck."

"What?"

"You got all of us too. And the Widow Douglas."

"What do you mean?"

"We're your family now."

Huck pondered this for a moment. "You think so?"

"Sure. So you can come on home now."

Huck wiped his shirtsleeve across his face and sniffled. "Yeah, I guess I can, can't I."

"Sure. And don't forget the gang. We can be robbers and pirates-"

"And I can be in the parade with you and Jim, right?"

"Uh, no. Parades are only for important people." Tom laughed as Huck faked a punch at his jaw.

"Huck, I need to ask you something."

"What?"

"I've been thinking. What are you going to do with your six thousand dollars?"

"I don't know. Ever since we found Injun Joe's treasure it ain't been nothing but a powerful lot of trouble. I could buy everything I need and not hardly scratch it, and never need any more, except for circuses and the like. How's a body to spend that kind of money?"

"That's what I've been thinking. I was terrible mean to Jim and I want to make it up to him."

"Well, you done gave him forty dollars. What else could he need?"

"I want to buy his wife and young'uns."

"What in the world do you want with three slaves of your own?"

"You dim-wit, I don't want them for myself."

"Well then, who you buying them for?"

"I want to buy them and set them free."

9

Tom let it soak in for a minute before he continued. "Huck, a slave woman and two young'uns, and one of them deaf and dumb, shouldn't fetch more than about a thousand dollars all together. That's not more than three or four hundred dollars to both of us, on the halves, if you was willing to go in with me."

Huck leaned forward, elbows on his knees, rocking the chair onto its front legs, apparently deep in thought.

"Well, Huck..."

Huck jumped to his feet, his chair falling over backwards with a loud bang, and bolted for the door. He tripped over the turned-up edge of the rug and fell to his knees, his hands slapping the floor.

"Shhh, Huck. You'll wake everybody up. Where you going anyway?"

Huck stood up. "I'm going to tell Jim that not only is he a free man, but they're a free family!"

Tom held up his hands. "Hold on. Let's wait till morning. The shock of it all may rattle his brain and send him off running all the way back home. Besides, we've got a lot of planning to do and a lot of arrangements to make. We'll tell him at breakfast, make a big show of it."

Huck grinned. "That'd be your way, Tom. That'd be your way."

Jim and Huck carried Tom downstairs for breakfast. Aunt Sally wanted to serve him in bed, but Tom insisted on joining the family around the big table in the kitchen.

Tom and Huck grinned at each other and fidgeted in their seats as Uncle Silas sent up a mighty powerful prayer over the food. When he finished praying, Tom pronounced that he and Huck had an announcement to make. Jim was called in off the back porch, where he was taking his breakfast with the slaves, since the announcement was about him.

When Tom finished, poor Jim sat right down in the middle of the floor. He couldn't have moved even if a ghost had been chasing him.

Everybody jumped up and was running back and forth from Tom to Huck congratulating them for such an idea. Tears poured down Aunt Sally's cheeks. She swore up and down that no matter what else Tom did bad from that point on, she was certain he would go to Heaven for such an unselfish act, even with Jim not being white. And Huck might make it, too. Uncle Silas wasn't going to be happy until everybody sat back down at the table while he offered up another prayer.

The family began passing the food around the table. No one noticed as Jim, still sitting in the floor, raised his face skyward, his eyes closed in supplication. "Praise be to the Lord," he said. "What's old Jim done to deserve this?"

There were, as Tom said, a lot of arrangements to make. Jim was going to have to make the trip alone, so they drew up papers of introduction for the steamboat captain so no one would mistake Jim for a runaway. They also wrote a letter to the family over in Constantinople, Missouri that owned Jim's family, offering to buy them. And Huck had Uncle Silas help him write a letter to Judge Thatcher, who was holding his six thousand dollars in safekeeping, authorizing him to close his part of the deal.

After lunch, Uncle Silas took Huck and Jim into town. With his forty dollars from Tom, Jim got a new set of store-bought clothes. He held his head high as they walked down the street.

News of the excitement at Uncle Silas's farm had spread quickly around Pikesville. Most of the people they met on the street recognized Jim as the captured runaway that had gotten his freedom. Jim tipped his new hat, just like Uncle Silas, every time they passed someone. No one acknowledged his greeting. He smiled just the same.

Sunday morning they all headed off to church, the family in the wagon, the slaves, and Jim, walking along the dusty road behind them. Fortunately, it was only four miles to the church.

When they arrived, Tom and Huck wanted Jim to sit up front with the white folk, but Aunt Sally said that wasn't biblical like. Something about being unequally yoked together, or something.

The service began and the congregation started in singing praises and shouting glory. A few of the members stood up and quoted a verse of scripture and testified. Some of their brief testimonies lasted about as long as a good sermon should last. The congregation was having such a good time it looked as though they didn't even need any preaching. But it didn't work; the preacher came on anyway.

Uncle Silas was the pastor of the Pikesville United Freewill Full Holiness Independent Missionary Baptist Church. Once he finished reading his sermon text about Daniel and the lion's den, he lit into Jim, everyone figured, by preaching about slaves that run off. He read over in the newer testament that whatsoever state you're in, to be content, and he reckoned that even though it weren't Arkansas, Missouri was a right good state. So Jim up and repented and swore not to ever run off again. And everybody shouted Hallelujah. It didn't occur to anybody to ask where he might run off *from* now, being as he was free.

Then Uncle Silas preached on the Ten Commandments, which didn't bother Huck much till he got to the part about stealing other people's slaves. He felt right guilty, but he figured Tom didn't feel guilty because he knew that Jim was free before he set out to steal him, so it didn't really count against him.

When the invitation was given for anyone that wanted to be baptized, Huck and Tom felt relieved, because that usually comes at the end of the service. And they didn't see any need, since they'd already had a bath the night before.

Reverend Silas finished up by taking up an offering, just to see how much the congregation loved the Lord. Tom was so proud of his uncle, he put in a whole silver dollar, without getting change back. He figured Uncle Silas was the best preacher ever. He could preach against things that God himself hadn't thought about being against.

After the service, the ladies laid out a feast that all day wasn't going to be long enough to finish. Tom hadn't seen such a spread since the mayor of St. Petersburg, the Right Honorable Mister Peters, supposedly of the original St. Petersburg Peters, had died. People came from all over to see that feast. Huck figured this had to be the best part of religion. He might have to consider attending more regular.

-3-

I t took all day Monday for Aunt Sally to get Jim's belongings packed for the trip. In reality, it only took about five minutes, but she kept going back and re-checking and re-packing a dozen times or more.

She also prepared a big feast for him to carry on his trip. But nobody thought about how he was going to carry it and, in all the commotion, they forgot to pack it when he left, so the family had enough leftovers to last all week.

Tuesday morning Huck, Aunt Sally, and Uncle Silas took Jim to town to catch his boat. Tom had to stay behind with the young'uns. He had been a little too active over the weekend and his fever was up.

Uncle Silas tied up the team and helped Aunt Sally from the wagon. Huck and Jim walked on ahead and stood by the landing as the *Colonel Crossman* approached the bank.

Jim was a bundle of nerves, standing there with his satchel in his hand. He would put the satchel down, take his hat off, shake hands with Huck, put his hand in his pocket, jingle the change left over from his forty dollars, put his hat back on, pick up the satchel, walk off toward the gangplank, turn around and come back to where Huck was standing, and start the whole ritual all over again. Huck couldn't help laughing at him.

"Huck, I won't never forget you and Tom, and what you done for old Jim. I won't never, never forget." He bent over and threw his arms around Huck, almost squeezing the breath out of him.

"Jim, he said, freeing himself from the embrace, "you don't have to worry about forgetting us. We'll be along in a few weeks, when Tom's leg heals up, and we'll go fishing and swimming and have a grand time."

"Well, just the same, you and Tom always done right by old Jim and was about the only ones that ever did, except Miss Watson by setting me free, Lord bless her. I always knowed she was a good one."

Jim took his hat off and bowed slightly to Aunt Sally and then followed Uncle Silas up the gangplank to meet the captain. After the introductions were made, and the letter about Jim being free was presented, the captain assured them that he would see Jim all the way home. Before leaving the boat, Uncle Silas, being a Christian sort of person and a preacher, shook Jim's hand and wished him luck.

Over the sound of the bells and the whistles, and the wheel slapping against the water as the boat backed away from the bank, Huck yelled, "Jim, don't you get off that boat till you get home!"

"Yes, sah, Huck, I'll do just that," Jim yelled back.

As they waved good-bye there were tears enough to go around. Uncle Silas pretended to have something in his eye and returned to the wagon to tend to the horses.

Huck looked around and saw some of the other travelers staring at the spectacle . . . three white people carrying on over a nigger. Huck remembered the hug, and his face reddened a little. He decided they could all go to blazes in a hurry.

15

Jim sat bolt upright in bed, his heart racing. The room was pitch black, except for a sliver of light from an outside lantern that peeked in between the curtains. The vibrations from the engines, the movement of the room, from somewhere the ringing of a bell. It took several minutes for him to remember where he was.

He opened the curtains halfway and looked out into the early morning darkness. It was nearly two hours till sunup, but he was wide-awake. He dressed and left his cabin.

He sat on a bench outside his cabin watching the day begin. The sky grew steadily brighter, as though the boat, by its progress, was moving closer to the light.

Other passengers began filing by, making their way to breakfast. But Jim didn't notice his hunger. He didn't think of food till a steward, carrying a covered tray, approached and stopped in front of him.

"Are you Jim?" he asked. "Of course you are. Captain sent this for you."

Jim jumped up, opened the door, and followed him in. The steward placed the tray on a table and turned to leave.

"Thank you, sah," Jim said. "That was right kind of you, bringing breakfast up to old Jim."

The steward smirked. "The Captain figured the white passengers wouldn't want to eat with you." He slammed the door on his way out.

Jim ate his breakfast, and the rest of his meals, alone in his cabin. But it didn't bother him much. He figured these folk weren't good people like Huck and Tom, anyway.

Jim spent the rest of the day on his bench. Each snag and island they passed reminded him of his journey down river with Huck. He sat quietly, not speaking to anyone else that day.

Storms rolled across the river all day Thursday. Jim sat on his bed and watched through the window as the lightning flashed. The river rose and the current grew stronger. The boat struggled, yawing from side to side, but kept churning its way north.

It was dark when Jim finally came out that night. He took a stroll around the boat but returned to his bench. There was still a light rain coming down, just enough moisture in the air that he could feel it on his skin as he sat under the cover of the upper deck.

He watched the reflection of the boat's lights on the water and dreamed about the reunion he would have with his family. He wanted to make a good life for them. He wondered if they should stay in Missouri or if they should make their way north to a free state. That was all too much for him. He would talk to Huck and Tom. They'd help him figure it out.

Jim looked up to see a tall, well-dressed man staring at him. He was leaning against the bulkhead trying to stay out of the rain. His white coat was pulled open and he had one hand in his pocket. With the other, he slowly stroked his mustache and goatee. He walked over to Jim and held out his hand.

"Excuse me. Are you the free slave that everyone is talking about?"

"Yes, sah, masa, I's Jim." He stood and took the extended hand.

17

"You don't have to call me master. My name is Potts." He pointed to the bench where Jim had been sitting. "Mind if I join you?"

"No, sah."

They sat down, with Jim turned sideways, eyeing Potts.

"Rain sure has cooled things off, hasn't it," Potts said.

"Yes, sah."

"Tell me, Jim, where're you headed?"

"Well, Mister Potts, sah, I's headed up to Missouri to my family, sah."

"Been a while since you've seen them?"

"Yes, sah, been a spell. But we's going to be together all the time now 'cause they's going to be free just like I is." Jim proceeded to tell Potts his story.

Potts listened, spellbound, as Jim recounted the story of his and Huck's flight down the Mississippi and of Tom's plan of escape from a simple log shed. Potts laughed in all the right places. Gasped at Tom getting shot. Breathed a sigh of relief when Tom was pronounced still among the living.

The more Potts smiled and nodded, the more Jim embellished. But in all fairness, that was probably the way Jim remembered it.

Jim had never met anyone, white or black, like Potts. He made Jim feel like an equal, an emotion a slave didn't often experience.

When Jim finished his tale he sat back and crossed his legs. Potts shook his head in disbelief.

"Jim, I wouldn't have believed it if I had heard it from anyone but you. That was some tale." He leaned back against the bulkhead and lapsed into silence.

After a few minutes, Potts continued. "Jim, this story of yours has me thinking. You could be a big help to me, if you would. You don't have to, now mind you, being a free man, but I could sure use your help with a little problem I have."

"What could poor old Jim do to help you?"

"Well, I'll tell you." He paused and glanced around. "Jim . . . I'm an abolitionist. You do know what that is, don't you?"

"Yes, sah. You go round stealing slaves and taking them up north so they can be free."

"Well, sometimes we do steal them." He grinned. "Sometimes we do it legal like, and sometimes we use a little trickery. Jim, there's a runaway slave being held in a jail up river from here, and I want to get him out and run him north-"

"No, sah! I ain't going to break into no jail and break out no slave. I get caught, sure enough, and then not only won't I be free no more. I'll be in jail, too. They'll hang poor Jim for sure."

"No, Jim, you don't understand. We're not going to break him out. They've advertised that they have him. We're going to pretend to be his master and pay the reward, it's only a hundred dollars, and they'll give him to us."

"Now, sah, how's they going to expect old Jim to be somebody's masa?"

"No, Jim, *I'm* going to pretend to be his master. I need you to pretend to be another one of my slaves that's come to help me take him home."

"I see now, sah. But I's mighty feared the High Sheriff here won't like being tricked by some free slave like Jim."

"Jim, you don't need to worry. I've done this several times. They really don't mind that much. They'd just as soon get rid of him, as long as someone has signed for him. And paid the reward."

"I don't know. Huck done told me not to get off this here boat, and I promised I wouldn't."

"That's sound advice, Jim, and I agree, except . . . well . . . don't you think your friends would want you to help another slave? Besides, we won't be off the boat more than about thirty minutes. Thirty minutes to help free another man."

Jim sat, bent over, his elbows on his knees, his left hand scratching behind his ear. He sat up straight and, with a determined nod, said, "Well, Mister Potts, sah, I reckon I don't mean to be selfish with this here freedom, so I believes I'll help."

"Good," Potts said, as he jumped to his feet. "We'll be there in about an hour. Meet me down by the gangplank when we tie up."

"Yes, sah, Mister Potts, I'll be there."

Jim stood by the railing straining for a glimpse of the lights from the town. He smiled as they rounded a bend in the river and the landing came into view. Thirty minutes from now the three of them would be back, an abolitionist, a free slave, and a slave running to freedom with nobody really chasing him. As soon as Mister Potts signed them papers for the High Sheriff.

The *Colonel Crossman* snuggled its bow up to the landing, its hull scraping the river bottom. The gangplank was lowered, with a loud plop, onto the muddy bank.

As they made their way up the bank, Potts whispered to Jim. "Now remember, for the next few minutes pretend you're my slave. Can you do that?"

"Yes, sah, Mister Potts, sah. I ain't been free so long that I forgot how to do that. Masa, sah."

"Good. Now follow me."

They strode down the main street for three or four blocks and turned down a side street. After two blocks, they turned into an alley and approached a side door.

"Jim, here we are. Keep your eyes down and act like a slave."

Jim nodded. Potts opened the door and motioned for Jim to enter. Jim heard the door close behind him and then the lights went out—probably caused by the sharp rap to the back of his head.

-5-

The sunlight blinded Jim. He rolled over on the floor and blinked his eyes, trying to focus on the objects in the room. Gradually, his senses began to clear.

He reached up to rub his aching head and the rattling of the chains startled him. He held his hands out in front of him. They were cuffed together. He ran his fingers down the chain to the fetters around his feet. He tried to scream but his mouth was gagged. In desperation he rolled back over towards the window.

"Be still, you uppity nigger. We've got four days till we get to Mississippi, so you need to get comfortable."

Jim sat up, recognized Potts, and passed out again. Throughout the morning, Jim teetered on the edge of consciousness. The smell of food finally brought him around. Potts, and some man Jim had never seen, were having their lunch. Jim watched them and, smelling the food, got more and more hungry.

Potts finally stopped eating long enough to address Jim. "If I ungag you, will you be quiet and eat?"

Jim nodded. Potts reached over with his pocketknife and cut the gag, nicking Jims ear in the process.

"Masa Potts, what happened? Did we get caught trying to trick the High Sheriff?"

"You really don't understand do you, boy?"

"No, sah. And you said we's going to Mississippi. This here boat is going clean up to Missouri. Why do we need to go to Mississippi and how's we going to get there?"

"You dolt. We changed boats last night. This one is headed south. I know a plantation owner down there that will pay a fair price for a strong, healthy slave like yourself."

"I ain't no slave! I's a free man!"

"Free, indeed." Potts took a few more bites and a long drag off a bottle. "You're going to find out what real work is, not playing houseboy for some old maid. Here," tossing Jim a chicken leg, "eat your food and figure it out for yourself."

Jim pinched his earlobe, trying to stop the bleeding. He couldn't figure it out. How did a free man get un-free? The only thing he knew for certain was that Huck was right. He shouldn't have got off the boat.

Four days later their boat pulled into Natchez. Potts and his friend loaded Jim onto a wagon for the seven-mile ride to the Willows Creek Plantation.

They arrived just before dusk and sent word to the owner, a Mr. Thibadeaux, that they were returning his runaway slave. While they waited, Potts and his friend helped Jim down from the wagon.

Thibadeaux stepped onto the front porch with a puzzled look on his face. "You say you have my runaway?"

"Yes, sir," Potts said. "And he's fit as a fiddle and sorry for his ways and ready to get back in the field. I believe the reward was listed at six hundred dollars?"

Thibadeaux smiled. "No, it was more like three hundred."

"Are you sure?" Potts asked. "I could have sworn it was closer to five."

Thibadeaux stepped off the porch and walked to the wagon for a closer inspection. He felt Jims arm and leg muscles and checked his eyes and teeth. "No. The highest reward I pay for *this kind* of runaway is four hundred dollars."

"Sold."

PART TWO
1856

Tom and Huck didn't know how much trouble they were in, but they figured it had to be bad. Aunt Polly and the Widow Douglas had brought them to Judge Thatcher's office together. The last time they were at the Judge's office was four years earlier, the summer that Jim had disappeared, when the Judge was drawing up papers to purchase Jim's wife, son Johnny, and daughter Lizabeth. And just as Tom and Huck had promised Jim, they set his family free. After they were granted their freedom they moved to St. Petersburg where Tom, Huck, and Johnny soon became inseparable. Today, as they waited on a bench outside the office, they stared at the "hanging" tree across the street at the courthouse.

"Tom, what'd they catch us doing this time?"

"I don't know. Has the widow not said anything to you?"

"Nope."

"Aunt Polly neither. I wish we knew, so we could get our story straight. They spring something on us, and it's hard to keep all the details in order."

"Yep. Especially when you're making them up."

Judge Thatcher opened the door and motioned for them to enter. "Gentlemen, please." Tom and Huck shuffled in. Their eyes darted from the widow to Aunt Polly looking for any sign. They sat down in two over-sized chairs in front of the Judge's desk. The Judge sat behind the desk, rocking slightly, his fingers drumming the arms of the chair.

"Boys," the Judge said, "I guess you're wondering why you're here." They nodded. "Well, we've been talking to the schoolmaster." Tom and Huck both lowered their heads and stared at the floor. "Mr. Dobbins says that you will be graduating next month."

Tom and Huck looked up. "We are?" Tom said.

"Yes."

"Both of us?" Huck said.

"Yes."

Tom and Huck grinned at each other.

"Boys," the Judge continued, "have you given any thought to your futures?" Their blank stares answered his question. "I thought not. Fortunately, these two fine ladies have. With their permission, I have taken the liberty of making employment arrangements for both of you. You will start as soon as the school term is up."

"Judge, sir," Tom said, "couldn't we wait till the summer is over?"

"No, sir. Mr. Dobbins plans to conduct the graduation ceremony on Tuesday," he glanced down at his calendar, "the seventeenth. You will start the following Monday."

The boys looked at Aunt Polly and the widow, hoping for a reprieve. None came.

"Huckleberry," the Judge said, "I've arranged for you to take a position with a steamboat company. You will start as a fireman's apprentice. A captain I know has assured me that, if you work hard, in four of five years he will start training you to be a pilot."

"Yes, sir. Thank you, sir." Huck sat up straight and smiled . One of the biggest smiles anyone had ever seen on his face.

"And Tom—"

"Yes, sir? Am I going to work for a steamboat company, too? You know it's always been my dream-"

"No, son, we've come up with something that we feel you'll be more suited for. You're going to come to work here with me."

Tom's mouth fell open. "Law? Me?" The Judge nodded. "Study law? Me?" The Judge nodded again.

"Tom," Aunt Polly said, "the Judge and I have talked about this at great length. We feel that this is the best thing for you."

Huck couldn't quit smiling over his great fortune. Tom couldn't take his eyes off the shelves lined with books, except to close them and pray that this was all just a bad dream.

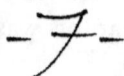

Huck lie in bed, half asleep, listening to the sounds of the night. Bullfrogs with their deep bass seemed to be singing lead. He wondered how they kept such good time.

From somewhere close by, a tom cat howled, startling him fully awake. *Darn cat,* he thought, *I was almost asleep.* The cat howled again. Huck turned over, his back to the window, determined to go to sleep. A rock against the window pane jolted him upright.

He tiptoed to the window and jerked it open, just in time for the next rock to whiz by his ear. There was no moon and he was unable to see anything in the pitch black, but he knew who it was.

"Tom!" he hissed.

"Good lord, Huck," Tom said in a hushed voice, "I was beginning to think you were dead. I've been out here meowing my head off for ten minutes."

"Just a minute." Huck pulled on his pants and slid out onto the porch roof and shinnied down the trellis. He followed Tom down the street a safe distance from the house.

"Now, what the blazes do you want?"

"Get your stuff, we're getting out of here."

"What?"

"You heard me, we're cutting out."

"What are you talking about?"

"Heading out west. We'll try our hand at prospecting, get rich panning for gold."

"Tom, you don't know anything about prospecting. When did you come up with this idea?"

"I've always wanted to try it-"

"Well, you've never said anything to me about it."

"Sure I did. Anyway, I've got to do *something*. Judge Thatcher and Aunt Polly are going to be the death of me."

"Oh, I see. You're just mad 'cause you didn't get the job you wanted."

"Dang right! And you would be, too, if you was stuck in a library full of law books." He slung the remaining pebbles in his hand against the fence. "Who in their right mind would do all that reading."

Huck sat down, his back against a tree. He scooped up a handful of dirt with his right hand and let it slowly funnel out of his clinched fist into his open left hand. He repeated this several times, switching hands, while he considered what to do.

"Tom, listen, we can't cut out now. We graduate in four days, and besides, we've got the town dance Saturday night. You don't want to miss that."

"I don't give two hoots about no dance."

"Well, what about your Aunt Polly? She'll be worried sick."

"Aw . . . she'll be okay. I'll send her a letter, tell her where I am."

"Tom, no, this ain't right. We've got to wait a few days. Give things a try . . . see how things work out. We can always cut out later - "

"No! Huck, I'm leaving tonight, right now. Now, are you coming with me or not?"

Huck didn't hesitate. "No. I'm gonna at least graduate Tuesday. No one I know has ever finished anything . . . I'll be the first. Then I'll see how things play out."

Tom glared at Huck. "I don't know what's happened to you. Used to be you'd jump at the chance to do something exciting like this."

"Tom, I'm still up for it, just not now."

31

"Well, if that's the way it's gonna be," he squatted down beside Huck and held out his hand, "I guess this is goodbye. Don't know when, if ever, I'll see you again."

Huck laughed and slapped Tom's hand away. He stood up and dusted off the seat of his pants. "You'll be back. I know you too well."

Huck! Huck! Wait up!" Huck turned to see Sid chasing after him.

Sid ran up and grabbed Huck by the arm. "I've been looking all over for you," he said after he caught his breath.

He removed the pipe from his mouth. "What's the matter?"

"Tom's run off, or something. His things are gone . . . like he's vanished into thin air."

Huck put the pipe stem between his teeth and smiled. He turned and continued down the street. "Don't worry about Tom, Sid, he'll show up."

Sid followed after him. "How do you know? You know where he's gone?"

"No, not exactly. But he'll be back, I promise."

"Huck . . . Aunt Polly is worried terrible. Mrs. Douglas has been at the house for hours trying to console her."

Huck stopped and faced Sid. "Mrs. Douglas is at your house?"

"Yes."

Huck shook his head in disgust. "Tom Sawyer, if you make me miss the dance . . . "

"What?"

"Nothing, Sid. Come on, let's go calm down those ladies."

Aunt Polly jerked open the front door before Huck and Sid made it up the steps. She threw her arms around Huck's neck. "Oh, Sid, you found him! Huck, tell me you know where Tom has gone off to!"

Huck gave her a peck on the cheek and stepped back. He grinned at Mrs. Douglas. "Hello, ladies. Well . . . no . . . I don't know exactly where he's gone- "

"What do you mean?" interrupted Mrs. Douglas.

Huck laughed.

"Huck," said Aunt Polly, "this isn't funny. You know something. What is it?"

"Have you seen Tom?" asked Mrs. Douglas.

"Yes, ma'am. I saw him last night, or I guess it was this morning."

"And . . . what did he say?"

"He said that he was running off."

"Oh, Lord help me!" said Aunt Polly as she collapsed on the sofa. Mrs. Douglas rushed to her side and tried to console her.

"Sid, fetch me a wet cloth from the kitchen." She sat patting Aunt Polly's hands until Sid returned from the kitchen.

"Huck," Mrs. Douglas said as she dabbed Aunt Polly's brow with the cool cloth, "Tom told you he was going to run off?"

"Yes, ma'am."

"And you didn't try to stop him?"

"Oh, no, ma'am, I tried. He just wouldn't listen to me."

"And you didn't think you should tell someone?"

"No, ma'am. Why should I? Tom's run off plenty of times."

Aunt Polly pulled Mrs. Douglas's hand away from her face. "But not in a long time. I thought I was finally through with all that . . . that he had grown up."

"I'm sorry, Aunt Polly, I didn't think. But I wouldn't worry about Tom." He sat down in a chair facing the two ladies. "Aunt Polly . . . Mrs. Douglas . . . do ya'll trust me?"

The ladies glanced at each other. "Well, yes we do, Huck, you know that," said Mrs. Douglas.

"Good. Then believe me, Tom will be back. And I have a suggestion to make . . . if you want to help him grow up some."

"What's that, Huck?" Aunt Polly asked.

"When he comes home, and he will, don't let on that you've even missed him. Act like nothing's wrong. Don't ever tell him you were worried."

A smile crept across Aunt Polly's face. She nodded her head lightly. "I understand."

The dance was in full swing when Huck arrived. He had left Aunt Polly's and returned to Mrs. Douglas's to retrieve a bottle that he kept hidden for special occasions. He was disappointed when he saw Judge Thatcher standing guard over the punch bowl.

He saw Becky Thatcher in her usual place . . . in the center of the dance floor. When he caught her eye, he smiled and waved. She smiled back. Her dance card was usually full but she would always save a few dances for him. Two dances later, he got his turn.

The spectators at the dance always commented on his dance skills. They always wondered how he learned. They didn't know about the hours he spent in his room practicing for these dances with Becky. And they would never know.

When Huck danced with Becky, he felt like he was on top of the world . . . literally. He had heard that the air on high mountains was sometimes too thin to breathe and when she was in his arms, he couldn't breathe. And he usually had trouble finding the right things to say. Tonight was no different.

Finally, during the band's intermission, she joined him for a cup of punch.

"Becky, you look lovely tonight."

"Thanks, Huck. You do, too, all dressed-up."

"You sure do seem to be having a good time."

"I am. Always do. I love to dance."

"Well, I thought you might be worried . . . about Tom."

"I was. Mary got here before you did and told me you knew something about it and you had told Aunt Polly that everything was okay. Do you think he'll be here tonight?"

"I don't know. I don't know exactly when he'll be back - "

"Well, if he doesn't make it tonight, it'll be his loss. And I'll just have to make you walk me home."

Huck could hardly believe his luck. "Well . . . if you need me to - "

Becky jumped up and ran across the room to speak to a classmate.

"I'd be glad to escort you home," he finished.

On the way home, they walked arm-in-arm. They chatted all the way home. Or at least Becky chatted while Huck listened. At the front door, Becky gave him a kiss on the cheek. Huck was soaring.

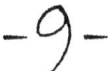

All eight of the graduates met in the adult Sunday School classroom, waiting to march into the auditorium. Or at least seven of them did. Tom, so far, was absent.

Mr. Dobbins was so nervous, he couldn't remember the students' names. It was "you there, quit fidgeting," or "young lady, quit giggling," or "boy, keep your hands to yourself."

The only name he seemed to remember was Tom's. And Huck was sure that some of the things he heard Mr. Dobbins muttering under his breath about Tom were things best not said in church.

Becky turned to Huck with a desperate look and mouthed silently, "Where's Tom?" Huck just smiled, held his hand up and signaled, "okay."

The organist began the processional and the graduates filed out. Becky Thatcher, as everyone expected, was the Valedictorian. And since she was the local judge's daughter, anybody that was anybody was there. And there was also interest in Tom and Huck, the two somewhat famous local boys. There had been much speculation, and even some wagering, about their chances of marching today.

The church was packed, with only the front pew vacant, reserved for the graduating class. Huck was visibly shaken by the large crowd. Becky, seated beside Huck, was still glancing around hoping to see Tom. And he didn't disappoint.

Just as Mr. Dobbins was approaching the pulpit to begin the ceremony, the front doors swung open wide. Tom, dressed in his Sunday best, marched straight down the middle aisle. He looked from side to side, making his apologies in whispered tones, and joined his class on the front row.

Huck leaned over to Becky and whispered, "Only Tom."

After the ceremony, as Huck was leaving with Mrs. Douglas, Becky hollered after him. "Huck . . . just a minute. I need to ask you something." She glanced around to make sure Tom wasn't near. "Huck, how did you know that Tom would come back?"

He grinned. "Because I know Tom. When I refused to run off with him, I knew he'd have no one to show out for. He *had* to come back."

PART THREE
1857

-10-

Tom buried his face in his hands and groaned. He rubbed his eyes, then ran his fingers through his hair. He sat up, leaned back, and stretched.

He eyed the stack of law books piled across the table in front of him. Dozens of pieces of paper sticking out from the edges bookmarked the cases the Judge wanted him to review.

A year of this, being cooped up in an office all day, days not spent fishing, or swimming, or rafting the Mississippi, had nearly killed him. Or at least nearly killed his will to live.

But there had been one advantage to this year spent in Judge Thatcher's office: Becky. She came by the office almost every day to bring her father his lunch. The three of them would eat together in the office, or when the weather was agreeable, in the shade on the courthouse lawn.

They often took short strolls after lunch. When the Judge wasn't looking, Tom and Becky would take each other's hand for a quick squeeze.

Tom checked the grandfather clock by the front door. Quarter to twelve. He stood up slowly and, holding onto the table, limped towards the back of the office and slipped behind the bookcase.

The Judge looked up from his desk. "Son," he said.

Tom stuck his head around the end of the bookcase. "Yes, sir?"

"Are you okay? Why are you limping?"

"Oh . . . I'm fine. Just got an in-grown toenail that hurts something terrible."

"Do you need to go see Doc?"

"No, sir, I'll be fine."

"Good. Here . . . run these to the courthouse . . . before the clerk goes to lunch. They have to be filed today."

"Yes, sir." Tom limped across the office, holding onto every piece of furniture he passed, grimacing in pain. He took the papers from the Judge and limped towards the front door. "Ouch!" He leaned against the door, holding his foot in the air.

"Oh . . . bother . . . here," said the Judge, "I'll do it myself." He stomped to the door and took the papers from Tom. "Get back to your books. And get that toe looked at this afternoon."

"Yes, sir." Tom returned to the table and leaned back in his chair, hands behind his head, smiling.

Promptly at twelve, Becky entered, basket in hand. Tom quickly cleared away the books on the table.

"Where's Daddy?"

"He went to the courthouse."

Becky glanced around the office. Tom looked at her and nodded. He grinned and started around the table towards her. She smiled and backed away.

"Now, Tom, you behave."

"I will. I swear." He held up his right hand as though taking an oath. "I just want to hold your hand for a minute."

She pointed a finger at him. "I know your hand-holding, Tom Sawyer. You'll try to get a kiss . . . right here in Daddy's office."

She ducked around one end of the bookcase; Tom faked after her and darted around the other end. She ran full into his arms as she turned the corner.

"Now," he said, "I believe you said something about a kiss?"

"Tom," she giggled and pushed lightly against his chest, "Daddy'll be back any minute. Now you let me go -"

"No, not till I get that kiss. Don't worry, it'll be several minutes before he's back. We'll have lunch spread out and he'll never know a thing."

"Tom . . . oh, alright." Becky giggled again. "But just one, and a quick one."

She leaned into him for the kiss. Tom put his hand behind her head and pressed his lips to hers. She pulled back but he refused to release her. She pushed again on his chest, but not hard. After several seconds, she wrapped her arms around his neck.

"Blasted clerk went to lunch early -"

Tom and Becky jerked apart. Judge Thatcher stood in the open doorway, mouth gaped open.

Afterwards, Tom ran all the errands for the Judge, sore toe or not.

-11-

The Widow Douglas took Huck in and treated him like he was her own son. This boy, who had never had a solid roof over his head, who had never had a real family, suddenly found himself living in one of the finest homes in town with one of the most loving women around.

He had also never had any rules to live by. He came and went as he pleased. He smoked his pipe. Sometimes he fished for his dinner, sometimes he stole for his dinner. He didn't have to go to school and he only bathed when he happened to go swimming. But the widow changed most of that.

At first Huck resented her intrusion into his life of leisure. He would tolerate all the restrictions of civilized life for a few weeks, then he'd run off. Tom would find him after a few days and tell him how the widow was worrying and crying and praying over him and Huck would go back home. She never scolded him for running off, just took him back with open arms.

The weeks turned into months and his stays with the widow got longer and the times he ran off got farther apart. Eventually, he stayed.

Without locking the door once to keep him from running off, the widow was able to fulfill Huck's worst nightmare . . . she made him respectable. And then came graduation.

It had been just a little over twelve months since Huck had finished school. In that time, he had been promoted to fireman. A boiler explosion that nearly sank their boat had created the opportunity for the promotion. He was asleep in his bunk when the previous fireman had been killed.

Huck frequently passed through St. Petersburg but most of his visits were short. Once, after the explosion, he had been able to stay for two whole weeks while their boat was being repaired. Usually, a dinner at home with the widow or a quick lunch with Tom was all his schedule allowed. On a good visit he'd also have time to stop by Becky's house. Today was a good visit.

Huck studied his reflection in the glass. He pushed his hair behind his ears with his right hand. His left palm was sweating around the stems of the flowers he had picked from the roadside.

He stood on one foot and wiped his shoe on the back of his pants leg; changed feet and cleaned the other shoe. He took a deep breath, hid the flowers behind his back, and gave the doorbell a twist.

Mrs. Thatcher smiled as she opened the door. "Huckleberry, how good to see you again."

"Hello, Mrs. Thatcher. Good to see you, too, ma'am."

"Won't you come in?"

Huck stepped into the foyer. Mrs. Thatcher walked over to the bottom of the stairs.

"Becky!" she yelled. "Huck's here!" She turned back to Huck. "She'll be down in a few minutes. You can wait in the parlor."

"If it's alright with you, ma'am, I'll just wait out on the porch."

"Okay. She shouldn't be long."

Huck went back outside, crossed the porch, and sat down in the swing. He leaned forward, his elbows on his knees, swaying gently from side to side.

"Huck!" Becky bounded out the door and ran across the porch. "Huck! You're home!" He jumped up and met her halfway. She threw her arms around his neck; he picked her up and swung her around.

"When did you get home?" she said, when he sat her down.

"About an hour ago."

"It is so good to see you. Oh me . . . I feel so guilty . . . I haven't been by to see Mrs. Douglas lately. How is she?"

"I don't know. Haven't been by there yet."

"Huck, you came here first? How sweet." She reached out for the flowers. "Are those for me?"

He had forgotten the flowers. "Uh . . . yes."

"Thank you. They're pretty." She held them close to her face, enjoying the fragrance. "Did you see Tom when you came through town?"

"Nope. Didn't see anyone, wasn't looking."

"I'm so glad you came by. How long can you stay?"

"I have to leave around sundown."

"Well, at least we'll have time for dinner together."

They sat down in the swing and talked for several minutes. Becky had at least two dozen questions about steamboats, and Huck was more than glad to elaborate. There was finally a lull in the conversation and Huck took the opportunity.

"Becky, I need to ask you something."

"Yes?"

"Becky," he paused and pulled at his collar, "Becky, we've known each other a long time -"

"Yes, we have."

"Please, let me finish. We've known each other a long time. You know that I don't come from an important family like yours-"

"Oh, Huck, you know that doesn't matter."

"Please. Anyway, my position in life is improving. I think I'm going to be training to be a pilot in a year or so, the Captain says so. And I've still got my half of the treasure. I've been thinking about maybe buying a house of my own -"

"Good for you, Huck."

"Becky, please, let me finish. What I wanted to ask was, well . . . surely you know by now the way I feel about you

46

and . . . well . . . do you think that there is any way you could ever find it in your heart to love me?"

"I do love you -"

"Oh, Becky!" He grabbed her in a tight embrace, put one hand to her cheek and kissed her on the lips.

She pushed against his chest, freeing herself from his embrace and slapped him. The slap stung her hand and brought tears to his eyes. "Huck! What are you doing?"

He jumped to his feet, holding his face. "I . . . I . . ."

"Huck . . . why did you do that?"

"Becky, I . . . I'm sorry. I don't know why . . . it's just . . . well . . . you said you love me -"

"I do. I love you like a . . . brother or something."

The blood crept up his neck and flushed his cheeks.

"Becky . . . I guess I just misunderstood. It's just . . . well . . . whenever we're together, you always seem to enjoy being with me."

"Yes, I always enjoy being with you."

"When we . . . have town dances . . . you always dance with me -"

"I dance with everybody, Huck, I love to dance."

"But . . . you're always hugging on me."

She smiled. "I don't mean anything by it -"

"But you . . . *kiss* me."

"Yes, on the cheek." She stood and took his hands in hers. "Huck, you're one of my dearest friends."

"You said we could have dinner together tonight. I thought you wanted to spend time -"

"Yes, I said we could have dinner together tonight. We . . . the three of us . . . me, you, and Tom."

He pulled away from her. "Tom?"

"Yes."

His eyes narrowed. "It's always Tom, isn't it?"

"Yes, it is."

"But I don't see a ring on your finger."

"That doesn't matter. You should know that. It's always been Tom, always will be."

He turned and jumped down the steps and strode towards the front gate.

"Huck, where are you going?" she yelled.

He looked back. "I guess I only saw what I wanted to see." Without closing the gate, he turned in the direction of the widow's house. "It's obvious I don't belong here."

-12-

Huck! Huck!"

Huck had just stepped onto the gangplank. He turned to see Tom running toward him. Tom ran up and grabbed him by the arm.

"Where're you going, Huck?"

Huck jerked his arm free. "None of your business."

"What's wrong?"

"As if you don't know."

"What are you talking about? All I know is that I went by Becky's and she was all upset, insisted that I find you. I've been looking all over for you. What's this all about?"

"Like I said . . . as if you don't know."

Tom stared at Huck, Huck glared back. Tom began to realize.

"It's Becky," Tom said.

Huck looked away.

"You're sweet on her."

"That's none of your business, either."

"Yes it is my business, Huck . . . she's my girl. Listen, I've known all along how you feel, but," he laughed, "well, it's just funny."

Huck stepped close to Tom, their noses almost touching. "What's funny about it?"

Tom stepped back. "It's just . . . you . . . and *Becky*? Everybody thinks it's funny."

"Who? Who thinks it's funny?"

"Um . . . everybody. I mean . . . her family . . . being who they are . . . judges and lawyers. And you -"

Huck stepped close again. "What . . . am I not good enough for her?"

Tom looked up. "Huck, you better get out of my face."

Huck shoved Tom, who retreated a couple more steps. Huck continued his advance. Once again they faced each other, toe-to-toe.

"Tom Sawyer, you've always thought you were better than me. You sit up there in your office all duded up in your fancy clothes while I'm down in that stinking engine room shoveling coal. You still think you're better than me. Well, you're not. And I'm going to prove it. Prove it to you. To everybody. To her. When I come back, you'll see. This isn't over, not by a long shot."

Tom shoved the larger man away. "Huck, we've been friends a long time . . . but you stay away from her."

Huck's fist struck just under Toms left eye and sent him sprawling in the dirt. Huck boarded without looking back.

-13-

Tom locked the door to the Judge's office and pocketed the key. He whistled as he walked in the direction of Becky's house. He didn't see the Widow Douglas as she came out of the mercantile store.

"Thomas Sawyer, how dare you walk past me without speaking."

He turned back. "Oh, hello, Mrs. Douglas. Didn't see you. How are you today?"

"I'm fine. Thanks for asking. Why, Thomas, what has happened to you?"

He touched his left cheek. His jaw still ached from the punch.

"I . . . got into a little fight."

"Shame on you, Thomas Sawyer. And at your age. I thought Polly was raising you better than that."

"Well, it wasn't my fault. I just got punched."

"Who was the ruffian that did this to you?"

"Oh, just a friend."

"Some friend." She reached up and touched the bruise. He grimaced and pulled away. "How are you treating it?"

"I'm not doing anything. I figure it'll get better on its own."

"Nonsense. You tell your aunt to use a piece of calf's liver, with pepper on it. That'll take the swelling right out."

"Yes, ma'am, I'll tell her."

"And remember the pepper, that's the most important part."

"Yes, ma'am."

"I'm glad I ran into you. I wanted to invite your family for Sunday dinner. Do you think you could join me?"

"I'm sure we can, Mrs. Douglas. Dinner at your house is always a treat. I'll be sure to tell Aunt Polly."

"Good. And you may bring your young lady friend, too."

"Becky Thatcher, ma'am."

"I know who she is. Everybody in town knows about you two. They'd be blind not to." Tom blushed. "Please bring her. It'll be nice to have some young people around the house. I'm afraid I'm going to be so lonely now that Huck has left for New Orleans. He is such a fine young man. He was the son me and Mr. Douglas never had."

"What?"

"I said he was the son -"

"No, before that. The part about New Orleans."

"Yes. He left two days ago."

"Left? When's he coming back?"

"I don't know. Not for a while. Said it had always been his dream to sail the ocean, see the world. I tried to talk him out of it. But he insisted that it was time."

Tom stared at her, his mouth open.

"Thomas, you didn't know?"

"I knew he left, but I didn't know he . . . *left*."

"I'm sorry. I assumed you knew."

He shook his head. She reached up, pointing to his cheek. He nodded.

PART FOUR
1860

-14-

To Tom's surprise, the law was a career apparently created just for him. In the past four years, he had discovered that the law wasn't just rules. It was about how to twist those rules and make them work for you. It was about how to make others believe the rule meant something entirely different that it appeared to. He had been a lawyer all his life and hadn't even known it.

And Judge Thatcher realized a couple things, too. First, that his law practice in St. Petersburg, jointly operated with his brother, Jeff, did not have enough business for three lawyers. There was barely enough for two. And secondly, that a lawyer of Tom's potential needed a larger stage to perform on.

So, after three years training Tom, the Judge sent him to St. Louis to join the firm of Whittingham & Burke, Esquires. With Tom's special talents, the move had been a profitable one. After only a year with the firm, he was well on his way to becoming a junior partner.

The Judge also had an ulterior motive for sending Tom to St. Louis. He was concerned about Tom and Becky. Their childhood crushes had developed into an adult romance. He wanted them to separate for a while, just to be sure of their feelings. The distance and the year apart had done nothing to dampen their love for each other.

"Hurry up, Tom! You're going to miss your boat." Albert, the office clerk, was standing in the doorway holding Tom's hat and coat.

Tom stood, bent over his desk, making notes in a file. "I'm hurrying as fast as I can! You've got to get this recorded at the courthouse tomorrow or -"

"Tom, go!" Tom jerked up instinctively at the voice. Whittingham, the senior partner had stepped into his office. He took the coat from Albert and held it up. "Go! We've been in this business for years . . . we can certainly manage without you for a couple weeks. We know all about your cases . . . now . . . go!"

Tom laid his pen down and glanced around the office.

"Go!"

Tom stepped quickly around his desk, stuck his arm out and Mr. Whittingham helped him with his coat. While Tom adjusted the coat, Albert placed his hat on his head, backwards and down low over his eyes. Tom adjusted his hat and stepped around Albert and Mr. Whittingham. He picked up his valise that was propped against the coat rack and checked his pocket for his tickets. He smiled at the two gentlemen, turned, and left without another word.

"Hmmph," Albert grunted. "He could have at least said goodbye."

Whittingham patted Albert on the back and lightly pushed him towards Tom's desk. "Son, he has other things on his mind right now. And I don't blame him in the least."

-15-

It was two o'clock in the morning when the boat tied up at the dock. There were only a handful of passengers disembarking at St. Petersburg, and Tom was first in line.

The wind had a stiff bite to it, blowing the falling snow straight into Tom's face. He pulled his coat collar up tighter against his neck and made his way down the inclined gangplank. He had to walk slowly, holding onto the railing with one hand, his valise in the other, stepping sideways to keep his balance.

As he headed up the hill to Main Street, the wind blew the snow on the ground along in waves, like ripples in a pond. Tom hated winter, but he loved snow. If it was going to be cold, he'd say, he at least wanted it white. But right now he was freezing and couldn't wait to get to Aunt Polly's. He knew there'd be a big fire and probably some hot chocolate waiting. He knew that, even at this ungodly hour, she'd be waiting up for him.

"Where do you think you're going, Sawyer?" A man stepped out of the shadows, bundled up in a long coat with a hat pulled down tight and a scarf almost completely covering his face. He had been standing against a building, blocking some of the wind. With the howling wind, it took Tom a few seconds to recognize his voice.

"Ben Rogers, you idiot, what are doing out in this weather?"

"Now what kind of friend would I be if I didn't meet your boat? I've just about caught my death, too . . . I've been standing out here all day long, waiting on your sorry self -"

"You have not. Even you're not stupid enough to do that."

"Well . . . now that's a compliment if I've ever heard one, or at least as much a compliment as anyone's ever going to hear from Tom Sawyer." He reached out and took Tom's valise. "Nah, I hurried down here when I heard the whistle. Now, let's get to Aunt Polly's before we both die out here."

They walked in silence, heads bowed against the wind, to only the sounds of the wind and the crunching of their footsteps in the snow.

Christmas decorations hung in most of the store fronts. With the lights out in almost all of the stores, it was difficult to make out any details. But Tom could probably describe most of them from memory. Most of the stores were decorated in the same style year after year.

As they made their way up the hill to Aunt Polly's, the houses they passed were dark. Tom could call the names of probably everyone that lie sleeping in every house they passed.

He couldn't help but think that so many things never change. This had been his life one time. If he had stayed, it would have remained so . . . never changing much. But he had moved on, and everything was about to change even more. He smiled. I made it, he thought, I made it.

The lights shining brightly in every window of the house guided the way to Aunt Polly's. Stepping up on the porch, Tom could see the fire and could hear the chatter of voices. As he and Ben stomped the snow off their boots, the door was jerked open wide.

"Tom!" Mary rushed out onto the porch and grabbed him, throwing her arms around him. She stepped back quickly. "Get in here," she said as she pulled him inside.

It had only been a few months since Tom had been home for a visit, but everyone acted like it had been years. Aunt Polly cried, of course, as she hurried to the kitchen to fetch the hot chocolate. Sid shook Tom's hand, and even managed a quick hug, both he and Tom acting like the two half-brothers hadn't been mortal enemies most of their lives. Their cousin Mary helped Tom with his coat, draping it across a chair near the fire. Ben, ignored, quietly removed his coat, hat, and scarf and tossed them on the couch.

The sight of a beautiful young lady sitting at the end of the couch caught Tom's attention. Mary noticed him staring at her and stopped chattering.

Ben stepped between Tom and the young lady, glancing back and forth from one to the other. "Becky," he said, "I have delivered him as requested."

"Thank you, Ben."

"Delivered me? What's that supposed to mean?"

Ben smiled. "I was under strict orders to deliver you here tonight, and also to keep a close watch on you for the next two days."

"Why?" Tom asked.

Becky stood up and walked into Tom's open arms. "Because I know your reputation for running off," she said.

Tom brushed a lock of hair away from her eyes. "Not this time." He kissed her lightly on the cheek and whispered into her ear. "And never again."

Tom could not stand this close to Becky and not kiss her. The kiss lasted longer than Aunt Polly thought was proper. "Ahem," she said as she placed the tray on the table in front of the fireplace. "Not for two more days, young man. Not for two more days."

-16-

The ceremony had been scheduled for early afternoon on Christmas day. Judge Thatcher, of course, was presiding, with his brother, Jeff, giving away the bride. Becky's best friend from school, Amy Lawrence, was serving as bridesmaid. Ben was to be Tom's Best Man.

The two parties made their preparations in separate Sunday School classrooms . . . the groom in one behind the choir loft . . . the bride in one at the front of the church. The church was slowly filling up. It had stopped snowing, the sky was a deep winter blue, but several inches still blanketed the town, making traveling a little tricky. Still, a full house was expected.

Becky turned from side to side, examining herself in the floor-length mirror that had been delivered to the church for the wedding. Amy fussed over her, straightening her train and adjusting her veil.

"Becky, you have just got to be the most beautiful bride ever!"

Becky blushed. "Well, maybe until you get married. You'll be prettier."

"Nonsense!" Amy reached under her veil and adjusted a curl. "Tom is such a lucky guy."

Becky took Amy's hand and pulled her close. "I feel so happy, I could just bust!"

"Well, you should. You two were made for each other. And I'm happy for you. But I'm sad, too . . . I'm losing my best friend. You'll be way down in St. Louis -"

"But you can come and visit anytime. You and . . . Ben."

Amy shook her head. "That silly thing hasn't even asked yet."

"Tom says he wants to. He's just nervous. You should encourage him a little."

"Encourage him! I've done everything but spell it out for him. I feel sometimes that I'm going to have to drag him to the altar."

"Well, he'll walk there today with Tom . . . and Daddy's here . . . so we could just have a double wedding."

Amy laughed. "I could just see the look on his face when the Judge says 'Oh, by the way, Ben, do you take Amy?'"

Becky laughed. "In due time, Amy. Ben'll have to be a fool not to want you."

Amy paused and gave Becky a solemn look. "Becky, are you nervous?"

Becky thought for a moment. "Surprisingly, no, not at all."

"Are you sure? Tom is . . . a character . . . he can be a handful."

"Oh, I can handle him alright. How do you think he ever got up the nerve to ask me to marry him? I had to *encourage* him, too. I'm not worried in the least." Becky smiled and nudged Amy playfully with her elbow. "I can handle Tom . . . in every way."

Amy giggled, but she still blushed.

Tom and Ben had to check each other's outfits and hair. Nobody had thought to provide them with a mirror.

61

While they waited, Ben sat in a chair in the corner of the room. He laughed silently at Tom pacing the room like a caged lion.

"Nervous, buddy?"

"Who, me? Nah, not at all. Why do you ask?"

"Just wondered. You're about to wear a hole in the rug, pacing around like that."

A tap at the door startled Tom. Jeff Thatcher stuck his head in the door. "Just a couple more minutes, boys. Just checking to see if you're ready."

After Jeff left, Ben stood up and held out his hand to Tom. "Tom, just want you to know how proud I am to be your Best Man. I know how close you and Huck were, and you'd probably rather he -"

Tom shook his head, interrupting him. "No, Ben, I'm honored that you would do this for me. Huck and I were close . . . but he made his choice. If he had feelings for Becky, he should have stayed and fought for her, instead of running off." Tom grinned. "He would have lost, of course, but still, he should have taken it like a man. No, like I said, he made his choice. And I'm glad you're here. Besides, someday soon, I'll be doing the same for you."

"Whew . . . I don't know. The thought of getting married scares me to death. Besides, the only girl I'd be interested in is Amy, and I'm not sure she'd even consider it."

Tom laughed. "Ben, of course she would. You're a great guy. Both of us are. Those girls would be crazy not to jump at a chance to marry us. Do like I did . . . just take charge and do it. Don't take no for an answer."

PART FIVE
1863

-17-

"Left! Left! Left!" Lieutenant Thomas Sawyer sounded out the cadence. "Left! Left! Stay in line there! Eyes forward! Platoon . . . halt!"

The platoon came to a halt. A private missed the count and stepped on the heels of the man in front of him. The two men shoved each other. Someone cracked a joke and most of the platoon laughed.

"Quiet in the ranks! Good Lord, you'd think this was the first time we'd done this. Men, we've been going over this for weeks. Didn't your mothers teach you anything? You can't even walk in a straight line."

"We're walking straight to our graves," said one soldier.

Tom stepped over to the offending man. "What did you say, soldier?"

"I said we're walking straight and brave, sir."

"That's what I thought you said." Tom began pacing up and down, straightening uniforms, switching guns to the correct shoulders, and delivering a generally good tongue lashing. He stopped in front of one man who was particularly out of uniform.

"Soldier," Tom said, looking down at his feet, "soldier, you're barefoot."

"Yes, sir."

"Were you not issued new boots?"

"Yes, sir."

"Did you lose them?"

"No, sir."

"Were they stolen?"

"No, sir."

The snickers began again.

"Then where are they?"

"In my tent, sir."

"And why are they in your tent?"

"'Cause they hurt my feet something terrible when I wear them."

The platoon burst out laughing. Tom tried to glare at his men but couldn't keep a straight face.

"Son, where are you from, Alabama?"

"No, sir. Tennessee," the soldier said proudly.

Tom raised his eyebrows and smiled as if that explained everything. "Soldier, you're going to be glad you've got those boots come winter."

"Ah, Lieutenant, everybody knows this war'll be over before winter."

Nobody laughed this time. That had been said before. That was two winters ago.

"Soldier, have those boots on tomorrow." Tom smiled and shook his head. "Put gravel in them till you get used to them, if you have to."

"All right men, we've been at this all day. Now let's see if we can get it right. Column of twos!" Tom stepped to the front of the column as the men shifted position. "Left face!"

Tom's squad, 2nd Platoon, F Company, was part of the 24th Georgia Volunteer Infantry Regiment. Their regiment was attached to Colonel John Fulton's brigade.

The 2nd Platoon, for all its laxness, was really a well-trained unit. Tom pushed them hard, and they did all he asked.

"Platoon . . . load!" The rifle butts hit the ground in unison. The ramrods rattled as the men went through the motions of loading. "Front line . . . kneel! Ready! Aim! Fire!" The hammers clicked on the empty rifles. "Re-load! Fire at will!"

Target practice was limited for Fulton's brigade. The ammunition was needed for the real fight. That didn't stop Tom, though. Two or three times a week he led his men in "aim" practice.

They would aim at an imaginary enemy, pull the trigger, and go through the motion of reloading. The sound of the hammers clicking on the empty rifles soon earned 2nd Platoon the nickname of Sawyer's Snappers. The nickname embarrassed his men, but Tom wore it as a badge of honor.

Tom knew his men wondered if he was crazy. But the drills kept them busy and out of trouble. Except for the fights they got into with the other companies that laughed at them. Maybe that, too, he thought, would help in battle.

"Cease fire!" The front line rose to their feet and, without an order, the platoon shouldered their rifles. "Right face! Column of fours!" Tom waited as they lined up four-abreast.

"Finally . . . that looked good." The men smiled. "That's enough for today. Let's get back to the fort." He wheeled around. "Forward . . . march!"

Several of his men strutted, their heads held extra high, swinging their arms wildly back and forth . . . mocking Tom. Their comrades laughed silently.

-18-

The *Spirit of the Storm* plowed its way through the waves, lumbering along at eleven knots. The one-hundred-seventy foot side-wheeler rode low in the water, its hold full and the deck piled high with cargo.

The sky was clear and visibility was all the way to the horizon. Even though the ship was painted a dull gray from bow to stern, its two smokestacks made a perfect silhouette against the afternoon sky. Not exactly ideal conditions for this cruise.

The Second Officer paced the pilothouse, spyglass in hand, scanning the horizon. Every few minutes crewmembers scurried in and out with information from throughout the ship.

The First Mate, Johnny Watson, stood at the starboard rail, pulling duty as a lookout. Johnny was one of the few, if not the only, Negro First Mates serving his country. After his father, Jim, had disappeared, and Huck and Tom purchased Johnny, his mother, and his sister Lizabeth and set them free, Tom had suggested that Johnny's family take Miss Watson's name for their own, in honor of her freeing his dad. That was eleven years ago, and Jim had not been heard from since.

The captain stood in the pilothouse, his hands behind his back holding his unlit pipe, staring straight ahead, as they approached Mobile Bay. At just over six feet tall, muscular, and with his black hair falling almost to his shoulders, Captain Huckleberry Finn was an imposing figure.

After he had headed down the Mississippi to New Orleans, Huck had signed on to a merchant ship. As soon as he learned the sea, he made a down payment, with his share of Injun Joe's gold, on the *Spirit of the Storm*. When he became the master of his own ship, he knew there was only one man that he trusted enough to be his First Mate . . . Johnny Watson. The two had sailed together for four years now. The last two as blockade runners for the Confederacy.

Even though they were expecting it, the shout still startled them. "Land ho, dead ahead!"

All eyes turned north, straining for a glimpse of land. The crew knew the islands around Mobile well. Within a few minutes they would be able to identify this one. Huck knew from his charts which island it was supposed to be.

"Maintain watch," Huck ordered, without changing his stance. The Second Officer began shouting orders, reminding the lookouts of their duties. They were nearing the outer islands, and the most dangerous part of the voyage. There were too many places around these islands for the Yanks to hide.

Huck stood to lose everything if they crossed a blockader. If he couldn't outrun the Yanks, Huck would have to scuttle his ship to keep it from falling into enemy hands. He knew that no Yankee would ever stand on the deck of his ship.

He had another reason for not wanting to get captured. A Confederate agent had approached him in Nassau and asked him to deliver a pouch to Colonel Powell at Ft. Morgan in Mobile. It contained information that could cost several Confederate spies their lives if it fell into the wrong hands. And should end the careers of a few Yankee spies, if it made it to the Colonel. And could get Huck hanged if found in his possession.

This wasn't the first time Captain Finn had delivered more than weapons and ammunition for the cause. For the past year, he had smuggled pouches and coded messages between Savannah and Mobile and agents in the islands. He never told

Johnny or the crew because he didn't want to implicate them, but his crew's reputation as hell-raisers provided an excellent cover. Nobody could expect such a rough bunch to be trustworthy.

"Capt'n," Johnny said, as he entered the pilothouse, "it's West Sand Island."

Huck nodded and motioned for Johnny to join him at the chart table.

"Good," Huck said. "Come to port five degrees, clear the island to the west. We'll run up through Little Pelican Channel this time."

There were only two approaches to Mobile Bay. One was by hugging the shoreline through Grant Pass. Huck didn't like using the shallow waters of the Pass. Too many runners had hung up on the sandbars and been blasted to pieces by the surf or the Yankees before they could free themselves.

The other approach was through the mouth of the bay between Mobile Point to the east and Dauphin Island to the west. The entrance to the bay was guarded by two Confederate forts, Ft. Morgan on Mobile Point, and Ft. Gaines on Dauphin Island. It was also protected by a massive minefield. The only opening was a gap a few hundred yards wide next to Ft. Morgan.

Huck hoped to reach this gap and make it into the bay before being sighted by the Yanks. If that failed, he would try to reach the safety of Ft. Gaines. They could anchor there, outside the minefield, until the enemy was driven away by the forts guns.

Within an hour they reached the north end of West Sand Island, the last cover they would have before the final dash across the open waters to Ft. Morgan, the jumping-off point. Pass the point, and they were committed.

"Ship to starboard!" The alarm sent Huck and Johnny scurrying to the starboard railing. The ship surprised them by coming around the opposite side of the island.

Johnny raised his spyglass and surveyed the approaching ship. Its flag, the Stars and Stripes, was flying high. "It's Union all right. Looks like the *Albatross*." They had crossed paths with her before but had never been close enough for her guns to reach them. The *Albatross*, running almost parallel to them, was trying to cut off any chance of reaching Ft. Morgan.

"Full speed ahead!" Huck shouted. The Second Officer relayed the command to the engine room. The fires had been kept at the maximum temperature in anticipation of the order. The engineer answered the bells and almost immediately they felt the ship begin to pick up speed.

Huck watched the Union ship while Johnny shouted orders. After a few minutes, Huck turned to Johnny and shook his head. "Mr. Watson, have the crew stand ready to man the pumps. Report all damage to me at once."

Johnny's order sent a crewman hurrying below to relay the message. He looked at Huck, his brow furrowed in concern. "Capt'n, you expect they'll catch up to us?"

Huck nodded.

"I'll have the crew prepare to throw some of the cargo overboard, to pick up speed-"

"The hell you will," Huck shouted.

"You don't think-"

"No, I don't."

Johnny collapsed his spyglass and put it in his pocket. "Shall I ready the lifeboats then, Capt'n?"

"Hell no! No member of my crew is abandoning ship while she's still floating."

"I just thought we should be ready if—"

"I know what you thought. But if we have to, we'll sail this boat straight to hell to keep the Yanks from getting it. No surrender, no abandoning ship, no cargo overboard."

"Aye, aye, Capt'n. Then I guess it's Ft. Morgan . . . or the gates of hell."

"Damn straight. We're not stopping for anybody but the devil or St. Peter." He grinned. "And I think you know who this crew is closer to."

"Aye, I guess you're right about that. But, if you don't mind, I think I'll say a little prayer anyway, just in case someone up there is listening."

A loud boom from the warship indicated that the time for talking was over. The shell fell short by over a hundred yards, and astern by almost as much.

Huck grinned. "If that was their best shot, you may not have to bother the Lord after all. Let's find out, Mr. Watson. Strike the Union Jack. Run up our flag. I don't think they believe we're British anyway, do you?"

"No, old chap, I don't believe they do," Johnny said with his best British accent. "Praise the Lord and damn the cannons! Let's give it a stretch!"

The deck crew cheered and started shouting in defiance when they saw the Stars and Bars unfurled. Sharp commands from Johnny, though, cut short their demonstration.

The first volley from the *Albatross* was not their best shot. The next shell struck the fore deck but bounced harmlessly into the sea. Another pierced the hull on the starboard side just at the water line. The sea began washing in with every wave.

A crewman rushed into the pilothouse. "Capt'n, we're taking on water by the barrel full!"

"Get those damn pumps going!" Huck yelled.

"Already on it, sir."

"Mr. Watson, get below and check the damage," Huck ordered.

"Aye, aye, Capt'n."

Johnny followed the crewman at a dead run down into the hold and found knee-deep water. "Where's the bosun's mate?" he yelled.

"He was standing right there when we got hit."

"You mean . . . "

"Yep. He's down there under the water somewhere, what's left of him."

"Damn!" Johnny exclaimed. He bent over and looked out the hole in the hull, watching the water flow in. "Keep those pumps going or we'll all be getting it."

The ship shuddered as the next round of shells found their mark. One shell shattered the starboard paddle-box and rattled around the wheel until it splashed into the water. Another struck the aft smokestack. The explosion clipped off the top half of the stack, leaving it dangling above the deck still attached on one side.

Huck zigzagged the ship, trying to keep the *Albatross* guessing. They were able to dodge several rounds, but some still found their mark. The ship groaned with each solid hit.

The ship reeled to port with the next volley. The force of the shell knocked Johnny and several of the crew from their feet. Johnny fell face-first into the water. He came up coughing and sputtering, wiping the saltwater from his eyes. The sound of the main mast crashing onto the deck terrified them.

"What was that?" Johnny shouted. Two crewmen waded over, grabbed him, and pulled him to his feet. He sloshed his way to the companionway and headed topside. He was almost knocked back down by a crewman rushing to find him.

"Mr. Watson, come quick! Capt'n's down!"

"What?!"

"Pilothouse is gone! Blowed up!"

-19-

Three crewmen were already working frantically to free Huck and the Second Officer. Johnny climbed through the rubble that had been the pilothouse. He glanced at Huck's lifeless form as he was dragged clear. He couldn't tell if he was dead or alive. And he didn't have time to find out.

Johnny started shouting orders. "Clear the deck cargo, throw it overboard! We've got to make more speed! Now!" He thought about Huck's order. "Sorry, Huck," he said to himself, "they're picking us apart. We'll be floating into Mobile in little pieces. It's part of a cargo or no cargo at all."

To Johnny's amazement, the helm was intact. He gave it a pull to the left and the ship responded. They could still steer. He grabbed the helm with both hands and turned hard to port, showing the Yanks his stern, giving them a smaller target. Johnny would run for Ft. Gaines and Dauphin Island now. They would be under the protection of their guns before the *Albatross* would get a chance to put another broadside into them.

The Union gunboat turned to port to give chase. This captain was determined to get his prize. But Johnny was just as determined. And so was the crew. They fought the fires on deck and the water in the hold with a vengeance.

The *Spirit of the Storm* rode higher as the deck cargo was cleared. This slowed the water pouring in through the hole in the hull. They began to gain on the *Albatross*. Another fifteen minutes. If only the pumps held out.

"Off the port bow, another Yankee ship!" The warning was too late. Another broadside struck the *Spirit of the Storm*. Johnny lost his balance and would have fallen if he hadn't had both hands on the helm.

One shell pierced the hull and another clipped the aft mast. It collapsed over the port side. Its reefed sails started unfolding in the water, slowing the ship as if they had dropped anchor. The crew attacked the rigging with knives and axes trying to cut it free.

Johnny looked in disbelief at this new ship. "What the hell else can go wrong," he cursed in desperation. He looked behind him at the *Albatross*, gaining on them now, and at the new enemy ship, which he knew was hurrying to re-load and finish them off.

He had no choice. They would have to turn once again, forcing the new ship to sail towards Dauphin Island, putting them within reach of the forts guns. The new ship would have to pull out of the fight. This would make it a one-on-one fight again, but it would give the *Albatross* one more shot at them.

Johnny turned hard to starboard, across the *Albatross's* bow. The Yank responded just as Johnny expected, also turning to starboard. The next broadside missed by fifty yards. He knew they wouldn't miss again.

Johnny held the ship on a course towards the minefield. He knew exactly how long it took for the enemy to re-load. He counted the seconds out loud. When he counted down to three, he spun the helm hard to the left, turning once again towards Ft. Gaines. At that instant, the *Albatross* unleashed another volley. All but one of the shells missed to either side of the ship.

It was then that Johnny's strategy paid off. While the Yankee ship was turned to deliver its broadside, Ft. Morgan opened up on them. Twelve guns from the fort fired and three struck their target. The *Albatross* had to break off the chase.

The crewmen on deck, realizing that the battle was over, began cheering. But their celebration was short-lived. They were still in danger. The fires on deck were close to barrels of gunpowder, and two holes in the hull were still pouring in seawater. Johnny began shouting orders.

"Run hoses from the pumps to the fires on deck! Where's the doctor? Get me an injury report!"

Johnny turned the ship back towards Ft. Morgan and gave the order to reduce speed. The engines had held. As he turned north and headed into the bay, the slower speed and calmer water slowed the flow of water in through the holes in the hull. The *Spirit of the Storm* made it home again. The worst beating she had ever taken, but still afloat.

Before sunset, the ship tied up at the dock in Mobile. A large portion of its cargo had been thrown overboard, its sail rigging and one smokestack were gone, the deckhouses were leveled and burned, and there were two holes in its hull. The bosun's mate was dead, and the Captain and Second Officer were down with serious injuries. There were also several minor injuries among the crew.

A crowd gathered to watch her limp in. Smoke was coming out of her in all the wrong places. And as amazing as it was that she was still afloat, the most startling part was Johnny standing amidships, shouting orders. A black man, standing on the deck of a Confederate ship, in charge of a crew of white men.

"Help with those lines," Johnny yelled. "We need a wagon to the hospital! Quick!" The dock burst into activity. The mariners in the crowd were trained to react to situations, not stand around making political observations. A ship was in distress. Within minutes, the *Spirit of the Storm* was secured.

After the commotion settled down, the harbormaster came aboard. He approached Johnny with a curious look on his face. "Are you the Captain," he asked.

"No, sir. I'm Johnny Watson, First Mate. That was the Captain that was carried off to the hospital."

"Oh." He seemed relieved. "Well," he waved his hand at the mess on deck, "it looks like you're out of commission."

"Nah. Just needs some patching up, a little paint here and there. She'll be better than ever," Johnny said.

"Patching up? Boy, this doesn't even look like a boat. It's just a hole in the water with some wood stuck in it. You better get her unloaded before she sinks."

Johnny grinned. "That's just what I was thinking."

The dockhands and Huck's crew worked through the night unloading the remaining cargo. The lightened ship raised the holes above the water line and the pumps began to gain. By the time she was unloaded, most of the water had been pumped out.

Johnny finished inspecting the ship as the sun rose over the exhausted crew. Most of the men had collapsed on the fore deck where they had been working. As Johnny approached, they began rising to their feet.

He went from man to man, shaking hands and patting them on the back. "Good work" he said to each man.

"Mr. Watson," spoke up one crewmember, "you saved us back there, sir."

"No, men, you saved yourself. Fast action and daring under attack-"

"Mr. Watson . . . *you* did it. You took over and outmaneuvered those bastards. We'd be on the bottom if it weren't for you."

Johnny smiled at the crew. "Men, we all did good back there. Now get some rest. We'll clean this mess up later." He turned to leave.

"Attention on deck!"

Johnny turned back and faced the crew, all standing at attention and saluting. He pulled himself erect and snapped a salute in return.

He was proud of this crew. They were good men, even if they were white.

-20-

"om! Tom!" Becky had been calling for several minutes.
Supper was on the table and getting cold.

She went through the same routine almost every night.
Tom would take a book and find some quiet place and read for
hours. Becky would prepare their meal and then try to find him.
It frustrated her, but she learned a long time ago that it was
useless to say anything.

They had been married for nearly three years, still with no
children. She was beginning to be a little concerned, but not
really worried. And Tom seemed to be in no hurry.

Tom had been practicing law in Atlanta for eleven months.
He had worked at Whittingham & Burke until the autumn of
62 when Whittingham got caught bending the rules just a little
too far in a real estate case. It seems that he and the presiding
judge had been silent partners with the defendant. It wouldn't
have been so rough on Whittingham, except that he
represented the plaintiff. They both swore later that they would
have been able to maintain a professional level of objectivity.

The firm announced that Whittingham would be resigning,
for health reasons. Although Tom couldn't have known about
the dealings of Whittingham and the judge, since he had
worked closely with Whittingham, his services, too, would no
longer be required.

Whittingham, who was basically an honest man, for an attorney, felt guilty about Tom's plight. He arranged a position for Tom in Atlanta with his cousin, who was also an attorney. This provided Tom a wonderful opportunity away from the scandal in St. Louis, in a growing Southern metropolis. The opportunities were boundless.

Five months after Tom and Becky moved to Atlanta, on Valentine's Day, Judge Thatcher died in his sleep. Tom lost the only real father he had ever known.

This night, Becky found him on the back porch swing enjoying the light afternoon breeze. She ran her fingers through his hair. He hardly noticed. She began kissing his forehead and cheeks playfully. He looked up, pretending to be annoyed. While she had his attention, she kissed him lightly on the lips and grabbed the book out of his hand and hid it behind her back. "Come to dinner right now, Thomas Sawyer."

"Hey, I was reading that."

"Later. After supper. Now move."

For most of the meal, she was able to keep him from talking about his law cases or his military training. He studied all the military books he could find, and then he talked to Becky about them over their meals. She usually pretended to listen, just watching his eyes light up. But not tonight.

"Becky, I was reading Hardee's book on infantry tactics -"

"Tom," she interrupted, "I don't want to talk about the war, or armies, or navies, or anything else scary or sad. I don't think I can take any more . . . if I have to listen to one more . . . just not tonight, okay?"

"I'm sorry. I didn't mean -"

"Fine." She held up her hands. "Okay. It's okay."

"Okay . . . what do you want to talk about then?"

She shrugged and then smiled. "You'll never guess what I received in the mail today."

"What?"

"An invitation from the fort."

"From the fort? An invitation to what? Do they want you to join the regiment?"

"No, they want me to take over the regiment. As a matter of fact, by order of President Davis, all regiments will now be commanded by women."

"I can picture it now," Tom said. "Divisions lined up against each other, thousands of men, having a sewing contest or a bake-off. The terror of it all. Of course, when one side was declared the winner, that's when the real fighting would start."

"Very funny, general. What do you plan on doing when you go into battle? March circles around the enemy until they get dizzy watching you and fall down? Or maybe you could just throw your books at the Yanks."

Becky could tell that her joke had smarted. She tried to apologize. "Tom, I'm sorry. I know -"

"Becky, I'm doing all I know to do-"

"I know, and I said I'm sorry. I'm sure you and your men will do bravely, that's not what I meant. But I don't want to talk about it anymore. Besides, you'll want to know what I really received an invitation to."

"I'm afraid to guess again."

"A ball. Mrs. Fulton is throwing a ball. Doesn't that sound great? You can dress up in your pretty little uniform and I'll get out my best dress. We'll have a wonderful time."

"I don't want to go to a ball."

"Tom Sawyer, you know you'll have a good time. Strutting around in your uniform - "

"I do cut a fine figure, don't I?" He hopped up, pulled himself erect, and started marching around the table. His exaggerated motions made Becky laugh. At one turn, he spun and began marching backwards. He tripped over his chair and fell flat on his back onto the floor. He jumped up, righted the chair, and plopped down as if nothing had happened. Becky was laughing so hard she was crying.

"Ma'am, I'd be honored to accompany you to the ball."

Becky dried her cheeks on her sleeve. "Thank you, Mr. Grace. I'm sure that at least *I'll* have a good time. Watching you on the dance floor, that is."

Tom crossed his eyes and stuck out his tongue. Becky cracked up again.

They laughed and talked until the sun began to set. Becky did her best to control the conversation. When the officer's staff planned a shindig, something big was about to happen. And she knew it. But tonight, she had plans to take their minds off the war.

"Tom, you look tired. We need to get to bed early."

"No, I'm okay."

"Tom, we need to get to bed early."

"Why? We don't have anything special we have to get up early for."

"I know that, Tom. You're not listening." She smiled at him, a finger clenched lightly between her teeth.

"Oh," Tom said, her meaning finally dawning on him. "I'll help with the dishes."

-21-

When Tom awoke, he was shivering from the nip in the early morning air. Becky, with her back to him, was hogging the covers as usual. He raised the covers and snuggled close. Her warm body felt good to his.

He wrapped his arm around her waist and pulled her closer. She awoke, turned her head and smiled. She took his hand and pulled it up until it rested between her breasts. She gave him a light kiss and snuggled tighter into his arms. And went back to sleep.

He held her for almost an hour. He was unable to go back to sleep so he lay there watching the dark of the night fade away as the sunlight took over for another day. He wanted to memorize every sensation. The smell of the day when it's new. The sound of the animals as they begin to stir. The softness of his own bed. The even softer touch of his wife.

He didn't know how long the memories would have to hold him, but he was sure that it would be too long. He didn't want to ever move from where he was right now. But he knew he would soon be called to battle. He also knew he had to get to the office today.

He slowly pulled his arm free, paused to kiss Becky on the temple, and slid out of bed. He dressed as quietly as he could and was about to leave without waking her. She sat up in bed, the covers falling to her waist, exposing her bare torso.

"Tom Sawyer, you hurry home to me, you hear?"

He paused at the door, smiled and shook his head once. "Looking like that, you can count on it."

As he walked the seven blocks to the law offices of Killian & Killian he couldn't help joining in with the whistles of the birds. It was a clear, beautiful morning and, if last night was any indication, it was going to be a wonderful day.

He entered the office and gave a big hello to anyone who was listening. The partners were in the front office with a client. He threw up his hand as he walked by and headed down the hall to his office in the back.

It was small and unimpressive, but it was cozy. Especially when Becky brought lunch. And they didn't have to worry about getting caught kissing. The creaking floorboards in the hall provided plenty warning.

Tom took off his hat and threw it at the brass coat stand in the corner. As usual, he missed. He took off his coat, hung it up, and bent over and picked up his hat. One of these days he'd hit it.

The stack on his desk was small, and getting smaller. The partners were trying to help him clear up his outstanding cases. He was mostly handling real estate transactions and wills. Lots of wills these days. And a lot of will probating, too.

He heard footsteps in the hall and looked up as the younger Killian knocked at the door. "Dad would like you to join us, please."

Killian & Killian, a father and son firm, had been a flourishing practice for ten years. The elder Killian had practiced for fifteen years before that. The younger Killian was an only child and unmarried, with little prospects of either situation changing. He was as kind and gentle as a man could be, but unfortunately, when God was handing out ugly, he got a double portion.

Tom put his coat back on and joined the three men in the front office. "You wanted to see me?"

"Yes, come in. Tom, I want you to meet a friend of mine. This is Lucius Jackson. Lucius, this is Tom, the young man I was telling you about."

"Pleased to meet you, Tom."

"Likewise, Mr. Jackson."

"Tom," continued the elder Killian, motioning to a chair for Tom, "Lucius has a problem, and with your special talents, I believe you can help him."

"I'll be glad to try," Tom said as he took a seat.

"He's being sued. And his case starts today."

"Today?"

"Yes. Well . . . more correctly . . . in about forty-five minutes."

"Mr. Killian, there's no way I can be ready to start a trial in forty-five minutes. I know nothing about the case-"

"Tom, I have confidence in you. Just hear Lucius out."

"Mr. Sawyer, I was all set to go to the judge this morning and pay what I'm being sued for. I was waiting till the last minute, just to tick off Zeb, the man who's suing me. But the more I thought about it, the madder I got. I know I've waited awful late, but I'd like to try to put up some kind of fight, if you'll help me. It's the principle of the matter."

"Well, sir, I don't know if I can be of any help -"

"Tom, you'll do fine," interrupted the elder Killian. "Get your hat and walk with him to the courthouse. He can explain on the way."

If Tom was exasperated when he left the office, it was nothing compared to what he felt when he got to the courthouse. When the judge, the Honorable Floyd Phipps Phillips, asked Tom for any motions to be filed, he had none. When the judge asked him if he had any questions for potential jurors, he had none. However, Mr. Bazemore Cummings, the attorney for the plaintiff, took an hour asking all sorts of silly questions.

Finally, the judge asked if any of the jurors were kin to any of the parties. One juror indicated he was a cousin to Mr. Cummings. The judge asked if they were close cousins. The juror replied no, that they lived about fifteen miles apart. He was one of the twelve selected.

Bazemore Cummings took fifteen minutes to present his opening statement. Tom followed with a simple one sentence opening statement. "Gentlemen, I assure you that the facts in this case are nowhere near what Mr. Cummings has just outlined to you." He never left his table and sat down quickly. He was afraid to say more. He wasn't even sure what the facts of the case were.

-22-

M r. Cummings, are you ready to call your first witness?"

"Yes, your Honor. I'd like to call Doc Davis." A short, shabbily-dressed man stood at the back of the courtroom and came forward. He swore to tell the truth with the wrong hand raised in the air.

"Sir, please state your name."

"You oughta know it, you just called it."

"I know, but state it for the record."

"Doc Davis."

"Doc, do you practice veterinary medicine in the Atlanta area?"

"If you mean do I tend to sick animals hereabouts, yeah."

"Have you had occasion lately to visit Mr. Zeb Littleton's farm?"

"Yep."

"Did you tend to a sick pig?"

"Yep."

"Were you able to help this pig?"

"Nope."

"You had to put it down?"

"Yep."

"How long had he had this pig?"

"Just a few days. He had just bought it from Mr. Jackson there," he said, pointing to the defendant.

"How do you know he bought it from Mr. Jackson?"

"He showed me the bill of sale."

Mr. Cummings crossed to his table and retrieved a piece of paper. "Your Honor, I'd like to introduce this bill of sale. It describes one Yorkshire sow sold by Mr. Jackson to Mr. Littleton just six days before Doc's visit."

The judge read over the bill of sale. "So entered."

"Doc," Cummings continued, "were there any other pigs on Mr. Littleton's farm?"

"Yep."

"Were any of them sick?"

"Nope."

"Thank you. No more questions, your Honor."

The judge looked over the rim of his glasses at Tom. "Mr. Sawyer, do you have any questions for this witness?"

"Yes, your Honor." Tom picked up the bill of sale from Mr. Cummings' table and read over it as he approached the witness stand. "Mr. Davis, you say that Mr. Littleton showed you this bill of sale for one pig."

"Yep."

"This bill of sale describes one Yorkshire sow. Is that correct?"

"Yep."

"You testified that there were other pigs on the Littleton farm."

"Yep."

"Yorkshires?"

"Yep."

"How do you know that this was the particular pig that Mr. Jackson sold him?"

"Cause Zeb told me so."

"Have you ever had occasion to go to Mr. Jackson's farm?"

"Yep."

"Does he have any pigs there?"

"Yep, several."

"Yorkshires?"

"Yep."

"Wouldn't you say that all Yorkshires generally look alike?"

"Well, yes, pretty much."

"So you can't identify this particular pig by her color?"

"Well, no."

"How about her size? What size would you say this pig was, small, medium, or large?"

"I'd have to say medium."

"How much does a medium size pig weigh?"

"It depends."

"On what?"

"On how big it is."

There were a few snickers around the courtroom. The judge tapped his gavel on the bench. Tom leaned against the bench and rubbed his hand across his brow.

"Alright, Mr. Davis, how do you treat most of your patients?"

"Very well. I treat them right kindly."

"No. I mean what medical procedures do you use to ease their suffering?"

"Oh. Most of the bad sick ones I shoot."

"How about the ones that aren't bad sick?"

"No, I don't normally shoot them."

"Normally? But you have shot ones that weren't bad sick?"

"Yep."

"Why?"

"If they look like they're about to get bad sick, just to head off any suffering they may be facing."

"You shoot them to keep them from getting bad sick?"

"Yep, sometimes."

The snickers turned into laughter, which Judge Phillips quickly gaveled down. A stern look around the courtroom quieted the spectators. Most cases were boring affairs but this one was beginning to show promise.

Tom smiled, shook his head and returned to his table. He shuffled through his papers pretending to look for notes that didn't exist. "Tell me, do you ever tend to sick people," he asked.

"Sometimes, when there ain't no doctor around."

"Really?" Tom asked, not expecting that answer. "When you do tend to people, do you carry a gun?" More giggles from the audience.

"Why?"

"Just curious. Wondered if you'd ever had to shoot anyone."

"Yep, once."

"You're kidding?"

"Nope."

"Why, was he sick?" More snickers.

"No. I caught him trying to steal my bull."

"What'd you do?"

"We ate him."

"The man?"

"No, the bull."

"Why'd you eat the bull?"

"Cause I ain't too good a shot, off at a distance."

"Did he die?"

"Of course he died. I just told you we ate him."

"Not the bull, the man?"

"Yep."

Gasps of shock replaced the laughter.

"He did die?" Tom asked.

"Yep."

Tom was just as shocked as the spectators. "Did you get in trouble with the law?"

"For what?"

"Killing the man."

"I didn't kill him."

"You said he died."

"Yep, about five years later. Got drunk and fell off the balcony at a saloon. Broke his neck." The courtroom grew quiet as Doc lowered his head and shook it solemnly, as if remembering the poor man. "It was a terrible loss. He was my prize bull."

The judge was laughing with everyone else as he banged his gavel demanding silence.

Tom was dumbfounded. He stood by his table for a full minute before continuing. "Mr. Davis, let's get back to the pig in question. How did you know it was sick?"

"Because all it did was lay around."

"Well what do healthy pigs do?"

"Lay around, I guess."

"Then what made you think this pig was sick?"

"Well, she just didn't seem interested in nothing. I've noticed, if you talk to them, they'll perk up their ears sometimes."

"So pigs find what you have to say to be interesting?"

"Yep, I guess so."

"And you can tell this by their ears perking up?"

"Yep."

"When you talk to people, have you ever noticed their ears perking up?"

"Well of course not."

"Does that mean that everyone you talk to is sick, or that they just don't find your conversation interesting?"

The laughter that shook the courtroom was not going to be gaveled down this time. The judge didn't even try. He was laughing too hard.

"No more questions, your Honor."

After the courtroom reassumed a semblance of decorum, Mr. Bazemore Cummings called his next witness.

"Mr. Littleton, did you purchase a pig from Mr. Jackson?"

"Yes."

"How did this transaction come about?"

"I saw him at the general store and we got to talking about his pigs. I then went by his place and looked at this one pig and bought it."

"For fifty dollars?"

"Yes, fifty dollars."

"Did you take it home with you right then?"

"No. I was on my horse. He delivered it a couple days later in his wagon."

"Was it sick when you picked it out to purchase it?"

"No, of course not."

"Do you own other pigs?"

"Yes, Mr. Cummings, you know I do. Doc's done testified to that."

"I know. Just answer the question. Were any of your other pigs sick?"

"No."

"So the pig in question couldn't have caught anything from your pigs?"

"No."

"So, in your opinion, the pig was sick when it was delivered?"

"It had to be. I didn't buy no sick pig. He switched pigs on me. Brought me a sick one instead of the one I bought."

"Thank you, Mr. Littleton. No more questions, your Honor."

"Your witness, Mr. Sawyer."

"Thank you, your Honor." Tom approached the witness stand. "Mr. Littleton, you say that you met Mr. Jackson at the general store?"

"No, I met him about eight years ago at a stock sale."

"No, I mean the day you bought the pig, you ran into him at the general store."

"Yes."

"Was he trying to sell pigs?"

"No. He was buying feed."

"Who brought up the subject of you buying a pig from him?"

"I guess I did."

"Why?"

"Uh, well . . . because everybody knows he has some of the best pigs around."

"Is this the first time you've had dealings with Mr. Jackson?"

"Um . . . no."

"So you've bought stock from him before?"

"Yeah, I reckon."

"Has he ever sold you a sick animal before?"

91

"Well . . . no."

"Has he ever cheated you in any manner before?"

"No, I guess not."

"You testified that Mr. Jackson switched pigs on you. While you were looking at this pig, trying to decide to buy it, was it in a pen by itself?"

"No, it was running with the others."

"What did Mr. Jackson do, before you left his farm that day?"

"We herded it into his barn and put it in a stall by itself."

"And then you left?"

"Yep. Headed back to my place."

"While you were at his farm, did you see any sick pigs while you were examining the one you bought?"

"No."

"Mr. Davis has testified that all the pigs on Mr. Jackson's farm and on your farm are Yorkshires. Is that correct?"

"Yes."

"Do you have any other pigs that look like the one he sold you?"

"Well . . . "

"Mr. Littleton, Doc has already testified that all Yorkshires look pretty much alike."

"Well . . . yes. I have three that look just like it."

"So, you have four, or had, four pigs that look just alike?"

"Yes."

"Okay. Thank you. Now sir, how did the pig die?"

"Doc shot it."

"Why did he shoot it?"

"'Cause he said it was sick."

"What did you do with the pig?"

"I ate it."

"You ate all of it?"

"No, we gave some of it to Doc, for his bill."

"Tell me, are any of your family sick?"

"No."

"Are you aware of any of Doc's family being sick?"

"No. Why?"

"I'm just concerned that you might have gotten sick from eating a sick pig. How did it taste?"

"Fine."

"If you got to eat the pig anyway, why are you suing my client?"

"'Cause I didn't buy her for eating. I bought her for breeding."

"Did you tell my client why you were buying the pig?"

"No, 'tweren't none of his business."

"So my client didn't know if you were buying the pig to eat or to breed?"

"No, I guess not."

"So he made no promises about the taste or the breeding potential of the pig?"

"No."

"So why is Mr. Jackson responsible to you for the fifty dollars?"

"'Cause he knew the pig was sick."

"How do you know?"

"'Cause it was sick when he delivered it."

"How do you know?"

"'Cause Doc told me so."

"How do you know it was the same pig?"

"'Cause it's dead!"

Tom leaned over his table, shaking his head. "No more questions, your Honor," he said when the laughs died down again.

Judge Phillips looked at Mr. Cummings. "Call your next witness."

"We rest, your Honor."

"Good. Mr. Sawyer, call your first witness."

"I call Mr. Lucius Jackson to the stand," Tom said. The court was so distracted, the bailiff forgot to swear in Mr. Jackson.

"Mr. Jackson, did you sell Mr. Littleton a pig?"

"Yes."

"Was it sick?"

"Hell no!"

The judge gaveled down the laughs again. "Mr. Jackson, you will watch your language in my court."

"Sorry, your Honor. Hell no, *sir.*"

"No more questions, your Honor."

"Mr. Cummings, do you have any questions for this witness?"

"No, your Honor."

"Call your next witness, Mr. Sawyer."

"Defense rests, sir."

"Thank God . . . I mean, very well. We'll reconvene at one-thirty for closing arguments. Adjourned for lunch."

Tom walked the two blocks to his office. Both Killians were waiting in the front room.

"How's the case going?" asked the younger Killian, with a smile.

"If I had a horse whip, I'd take it to both of you. You set me up." Both Killians broke out laughing. "That Littleton, and his attorney, are idiots!" Tom was pacing back and forth angrily, his hands on his hips. "And that Doc Davis! Where do you find these people?" The elder Killian was fairly howling by now. Tom was trying to stay mad, but lost it, and joined in the laughter. "Why did you do this to me?"

"I told you, because of your special talents," said the elder Killian.

"And what are those? Being a sucker and looking foolish?"

"Relax, Tom," said the son. "You were probably the only one in the courtroom that didn't look like a fool. We knew this case was a bunch of manure, and who better to help spread it than Tom Sawyer? You've spent a lifetime doing just that."

Tom smiled and headed for the door. "I've got to go prepare my closing statement." He pointed a finger at both Killians. "I swear, I'll get you for this."

The judge gaveled the court back into session. "Mr. Cummings, we're ready for your closing statement."

"Thank you, your Honor. Gentlemen, I'll be brief." And then he spent the next twenty-five minutes not being brief. "To sum it up, you've heard the evidence. My client went to Mr. Jackson's farm and picked out and purchased a healthy pig. Two days later, according to testimony presented here, a sick pig was delivered, and four days after that, the animal had to be destroyed. Mr. Littleton purchased this pig for breeding purposes and has now been deprived of that possibility. Cut and dried. Plain and simple. I request that you find for my client. Thank you."

"Mr. Sawyer, are you ready?"

"Yes, your Honor." Tom approached the jury box and smiled. Not a big smile. Just a little one, to make sure they all understood the joke. "Gentlemen, you are in a rare position. This is one of those few occasions when the opposing attorneys are in agreement. This case *is* cut and dried. It is indeed plain and simple. However, Mr. Cummings has failed to remind you of a few points of interest. You know that Mr. Littleton picked out the pig he wanted to purchase. Mr. Littleton then testified that he saw no sick pigs at Mr. Jackson's. Both witnesses for the plaintiff have testified that there are no other pigs sick at this time at either farm. Mr. Littleton then testified that he had three other pigs that looked just like it, so there is no way he can be sure which pig was delivered and which ones were already there. We also have the uneducated testimony of the so-called vet that pronounced the pig sick. And finally, the only real evidence in this case, the alleged sick pig, has been eaten by the two witnesses for the plaintiff. I request that you find for my client. Thank you for your time and patience."

Tom and Mr. Jackson borrowed an office across the hall from the courtroom to wait for the jury. An hour and a half later the jury still had not returned. Tom was concerned but didn't show it. Mr. Jackson was agitated and couldn't hide it.

"What's taking them so long?" Jackson asked.

"This is really a very complicated case," Tom said, trying to sound lawyerly. "A lot of legal ramifications. Setting precedents and the like."

"It don't seem too complicated to me. He wants to have his pig and eat it too, you might say. Or my pig, that is."

"You shouldn't worry. I feel good about our legal position. You never know what a jury will do, though. But if we lose, we can always file an appeal." Tom began to imagine his revenge against the Killians.

There was a knock at the door. "They're back," said the clerk. As Tom and Jackson walked down the hall to the courtroom, they passed other attorneys milling about. "Good luck, Tom. This is a tough one, isn't it?" Other such lame remarks followed him back to the courtroom. Serious fun poked at him by his friends. His former friends. He just glared and tried to ignore them.

"Mr. Foreman, has the jury reached a verdict?" asked the judge after everyone was seated.

"Yes, your Honor, we have."

"And what is your verdict?"

"We find for the defendant."

"Thank you, gentlemen. Mr. Littleton, I am ordering you to pay court costs. See the clerk before you leave. Mr. Jackson, this case is dismissed. Court is adjourned."

Tom and Lucius shook hands. "Thank you, Tom. You did a wonderful job. Thank you so much."

"You're welcome, Lucius. This was a tough one, all right, but the jury did the right thing."

Lucius slapped Tom on the back. "Care to join me for a drink, Tom?"

"Thanks, but no. I've got to get back to the office. And you need to come by later to settle up."

"Sure. I'll see you after while."

Tom left the courtroom to return to his office. Outside, in the main hall, he ran into several lawyer friends.

"Old Tom has won another pig, er, I mean, *big*, case."

"Yeah, when he takes a case, he goes whole hog."

"You really brought home the bacon on this one, didn't you?"

"You and the missus can really live high on the hog after this win?"

"Very funny, boys," Tom said. "If you're not careful, I'll sue every one of you."

"For what?" one of them asked.

"For being full of what I've been spreading all day." The good-natured laughter echoed through the courthouse.

That afternoon, Jackson came by Tom's office. "Thanks again, Tom," he said.

"Anytime. Here's the bill for my service."

Jackson stared at the bill. "This is a bill for one hundred dollars!"

"Yes?"

"But I was only being sued for fifty dollars."

"Yes, but it's the principle of the matter. You won!"

-23-

Huck awoke. His head pounded with each heartbeat. He pressed the butts of his hands against his temples. It took several seconds for his vision and his thoughts to clear. The last he remembered, he was dodging cannonballs.

He tried to sit up but the movement brought searing pain to his stiff joints. He collapsed back onto the pillow.

With much effort, he rolled over on his side, dropped his legs over the edge of the bed, and pushed himself up. The sheet, streaked with bloodstains, both old and his own, was covering only his lap. He realized his clothes were gone.

As he gazed around the room, filled with sick and injured men, he was thankful that he didn't recognize anyone. Maybe his men had not been injured, he thought. Or maybe they hadn't survived to make it this far.

He heard a noise behind him and turned to see a young lady, smiling, her arms folded across her chest. He grabbed the sheet and tried to cover his buttocks.

She laughed. "Too late, Captain."

"Who are you?" he demanded, red-faced.

"I'm your nurse. As you can tell from your bandages, you had several injuries, all over your body." She smiled again. "We had to give you a good going over."

"Where am I?"

"You're in a hospital."

"No, *where* am I?"

"Oh. Don't worry, you're still among friends. You're in Mobile."

"Are any of my men here? Do you know if my ship made it in?"

"Well, obviously your ship made it in. You're here, aren't you? But I don't know about your men."

"Where are my clothes? I've got to get back to my ship," he said, looking around.

"Not until the doctor says you can go. Don't worry, you'll get your clothes back, what's left of them." She helped him turn back around in the bed and ease back onto his pillow. As she straightened his covers she said, "Now just lie back and rest until the doctor makes his rounds. Breakfast will be served soon."

Huck closed his eyes and prayed for sleep to return. He had to get some relief from this headache. He hadn't been asleep too long when two noisy orderlies began serving breakfast. The food wasn't worth waking up for. And besides, even chewing hurt.

After breakfast, he was able to nod off again. He slept off and on for most of the morning. Before noon, dressed in his tattered and bloodstained uniform, he was wheeled to the front entrance where a buggy was waiting to take him to the docks.

Huck had to ask the driver several times to slow the horses. Each bump in the road brought a new experience in pain. The driver stopped at the edge of the pier and helped him climb down. He hobbled to where the *Spirit of the Storm* was tied up.

He knew she had been damaged in the attack, but he was not prepared for what he saw. She appeared to be little more than a hull with one smokestack standing. Their brush with the Yanks had almost proved fatal. His cargo, precious to the Confederacy, had almost been sent to the bottom of the sea.

He came aboard without anyone noticing. The crew was still collapsed on the deck or below in exhausted sleep. The wreckage was scattered on the deck and on the dock where it had been piled. He dreaded going below to see the damage there. He was also afraid to find out how many of his men had been hurt.

He walked below, stepping over hoses, rubble, and sleeping men. He examined both holes in the hull. On the port side, away from the dock, he stuck his head through the gaping hole. He could have reached the water less than two feet below.

Huck then headed for his cabin. It was there that he found Johnny. While the crew rested, Johnny had begun surveying the damage. He was at Huck's desk writing his report when fatigue took over. He fell asleep on his papers.

Huck knocked on the door loudly.

"What?!" Johnny jerked awake in his chair, a scrap of writing paper stuck to his face. "What the . . . Huck!" He jumped up and rushed to Huck and, without thinking, greeted him with a tight hug.

"Oh, I'm sorry, Huck. Are you okay? Did I hurt you?"

"Well, I was okay. The doctor told me not to be getting squeezed to death, so I guess I'm done for now." He removed the paper still stuck to Johnny's face.

"Uh . . . sorry." Johnny stepped back to the desk and cleared away his writing. Huck took his seat.

"Capt'n, you look like hell."

"Thanks, I appreciate that." The smile left his face. "Johnny, why hasn't all this mess been cleaned up?"

"Huck . . . Capt'n . . . the men worked straight through the night, getting her unloaded . . . in case she sank. After the fight, and the fires, and bailing water, well . . . they just had nothing left. Once the boat was secure, I told them to get some rest."

"You did?"

"Yes, sir."

"Okay. But I want this mess squared away today. We've got to start putting her back together."

"Yes, sir."

Huck shifted his weight and tried to find a more comfortable position. "Well, tell me, what happened to me?"

"Yanks blew up the pilothouse. You're lucky you weren't killed."

100

"Then I guess it's okay for me to look like hell." He shuffled through the papers on his desk. "Is this the cargo manifest?"

"Yes."

Huck read over it. "I don't understand . . . what are these marks? Why is some of the cargo marked through?"

"That's the items we had to throw overboard. Mostly deck cargo -"

"Throw overboard! Damn it, Johnny, I do remember enough of the fight to know I gave you a direct order not to jettison any cargo-"

"Yes, but—"

"Don't but me, I gave you a direct order. Do you have any idea how much money you cost me? I know you're itching to be captain, and when you've got your own boat, you can throw cargo-"

"No, Huck, it's not that. I had to make a decision. Those ships were pounding us and if we didn't gain some speed—"

"Those ships? What do you mean?"

"What? Oh . . . yeah . . . you were out. Another Yankee ship showed up right after you got hit. We were getting it on two sides."

Huck looked through the manifest again and laid it aside. "Oh . . . I see." He reached into the bottom drawer of his desk. "You know what I need right now? A good stiff drink. Care to join me?"

"Now you know I don't drink much. The good book says we shouldn't, except on special occasions, like people getting born, or married, or dying or such."

"Speaking of dying, how many men . . ."

"Two. The bosun's mate and the Second Officer. The bosun's mate died instantly, the Second Officer hung on until just after we docked."

Huck thought about the two men he had lost. Good men. He slammed his fist down hard on his desk, startling Johnny. "Damn! Damn the Yankees! Why can't they just go home and

101

leave us the hell alone?" He massaged his forearm as he grimaced in pain.

"Johnny," Huck said, reaching for the bottle, "two of our friends are dead. That's special occasion enough for me."

"Yeah, me too, I guess."

Huck poured two glasses and the two men paused with their drinks in their hands. They thought of yesterday's ordeal and raised a silent toast to the dead.

After a few sips, Huck asked, "By the way, did you ever get around to saying that prayer yesterday?"

"Oh yeah, I prayed an awful big one."

"Well, it looks like it worked. Mostly. You should say another one and give thanks, even though we were pretty badly beaten up."

"I think you're right." Johnny sat his drink down and raised both hands in the air. "Praise be to the Lord, we done escaped from them damn Yankees!"

The crew began the task of cleaning up the rubble. They went about their duties without their usual banter. They'd lost two friends and it would take a while for them to come around. Huck knew to let them be.

Huck and Johnny finished their first survey of the ship. They were standing alone in the pulpit looking aft over what was left of the main deck. Huck just kept shaking his head.

"Damn, the old girl took a beating this time," Huck said.

"Yeah, but she's a solid boat. We'll put her back right."

Huck nodded in agreement. "Damn straight, we will." He leaned back against the rail, his hands in his pockets.

"Huck, we should have this mess cleaned up tomorrow. What do you want the men to do when we're cleared away?"

"Well, you can give some of them leave. They're pretty good at sailing ships but don't know much about building them. We're going to have to bring in some experts to help put her back together. Check with the harbormaster to see if he can recommend anyone."

"I'll get with him first thing in the morning."

"And tell the crew I'm going to treat them to dinner tomorrow. Don't look so surprised. If you don't mind, make the arrangements."

"Be glad to," Johnny said with a grin.

"And it doesn't *have* to be the most expensive place in town." He sat down on an empty crate, stretched out his legs and rubbed his aching muscles. "Johnny, I overheard some of the men talking about how you took over when I went down. You held them together and brought the ship in. They'll not be forgetting it."

"The crew saved themselves. I just did what you would have done."

"That's not what I hear. I swear, sometimes I think you're a better sailor than I am."

"Well, Huck, everybody knows *that*."

"Watch out now!" Huck leaned forward, placed his hands on his knees, and stood up with a grunt. "You can handle things for a while. I need some rest. I've got to take a boat down to Ft. Morgan in the morning on some pressing matters..."

"You going to deliver that pouch we brought in?"

Huck jerked his head around and stared at Johnny. "Yes . . . but how did you know about that?"

"We all know about that pouch, and all the others too, and the risks you take carrying them."

Huck glanced around at some of the crew working on deck. "Everybody knows?"

"Yeah. But don't worry, your secret's safe with us."

"It better be. Well, I'm going to the fort in the morning with my *secret* pouch. And I think I'll tell the Colonel you're a Yankee spy."

"Right. God save the Union!" Johnny gave a mock salute and headed off to the other end of the ship. Huck went below to his cabin.

-24-

The packet to Ft. Morgan was filled with soldiers. Most were returning to the fort of their own free will. Two were in shackles and under guard. Huck judged from their jovial manner, though, that they weren't in too much trouble. And a few green-faced trips to the rail indicated a couple days in the stockade might do them good.

When they arrived, a corporal escorted Huck to the Colonel's office. As they walked past a row of cannons, Huck admired the big guns that had come to his ship's rescue. He wished he'd been awake to hear them.

The Colonel had watched the struggle from the fort but didn't know the extent of the damage to Huck's ship. He was relieved to see that Huck wasn't seriously hurt.

"Captain Finn, long time, no see. Hope your welcome home wasn't too rough."

Huck shook his head. "Roughest yet. Knocked us out for a couple months, but we'll run again."

"Good, good. Any other injuries?"

"Killed two of my men."

"Sorry to hear it." The Colonel moved behind his desk and sat down, motioning for Huck to take a seat.

For the next half-hour they talked about the battle. When Huck finished with the details, the Colonel leaned back and put his hands behind his head.

"So," said the Colonel, "I'm sure you didn't come all the way down here to tell me about your little run-in with the Yanks. What can I do for you?"

"Colonel, a gentleman in Nassau asked me to deliver this to you." He leaned forward and handed the pouch to the Colonel.

The Colonel emptied the pouch onto his desk. He removed his reading glasses from his vest pocket, picked up a battered looking notebook from the pile, and stepped to the window for better light. After reading the first page he returned to his seat. As they sat across from each other, the Colonel seemed to be sizing him up.

"Captain, have you read this?"

"Some of it. I like to know what I'm getting into. Interesting reading."

"Does anyone else know you have this?"

"I didn't think so. But it seems my whole crew knew. It was locked in my cabin when I was hurt. It was still locked up when I got back to the ship yesterday afternoon."

"Do you think anyone read any of it?"

"No, I don't. They were pretty exhausted. I don't think anybody even thought about it. But don't worry, they're good men."

"They better be, or a lot of good people could wind up dead." The Colonel put the pouch and its contents in a drawer and locked it, pocketing the key. "Finn, would you care to join me for some lunch?"

"I'd like to, but I promised my men a night on the town, so I need to get on back."

"I understand, I'm afraid. I've heard about your crew's nights on the town. Send word if you need someone to bail you out."

"Thanks, Colonel. I'll remember that." The two men shook hands. As Huck pulled the door closed behind him, he saw the Colonel fumbling through his pockets for the desk key.

When Huck arrived back at the *Spirit of the Storm*, Johnny was waiting for him. "Huck, the crew went on ahead without us. Didn't want to wait. Said something about being thirsty. I've got a buggy waiting, so we can leave when you're ready."

"Sounds good, I'm starved. Let's see if we can catch up with them."

As they rode to the restaurant, they discussed the arrangements Johnny had made regarding the repairs to the ship. Huck didn't ask Johnny if he had read the notebook. He didn't have to. And Johnny didn't ask about the meeting with the Colonel.

As they entered the restaurant, Huck noticed one of his men, standing at a table in the back, waving to get his attention. Most of the conversation in the dining room stopped. The white soldiers and sailors watched Johnny as he followed Huck.

It didn't take long for an artillery master sergeant, filled with a little bit more beer than brains, to approach their table. The table grew quiet as everyone saw him glaring at Johnny.

"Can I help you, Sergeant?" Huck said.

"We don't share no meals with no nigger," he said.

Huck looked around, pretending to be confused. "What nigger?"

"That nigger sitting next to you."

Huck looked at Johnny and winked. "That ain't no nigger. That's my First Mate."

"Captain, I don't care if he's your brother, he's still a nigger!"

Huck turned and looked at Johnny. "Well, I'll be damned. Mr. Watson, now don't get upset, but you *are* a nigger."

"Nasuh, masa, suh, I'z ain't no nigger. I'z white jess like yu'z."

"Are you sure? This man seems to think you're a nigger and you do look like one."

"Yasuh, suh, I'z sure. I'z ain't no nigger."

Huck turned back to the sergeant. "I'm sorry, Sergeant, but I guess you're mistaken. He says he ain't no nigger."

For the second time in forty-eight hours, Huck received a blow to the head. This one sent him sprawling, flying from his

107

chair. The sergeant didn't get in a second blow, though. A wine bottle across his skull saw to that.

Huck woke up, flat of his back on a cot. Leaning his head back, he looked upside down at an important-looking officer. He rolled over, rose up on his elbow and looked through the bars at an old friend.

"Col. Powell, good to see you again. What are you doing behind bars?"

"I'm not behind bars, you drunk fool. You are."

"I was afraid you'd say that. I'm not sure, though, but I don't think drink did this. It couldn't have been any of your men, could it?"

"Why do you think I'm here? I've come to bail them out. At least the ones your crew didn't send to the hospital."

"Sorry about that."

"I bet you are. When I told you to let me know if you needed someone to bail you out, I assumed you knew I was joking."

"Well, I guess next time you'll have to be more specific." He rolled his feet off the cot and sat up, rubbing his head. "Between your men and the Yanks, I don't think I'll survive the week. You said something about bailing us out?"

"Yeah, this time. And there'd better not be a next time. This little display did over nine hundred dollars damage to the restaurant. I assume you and your men are good for your half?"

"Yes, sir, Colonel, we'll take care of it."

Col. Powell was waiting for Huck and Johnny when they left the jail.

Huck held out his hand. "Thanks for bailing us out, Colonel."

The Colonel ignored his offered hand. "Boys, you've got to quit busting up everything every time you come to town."

"But we didn't start it," Huck said. "It was probably some of your men—"

"I don't care who started it. Dammit, Finn, I know he's free and he's your friend," he said, pointing to Johnny. "He may even be a good man. But this is still Alabama and there's still a war on. You're going to get yourself or him or somebody killed. Now get your ship put back together and get out of town. And no more fights. Any more trouble and I'll restrict you and your men to your ship for the rest of your stay."

"Can you do that, Colonel?"

"Any more fights, and we'll sure as hell find out."

-25-

Becky was determined that this night was going to be perfect. Every detail would be checked and re-checked. And then checked again.

She had spent most of yesterday afternoon preparing his uniform. She was as proud of his lieutenant's bars as he was, and they would shine tonight.

Today, she would pamper herself. Her dress had been washed and every wrinkle ironed out. Her crinoline was re-hemmed with a delicate red lace. Just in case she kicked up her heels a little too high. Which she intended to do.

Her makeup would be simple. She didn't usually wear much, didn't need to. Tonight, just a touch of rouge to her lips and cheeks. Even though her cheeks would be rosy enough from the excitement and Tom would see to it that the rouge didn't stay on her lips too long. Probably not past the carriage ride to the dance. But she wouldn't mind.

The final, and most important, touch would be her hair. Many ladies preferred to wear theirs up, but Tom liked Becky's down. Every curl of her long blonde hair would be in place.

Becky lay in the tub, relaxing in the tepid water. Her wet hair hung over the edge, dripping lightly onto the floor. Lillian, her maid, dropped a towel on the floor and took her foot and dried it up.

Lillian was a free colored lady that worked for the Sawyers three days a week. She usually didn't work on Saturday, but today she wanted to help Becky get ready for the dance.

"Miss Becky, do you wants some more hot water?"

"No, Lillian, this is fine. It's just too hot today for a hot soak. I'm going to stay right here till it gets too cold to bear."

"Yessum, Miss Becky. I's gonna go make's some tea now. I'll lays your towel right here. You just call me when you's ready to get dressed."

"Tea sounds good, but you know what sounds even better? Lemonade. I'd love a glass of lemonade."

"Yessum, Miss Becky, I'll sees what I can do about that."

Becky wet the washcloth and draped it over her face. The lukewarm water felt good dripping on her neck and running down her chest.

About forty-five minutes later Lillian returned with two tall glasses of lemonade. Becky was curled up on the bed, wrapped in a towel.

"Alright Missy, time to get up. We gots to see to your hair right away. Mister Tom'll be home before you knows it." Becky just groaned and pulled a pillow over her head. Lillian quietly walked to the other side of the bed and tickled Becky's feet. Becky giggled and pulled her feet away.

"Quit that, Lillian," she said as she threw the pillow at her.

"Quit, indeed. If'n you don't get up, I'll take a hickory to them pretty legs. And I's sure Mister Tom won't want no hickory marks on them legs tonight."

"Lillian! How dare you?" Becky said, her face turning red.

"I dares just fine, Missy. Now you gets over here sos I can fix your hair."

Becky huffed and puffed all the way to the chair in front of her dresser, pretending to pout. Lillian had become more than a maid. She was a friend. Too many times, when she was supposed to be tending to her duties, she and Becky would wind up talking about their problems. More particularly, their men folk.

Lillian had never married. She was going to one time, but he was sold off to a plantation in South Carolina and they never saw each other again.

She had a brother that worked on a farm down in Albany. She got to see him once or twice a year. She was working hard to save up enough to buy his freedom. Tom had helped make the arrangements with his owner. Another year and a half and he would be free. Or sooner, if the Yankees hurried. She wasn't sure she liked the idea of all those Yankees coming to town, but she did like the sound of a proclamation that President Lincoln signed.

And Lillian listened when Becky talked. Recently though, most of their talks ended up with Becky in tears. She couldn't stop worrying about Tom going into battle. And it appeared that it would be soon.

"Miss Becky, your hairs done turned out just fine," Lillian said as she walked around in front of Becky to get the full effect. "Miss Becky," she gasped, "what's you crying for? I done told you that you looks just fine."

"Oh, Lillian, our time is getting so short. He'll be off to the war soon, I just know it." Becky buried her face in her hands.

"Now don't you crys no more. Mister Tom is gonna do just fine off at that old war. He's gonna do just fine."

"I'm just so scared. I don't want him to go."

"Missy, you knows that he gots to go. But he'll come home again, for sure."

"I wish I could be sure," Becky said, as she tried to stop crying.

"You can count on it. The good Lord'll bring home a man like Mister Tom. Ain't gots no need to leave him lying around no old battlefield. Don't make no sense. He'll be coming home all right. Now you stops that crying and messing up your pretty face. Mister Tom don't need to see you worrying so. Ain't no sense in that neither."

Lillian handed her the wet cloth from the bath and a towel. "Now wash up quick and put that pretty smile of yours back on. We gots to get you dressed. Mister Tom be home any minute."

"Oh, Lillian, I hope tonight is just perfect," Becky said, beginning to return to her usual bubbly self.

"It will be, Missy. I just knows it."

"I hope it don't rain. It's been a little cloudy today."

"Well, my old bones tells me it's gonna rain, but it shouldn't be till later tonight. Sos you be sure to carry a wrap for the ride home."

"Your old bones, indeed. You and your weather predictions."

"I's telling you to take a wrap. And don't sass old Lillian."

"Okay, okay. I'll take a wrap."

Becky got her mind off the war and started prattling a mile a minute about the dance. It was all Lillian could do to keep up with the "yes, Missys" and the "no, Missys."

Within thirty minutes, Becky was dressed and sitting by the window finishing her lemonade. When the carriage pulled up in front of the house, she hid behind the curtain so Tom couldn't see her.

All Tom had to remember to do was order the carriage. He was surprised that Becky had allowed him to do even that. He had spent the morning behind his desk at his office. Not that he had any cases to work on. He just didn't want to stay home.

His plan was to piddle around the office, take a long leisurely lunch and arrive at home just in time to dress and leave. He was afraid that if he arrived any earlier, he would get washed, ironed, and starched to death.

He slammed the front door and yelled "Becky, I'm home!" He wanted to be sure the ladies knew he was in the house. As he passed the parlor he saw Lillian collecting her things. "Hello, Lillian. Is it safe to come in yet?"

"Yessuh, Mister Tom, your lady's all ready. I's done my best and I's be leaving you alone now."

"Don't you want to wait and ride with us? We can drop you off at your place."

"How dares you, Mister Tom. Miss Becky don't want no other woman in her carriage tonight, even if'n she is an old colored woman."

"An old colored woman? Miss Lillian, you know you're the second-prettiest woman in Atlanta. What say I take you to the dance instead?"

"Mister Tom," she giggled, "don't make me have to take no hickory to you, too. Now you behave."

"Me *too*?"

"I swears, you two are the most misbehavenist young'uns I's ever did see. Now your clothes are all laid out in the kitchen. You gets yourself in there and gets dressed. And I's gonna gets myself on home."

"In the kitchen? I'm not dressing in the kitchen. I'm going up to my bedroom and dressing like a normal person."

"No suh, you ain't. Miss Becky wants to make her grand entrance, and you's gonna let her. Now do's like you done been told, and get in that kitchen and gets dressed."

"Yes, ma'am," Tom said, saluting, partly out of habit, partly out of fear of Lillian.

"You just hollers up at Miss Becky when you's dressed and go sit at the foot of the stairs. She'll be down directly."

Tom hurried into the kitchen and changed his clothes quickly. He didn't want to delay Becky's entrance any longer than necessary. He almost ran to the foot of the stairs.

"Becky, I'm ready! You can come down now!" He expected her to come bounding out of the bedroom instantly. But she didn't. He paced around for four or five minutes but finally gave up and sat down.

He didn't hear the bedroom door open. Becky was standing at the top of the stairs before he noticed. He jumped to his feet, one hand on the railing and one foot on the first step. His mouth dropped open. He had not seen her look this lovely since their wedding day.

Becky slowly descended the stairs, stopping two steps from the bottom. She reached out, placed her hand under his chin, and closed his mouth for him.

"Don't just stand there like a fool. Say something."

"I'm sorry," he said.

"For what?"

"We're not going to be able to go to the dance tonight."

"What?" she exclaimed.

"No, we can't go."

"Why? What's happened?" she asked, her hands on her hips.

"There's no way I'm letting you go out looking like that. I'm keeping you here all for myself," he grinned.

"Tom Sawyer, I oughta shoot you, scaring me like that, after all the trouble I've gone through to look good for you. Now let's get in that carriage and go have some fun. You did remember the carriage, didn't you?"

"Yes, your majesty."

"That's better. Now remember, walk two steps behind me at all times."

"Yes, your majesty."

It was a short ride to the hotel. Becky's lip rouge didn't survive the trip.

-26-

The ball was being held in the main dining room of the George Washington Hotel. Col. Fulton's wife had chaired the decoration committee. It really wasn't much of a committee. The Colonel had ordered a full platoon to assist her. When she got through with those soldiers, they weren't sure who was the harshest commanding officer, the Colonel or his wife.

Most of the furniture in the dining room had been carried upstairs and stored. Banners for each company, along with the brigade colors and the Stars and Bars, were hung from every available inch of wall space and draped over doorways.

In one corner of the lobby, between two rebel battle flags, stood three easels containing pictures of Robert E. Lee, Stonewall Jackson, and, of course, Colonel John Fulton. The third picture was maybe a stretch in some people's mind, but not to the men of the 24th Georgia.

Chairs were placed all around the walls and the refreshment tables, on one side of the room, were placed a few feet from the wall allowing for two serving lines. The three large floor-length windows on the opposite side of the room were left open to allow in the evening breeze and to permit the revelers to wander in and out from the veranda. The band was seated at the far end of the room. The center of the room was reserved for dancing.

When Tom and Becky arrived, the dance was already in full swing. Their carriage circled in and dropped them off at the front of the hotel. The receiving line extended out the door about four or five couples. Col. Fulton insisted that all his officers and wives parade by for a handshake and a pat on the back.

By the time they reached Col. Fulton, Becky's foot was already tapping time with the band. Tom wasn't much of a dancer, though he would do the slow ones. Becky would have to dance the jigs with the younger men. The ones that weren't as sophisticated as Tom. Or as scared.

"Lt. Sawyer, good to see you," said the Colonel.

"Sir, good to see you, too. Colonel, I don't know if you remember my wife-"

"Mrs. Sawyer, how good to see you again." The Colonel took her hand and bowed lightly over it. "Lieutenant, of course I remember her. You don't forget someone as lovely as she is. My dear girl, I've been meaning to ask . . . how did you get stuck with something as ugly as him?"

"Well, Colonel," she grinned, "pickings were mighty slim in Missouri. He was the best available."

"My condolences, ma'am."

"Thank you, Colonel."

"You're welcome. And call me John. With your permission, if I may be so bold, I'd appreciate it if you would do me the honor of saving me a dance."

"Okay . . . *John.*"

"Colonel," Tom said, taking Becky by the elbow and gently pushing her ahead, "if you're going to flirt with my wife, could you at least do it behind my back?"

The Colonel took Tom's offered hand. "Oh, I intend to do that, too," he laughed as he pumped Tom's arm. "I intend to do just that."

Tom led Becky toward the drink table. She slid her arm through his.

"The Colonel is a nice man, isn't he?" she said. "I really like him."

117

"Nice man, my eye. He's a big flirt. And I better not catch you dancing with him."

She pulled back. "Tom? Are you serious?"

He grinned. "Nah. It's just that everywhere I go . . . well . . . everywhere I take *you*, it's the same thing. All the men gawking, asking for dances, asking if they can get you something to drink. I swear, sometimes I wish I'd married an ugly girl."

She snuggled close and looked up into his eyes. "Really?"

He tried to look serious but couldn't. He laughed. "Nah."

The band started playing a slow tune and she started pulling him to the middle of the room. "Come on," she said.

"Can't we at least get some punch?" he asked, pointing to the drink table.

"No. Later. Dance with me now," she insisted. They danced through two slow songs and the way Becky looked up at him, he was glad he hadn't headed to the punch bowl first.

The band announced a jig and Tom excused himself. The lines were formed, the dancers joined hands, and the band took off at a clip. A tall, lanky, almost toothless fellow rocked back and forth, squeezing and jerking the concertina as if the outcome of the war depended on it. The fiddles and banjos were going at breakneck speed trying to keep up. The laughs and yells filled the grand old hotel.

Tom made his way to the punch bowl and received a knowing wink from the private that was serving the drinks. The punch seemed to have a little extra special flavoring. Not enough, though, to get Tom to dancing the jigs.

He crossed to the side of the room opposite the band to where Col. Fulton was talking to some of the other officers.

"Men," Tom heard the Colonel say, "I have never seen such a fight. They tore into each other. Such hollering and howling. They were clawing each other, covered in blood. The General bit his nose clean off. It was a fight to the death—"

"Bit his nose off?" Tom interrupted. "What battle was this?"

"Battle? It wasn't a battle. It was three weeks ago. I was out hunting with my coon dog, General, and he ran into a bobcat."

The Colonel and the other officers laughed at Tom's obvious misunderstanding.

"Oh. I thought you were talking about a recent battle," Tom explained, even though he didn't need to.

"Not tonight, Lieutenant. We talk about anything but the war. We've got good punch, good music, good friends, and lots of pretty ladies. Which reminds me, I've been promised a dance. If you'll excuse me, I'm going to go collect that promise. Keep Lt. Sawyer busy for a while, boys."

The Colonel handed his drink to Captain Tate, smoothed back his hair, adjusted his uniform, smiled at Tom, and joined the dance. The clapping and cheering by the officers just egged him on. He was a bad dancer, but at least he went all out.

Captain Tate nudged Tom with his elbow. "What do you think of our Colonel now?"

"Well, if he fights as well as he dances, we're in a lot of trouble. But at least we'll have fun watching it." Tom slapped the Captain on the back and headed off to the food table. It had been a long time since lunch and it was going to be a long night.

Tom fixed a plate of sliced ham, mashed potatoes, and fried tomatoes. After another trip past the punch bowl and the glassy-eyed private, he found a chair in a corner next to a frazzled-looking man leaning on a crutch. He placed his drink on the floor, crossed his legs and put his plate in his lap. He couldn't help grinning, wondering if this might be some of Mr. Littleton's famous pig.

Tom raised his fork to wave back at Becky, almost losing a piece of tomato. She waved every time she swung by, if she had a free hand. If not, she would roll her head to one side and try to get a glimpse of Tom, to make sure he wasn't getting jealous.

After a few bites and a swig of punch, Tom turned to speak to the man with the crutch. It was then that he realized the reason for the crutch. The man was missing a leg. Tom stopped with his mouth open, suddenly not knowing what to say. Fortunately, the man didn't acknowledge his attempt at conversation. Within a few minutes, Tom regained his composure and introduced himself to the man.

"They seem to be having a good time, don't they?" Tom said.

"Yeah, they do."

"I'm not much of a dancer, though, are you?"

"Uh, no," said the man, looking down at his folded pants leg. "At least not the fast stuff," he chuckled.

Tom couldn't hide his embarrassment. "I'm sorry. I didn't mean—"

"Don't worry, I needed a laugh. And that was about the dumbest thing anybody has said to me. And believe me, I've heard it all."

"How did you lose it?" Tom asked, trying to recover.

"I didn't lose it. I know exactly where it is. It's buried with about two hundred of my friends up in Tennessee. At least I walked away, sort of."

"It must have been a rough battle."

"Yep. That's why we we're running away from it."

"You were retreating?"

"Yeah. The Yanks were clobbering us on three sides. Our lines broke and it was every man for himself."

"That's when you got shot?"

"Shot? Hell, I didn't get shot. Damned quartermasters wagon ran over me. Cut my leg clean off. Smooth as a knife in butter. Been in the fighting over a year and no Yank had laid a hand on me. Done in by a wagon wheel."

Tom didn't know what to say. He took a few more bites and another sip of punch. The man stopped talking and was staring at him.

"Son, if you don't mind me saying, you don't look like you've seen much action."

"No, not yet. We've been training for about six months. We expect that we'll be called up any day now."

"What kind of training have you been doing?" asked the man.

"Well, the basic kind," Tom said, pulling on his collar. "You know, marching and target practice."

"Have you trained your men to shoot over their shoulders?"

"No. Why over their shoulders?"

"Over their shoulders as they're running from the Yanks."

"My men won't be running from the Yanks."

The man struggled to stand, propping on the chair and using the crutch to push himself up. He looked Tom in the eye without the slightest hint of a smile. "They will if they have any sense."

Tom sat quietly, thinking about the man's parting words. Becky took a break and stopped by the punch bowl. If she noticed the special flavoring in the punch, she didn't let on. When she sat beside Tom, she noticed that he was extra quiet. "What's the matter, hon?" she asked.

"Huh? Oh, nothing. I was just talking to an old soldier. He lost a leg. I guess I was just feeling sorry for him."

"Oh. Well, I don't want you in a bad mood tonight."

"No. No. I'm fine."

"Tom, if you want, I'll sit with you awhile."

"Uh-uh. No way. You're having a great time. And I love to watch you. How do you do it?"

"I just let the music move me around the floor."

"Well, that same music would move me till I tripped all over myself."

"You just have to learn to relax."

"I'm relaxed just fine. Now go. Go dance to your little heart's content."

"Okay, if you insist." She leaned over and gave him a peck on the cheek and returned to the dance line.

The party broke up just after midnight. The food was almost gone, and the punch bowl was empty. Tom and Becky were some of the last to leave. All of the band but one fiddle player had left. They had the floor to themselves for one final slow dance.

In the carriage, Tom held Becky tight. On the way home, it started to rain.

The next morning, a courier delivered the dispatch that Becky had feared and that her husband knew was well overdue. It was time for Tom to get into the war.

-27-

The fort was a forty-acre field just south of town. The only real structure on it was an old open-air shed about three times as big as a good-sized barn. The Baptists and the Methodists used to gather here, before the war, for their camp meetings. Not at the same time, of course. Since the war started, the sides had been boarded up to give a little more protection from the weather. Now it was used mostly for storing military supplies.

A couple of officers' tents were erected in front to serve as a headquarters. But Col. Fulton usually stayed in town at the house of a veteran who had gone off to the war last year and wouldn't be needing it anymore. The tents for the rest of the brigade were spread out behind the shed down by the creek.

The entire brigade, over three thousand men, was gathered here today. In the early morning darkness, dozens of campfires raised a glow over the hillside. Some of the men were taking down their tents, almost ready to pull out, while others were just beginning to stir about.

Camp was being broken a few companies at a time. It would take several trains to move the whole brigade and the first companies would move out before dawn for the short three-mile march to the depot. Company F would be among the first to leave.

Lt. Sawyer had already stowed his tent in the quartermaster's wagon and was finishing his last cup of coffee. He knocked out the last few drops against the butt of his hand and put the cup in his haversack.

Sergeant McDonnell was moving among the second platoon trying to hurry the men. It was a matter of pride to Tom that his platoon be ready before Captain Tate's. You also never wanted to make the Captain wait.

McDonnell found Tom warming his hands by the dying fire. "Lt., second platoon is ready, sir."

Tom stood and stretched. "Alright, get the men in formation, over there," he said, pointing to a clearing between the tents. "Right now."

Tom stood stolidly with his hands behind his back as the forty-eight men under his command fell into formation. They finished roll call before the first platoon fell in. Tom couldn't help smiling at the Captain.

After the first platoon finished roll call, Captain Tate shouted at Tom. "Lt., is second platoon ready?"

"Ready, sir! All men present and accounted for!"

"Well, don't just stand there—let's go catch a train!"

Tom saluted and turned and faced the men. "Company F, right face, column of fours, forward . . . march!"

They marched through the darkness. Past farmhouses that were barely more than specks of light where lanterns could be seen through windows.

Past recently harvested cornfields, the stalks trampled down, from which coveys of quail rushed up, startling the soldiers almost as much as they were startled.

As the dawn began to break, they passed half-picked fields of cotton whose white rows were being attacked by men, women, and children whose skin was as black as the night. Low, mournful singing could be heard, but none of the slaves paused to look up at the soldiers.

Only the dogs seemed to pay any attention. Some barked loudly, warning their masters of the advancing army. One farmer emerged from his house to curse at his dog for the commotion. A shrill yelp as the dog was disciplined brought laughs from the ranks.

As they entered the city, few passersby acknowledged their presence. Instead of heralding the untested heroes, many darted in an out between the companies hurrying off to their day's duties. The people of Atlanta had seen this too many times before.

But the soldiers still strutted proudly. Many of their wives and children were there to see them off so they had to put up a good show. Tom strutted more than most.

The procession came to a halt as the front of the line reached the depot. Once the engine finished hooking up to the additional cars on the sidetrack, they would fan out along the length of the train and board.

Tom knew that Becky would be among the crowd. He hoped he could find her and steal just one more kiss. He finally noticed her, standing on the west side of the street, squinting into the morning sun, trying to get a glimpse of him.

Tom started barking orders in a voice loud enough for her to hear, pretending he didn't know she was there. When he was sure she had heard him, he stopped and began looking through the crowd to find her. When their eyes met, he crossed the street, swept his hat off, threw his arm around her waist and, ignoring the watching crowd, pulled her close and kissed her. After a long kiss, he stepped back a step.

"Oh, excuse me, ma'am. I thought you were someone else. But if you don't mind my saying, that was a mighty good kiss. Is your husband in town?"

Taking her cue, she responded. "Why no sir, he's off at the war."

"Well, ma'am, I might be gone for a while and I was wondering, might I have another kiss, for luck?"

"Why sir, what kind of lady do you take me for?"

"This kind." He stepped close to her, put his hand under her chin, lifted her face up toward his, and kissed her gently. Their lips touched lightly as they stared into each other's eyes.

They were interrupted by a shout from the Captain.

"Lieutenant, time to board! Move your men up!"

"Yes, sir, Captain," Tom yelled back. He continued to stare into Becky's blue eyes. "Becky . . . I —"

"Sawyer! Move your ass!"

"Yes, sir, Captain," Tom said, as he put his hat back on and turned away from Becky.

"Tom Sawyer," she yelled after him, "you hurry home to me, you hear?"

He stopped and looked back one last time. "Looking like that," he said, "you can count on it."

-28-

The repairs to the *Spirit of the Storm* were almost complete. The holes in the hull were patched, the deck houses had been rebuilt, and a new coat of gray paint had been applied to the whole ship. And even though they hadn't been damaged in the fight, Huck had the engineer do some upgrades on the nine-year-old engines.

Huck had personally supervised the repairs to his ship. He had to know first-hand that she was ready to put to sea. The task had been very trying and, today, with the job winding down, he was taking it easy. He was perched atop the port paddle-box watching the installation of the new smokestack.

He was shirtless and his pants legs were rolled up, trying to stay as cool as possible. During the past few weeks, the heat had been almost unbearable. Several times a day, some unfortunate crewman would *fall* overboard. And of course, several of his brave comrades would dive in to rescue him. The crew had worked tirelessly so Huck tolerated these moments of respite. He had even fallen overboard a few times himself.

Jumping off the stern of his ship reminded Huck of the times he and Joey Harper had gone skinny-dipping off Jackson's Island. They had had some grand times growing up. He wondered what ever happened to Joey. He hadn't heard from him in several years.

Johnny startled him from his daydream. "Capt'n, the rest of the crew has arrived."

"Good. How many did we lose?" he said as he climbed down from the paddle-box.

"Four."

"Who?"

"Well, Smitty took a position on another boat."

"Good for him. Not a big loss."

"I'll have to agree. And young Williams heard that his brother got killed up in Virginia, so he decided to join the infantry and kill some Yanks. Clayton decided to go back to Mississippi and become a farmer again."

Huck laughed. "I just can't picture Clayton behind a plow."

"Me neither. He'll be back, I expect. And no one knows anything about Berry."

"Do we have enough replacements?"

"Three. We picked up one from the ship that came in two days ago. They're going to be doing some repairs for a while, and he didn't want to hang around in port. Also one of the local soldiers will be joining us. His term was up, and he thought he'd try his luck at sea."

"He isn't one of Col. Powell's men, is he?"

"I wasn't going to tell you that," Johnny said with a grin. "And we've got a young man, Douglas, from up around Knoxville."

"That's all? A veteran who's in a hurry to get out of town, and two landlubbers. Are you sure about this, Johnny?"

"We'll be all right. They seem real anxious to learn."

"Couldn't find anybody else, could you?"

"Not a soul," Johnny said, shaking his head. "Seems everybody is afraid to sail with you."

"Why?"

"For some strange reason, there's rumors going around that you're crazy."

Huck grinned and shook his head. "They're not rumors, Johnny."

At sunrise, the ship's whistle sent the crew scurrying from their berths. The cook had breakfast waiting. The men ate quickly and rushed to their posts. The new crewmen just tried to stay out of the way.

The deck was swarming with men. To the untrained eye, it would appear to be total chaos. But it was really a well-choreographed dance. A few key orders were shouted, but the men knew the routine.

As soon as they had enough steam, the *Spirit of the Storm* pulled away from the pier and headed south for a shakedown cruise to the mouth of the bay.

The ship weaved its way through the moorings, passing unmanned vessels, some of which appeared to have been abandoned. On a few, a single watchman could be seen stretched out on the deck, asleep at his post. One ship was making ready to move to the dock to be loaded. No one paid any attention to Huck's ship.

Within thirty minutes, they were at full speed. Huck had given the order to increase speed in increments: quarter-speed, half-speed, three-quarter-speed, and finally, full-speed. At each speed, he had received condition reports from men positioned throughout the ship.

Huck was standing in front of the pilothouse. From this position he could watch for snags and sandbars. And besides, he just loved the wind in his face.

The wind was low today and the water calm. A perfect day to push his ship to the limit.

"Capt'n," Johnny reported, "she's pushing fifteen, fifteen and a half knots. Pressure's holding good on the boilers. Looking good so far."

He removed his pipe from his mouth. "Good, Mr. Watson. Hold her right there till we get to the fort. If she's going to give, I'd rather it happen now. There does appear to be a slight tremor on the starboard side. Have the engineer look into it." Johnny nodded and relayed the order to a crewman who headed below.

The ship rode high and smooth all the way to the fort. Huck was about to give the order to turn around when a lookout yelled, "Capt'n, past the fort, I think it's a Yankee ship!"

Huck grabbed his spyglass and focused on the ship steaming by in the distance. The Stars and Stripes normally made his blood run cold. And hot at the same time. But today, it was just a banner on a distant vessel. "Not today, my Northern friend, not today," he muttered to himself. "Mr. Watson, come about. Take us back to the dock."

"Aye, Capt'n. Full stop!" Johnny shouted. The order to come about brought them to a near standstill. The port wheel continued to spin forward while the starboard wheel was reversed. The ship spun almost on its axis.

By mid-afternoon, the *Spirit of the Storm* was secured. There were smiles all around. They were back in business.

-29-

The train rolled along, headed north. It rocked from side to side as it picked up speed. The rattling as it crossed each joint of track became a consistent rhythm.

Many of the troops were already asleep. Some were finishing off their last portions of fresh food from home. From here on, it would be mostly hard tack.

For some of the younger men from farther out in the country, this was their first train ride. And maybe their last. Several sat and stared as the landscape flew past.

They had been rolling about an hour when Tom was summoned by Captain Tate. He joined the Captain in his car with the first platoon.

"You sent for me?"

"Yes, Lieutenant. Second platoon squared away back there?"

"Yes, sir. Settled down and resting." Tom sat on the bench opposite the Captain. "What are our orders?"

"Anxious to get into the fight?"

"Yep. I want to see if I can send some Yanks where they belong."

"Back north?"

"No. I had in mind a place that doesn't get quite that cold."

Captain Tate grinned and nodded in agreement. "Well, it looks like you'll get the chance to do just that." He handed

Tom a sheet of paper. "Colonel Fulton's taking us to join up with General Bushrod Johnson."

"Where's he?"

"He's with General Bragg and the Army of Tennessee just south of Chattanooga."

Tom looked down the list of the divisions they would be joining and let out a low whistle. "Capt'n, this is going to be big."

"Yep. Fifty thousand men, or better. Everybody that's anybody is going to be there, so we should have quite a party." He took the paper from Tom, folded it, and put it in his shirt pocket. "Tom, we've got a long ride ahead of us. We'll be making a few stops, so stay with your men and let me know if you have any problems. Try to keep their spirits up."

"I will," Tom laughed, "if I can keep them awake."

When Tom returned to his car he walked slowly down the aisle, taking time to look at each soldier. As with the first platoon, the men were sleeping, eating, or staring out the window. He came across one group of four, sitting facing each other, quietly playing cards. The hands were dealt onto a drumhead. As he walked by, a private spoke to him.

"Lieutenant, you look nervous."

"Why should I be nervous, Private Dollar?"

"We're going into battle in a few days."

"Oh that," Tom said. "Nothing to be worried about. We'll go to Chattanooga, kill some Yanks, and then go home again."

"Lieutenant?" asked Sergeant McDonnell, who looked a little pale and wasn't his usual boisterous self.

"Yes, Sergeant?"

"Are you scared?"

"Scared? Scared of what?"

"Dying."

"No, not really. Believe it or not, I've already been dead once. Even went to my own funeral."

"Look out boys, here comes another of Tom's tall tales," said Private Koch.

"No, seriously. Me and two other boys ran away from home and everybody thought we were dead. I sneaked back home one night and listened to them plan our funeral. We timed it just right, came marching down the aisle just as the preacher was declaring what good boys we'd been."

"Was everybody surprised?" asked the fourth card player, a Private Henderson.

"And how. They were so glad to see us they nearly beat us to death."

The four soldiers laughed lightly. A couple others that appeared to be asleep, with their hats pulled down low over their faces, could be seen smiling under the brims.

"Lieutenant," asked Dollar, "what's the scaredest you've ever been?"

"Oh that's easy. Once I was trapped for days in a cave with a murderer and my girlfriend."

"What happened?" asked Koch.

"When our candles burned out I tied one of them up and started kissing the other."

"Which one?"

"Well, when we were finally found, we hung my girlfriend and I married the murderer. Couldn't let a good kisser like that go to waste."

"Yeah, right," said the sergeant.

"So you were scared in the cave?" asked Henderson.

"No. I didn't get scared till later. My girlfriend's father was the local judge. He made us get married."

"Well," said Henderson, "that sounds like the proper thing to do, protecting her honor and all."

"Yeah, but we were only twelve."

The four card players laughed again.

"Lieutenant," said Dollar, "tell us about your wife."

"Yeah," said Koch, "I hear she's real easy on the eyes."

"Oh yeah," Tom said, "sure she's pretty. But she's a mean vicious woman. The Colonel was going to let me stay at home, but if I go face the Yanks, at least I'll have a chance."

They laughed again, but then grew quiet. Henderson spoke next.

"Lieutenant, what's going to happen in Chattanooga, really?"

"Sir," he said to the private who was almost twice his age, "we're going to win. We're going to defend our homes, our land, our families, our way of life. Men, we're trained, we're equipped, and we're going to be joining some of the best generals in this war. All we have to do is get our heads right and be ready to do this thing. Remember, a coward dies a thousand deaths."

"Or gets married just once," laughed the sergeant.

"What's that supposed to mean?" Tom asked, not getting the joke.

"I don't know, but it sounded funny."

Tom waved off the laughter and returned to his seat for some shuteye. He pulled his hat down low and closed his eyes. But he couldn't sleep.

These men . . . his men . . . were scared. The time they had spent together training now seemed like a game. But he must now lead them into battle. Some of them, maybe a lot, wouldn't be coming home.

He was scared. The games were over.

The train eased to a stop at Cass Station. Some of the men were already standing in the aisle before the train came to a stop. They had to grab the backs of the seats to keep from losing their balance as the car rocked back slightly.

"Men," Tom shouted, "we're taking on coal and water so we'll be here awhile. You can stretch your legs, but don't wander off too far. And you better come running at the first whistle."

Rumors had spread through the ranks about a saloon. The men were anxious to find out if they were true. Sergeant McDonnell waved at Tom as he stepped from the train. "Lieutenant, care to join us for a drink?"

"Well, the Captain did tell me to keep an eye on ya'll. Men, I've been training for months to lead you, so follow me."

Their spirits rose as they headed off in the direction of the saloon. They didn't know when they'd pass another one, so they had to take advantage of the opportunity.

As they passed the depot office they came to a small village of tents being used as a field hospital. The sides on most of the tents were rolled up to allow in the fresh air. Men were scattered around on cots waiting for the next train south.

Some of the wounded were seated on their cots, bent over, their heads in their hands. Several only had one hand to rest their head on.

Some sat staring straight ahead, as if in a trance. Others were nervously looking from side to side as if expecting the next attack. A few sat with bandages across their eyes, head erect, listening intently to the sounds around them, seeing nothing.

Tom's group stopped in the middle of the street. Their jovial conversation turned to stunned silence. As they stared at the human destruction before them, Tom felt the need to say something to his men.

"There sits the South's finest. Heroes every one," he said.

"Lieutenant," Henderson asked, "doesn't this make you want to run?"

"You better believe it, Henderson. Straight to the Yanks and make them bleed for this. This has been going on for over two years, and it's time we put a stop to it. If we hit them hard enough, maybe we can do just that."

Moans could be heard coming from several tents. Screams could be heard coming from one, a surgeon's tent.

They turned and continued towards the saloon. They still wanted that drink, but for a different reason now.

-30-

The first companies of the 24th Georgia Volunteers arrived in Ringgold before sunset. Orders were shouted, many in curses, as the men hurried to unload the train.

The companies began falling into formation in the middle of the street. Tom completed the roll call of F Company while Captain Tate met with the senior officers for their orders. He returned shortly with the good news.

"Men, we don't have far to march tonight. We're camping just outside of town. Lieutenant Sawyer, take the men down that road, about a half-mile. You'll see other troops already there. I'm to stay behind and assist the rest of the brigade as they roll in. I'll see you first light." They exchanged salutes and the Captain headed back to the depot.

As they made their way out of town, they passed a large tent erected in a clearing. Singing could be heard coming from inside. Private Dollar spoke up from the ranks.

"Lieutenant, what's going on over there?"

"Private, that looks like an old-fashioned camp meeting."

"A camp meeting?" Henderson said.

"Yep, a camp meeting. I've heard that some of these preachers follow the army around holding revivals," Tom explained.

"A camp meeting," Koch said. "You mean a bunch of Bible-bangers trying to save people?"

"That about sums it up," Tom answered.

"If they want to help save us," Koch continued, "they need to put down those Bibles and get a gun and come with us."

"They don't see things that way," Tom said. "They're more concerned about eternity than just winning some battle tomorrow."

"Lieutenant," Henderson asked, "you gonna go to the meeting?"

"I might drop by, just to see the show. Some of these holy-rollers can really get excited sometimes."

"Well, you won't catch me down there," Koch said. "That Jesus stuff scares me stiff. Who needs it?" Several of the men laughed, in agreement with him.

"Suit yourselves, boys," Tom said. "Just don't let the devil get you." Laughter rippled through the ranks again.

Camp was quiet this night. Very little conversation could be heard. A harmonica here, a jaws harp there. In the distance, someone strummed an out-of-tune guitar.

Before he turned in for the night, Tom decided to visit the big tent. Aunt Polly had been able to instill into him a little more fear of God than of Yankees. He figured it had been a while and he might need to take care of some things before he went into battle. Just in case.

The tent was packed. Tom had to stand in the back. He removed his hat and joined in with the lady leading the troops in a chorus of *Amazing Grace*. This congregation seemed to sing more earnestly than Tom remembered the congregation in St. Petersburg ever singing. Maybe they thought they were just a little closer to heaven. Or hell.

As the preacher took over and started describing the benefits of missing eternal hell fire, Tom let his eyes drift around the tent. In the flickering lantern light he saw some of the men who swore not to come. He smiled when he saw

Private Dollar sitting, listening intently, wiping tears from his cheeks.

Tom looked around for the rest of the poker foursome. He realized Private Koch was seated two rows in front of where he was standing. Koch was bent over in his seat with his face buried in his hands. He would rise up occasionally and look toward the pulpit. When the preacher asked for a show of hands requesting prayer, his was the first hand up.

Tom found another, Sergeant McDonnell, standing to the side, smiling and nodding his head in agreement with the proceedings. Tom wondered if the fourth partner was there. He looked around the tent but couldn't find him.

Everybody's attention was drawn down front where a salvation was happening. The preacher was standing over some lost soul with his hand on the penitent's head and his other hand holding a Bible in the air, poised as if to strike Satan out of him by force if he wavered at the last minute. Shouting from the front of the tent told Tom the struggle was over and the Lord had won.

The soldier stood up and was hugged by a group of saints dressed in gray. He turned and headed back to his seat. It was Private Henderson.

Probably wouldn't be any poker played in that tent tonight, Tom thought.

Morning found several thousand men breaking camp and preparing to march. Captain Tate approached a group from F Company standing around a campfire.

"Couter up, gentlemen. Let's go welcome the Yanks to Georgia."

"Where we headed, Capt'n?" Tom asked.

"West. Place called Chickamauga Creek"

"Chickamauga," said Sergeant McDonnell. "What kind of word is that?"

"Funny. Same question we asked the Colonel last night. It's Cherokee. It means river of death."

-31-

A knock at his cabin door interrupted Huck. He looked up from his cargo manifest.

"Capt'n, excuse me sir."

"Yes, Douglas."

"Sir, there's a Colonel Powell here to see you."

"Colonel Powell? Damn! What have you men done now? Show him below."

Colonel Powell stuck his head in the doorway and Douglas stepped aside. "I'm already below, Capt'n."

"Oh. Well, come on in and give me the bad news."

"I find it hard to believe myself, but that's not why I'm here," he said as they shook hands.

"Well, in that case, welcome. Take a load off," Huck said, motioning to a chair.

The two men sat, this time with Huck behind the desk.

"It looks like you're about ready to sail again. Headed back out soon?"

"We plan to leave by the end of the week. That should make you happy."

"Yeah, makes my job easier. I noticed you don't have any masts. You're not going to run without sails are you?"

"No. They're being remounted tomorrow. My engines have never failed, but it still feels good having a backup."

"I bet. Where're you headed?"

"Nassau. Should be able to pick up a return cargo quickly."

"Good. Good. By the way, I could swear I saw one of my men loading your boat. Are you stealing my men now?"

"Colonel, you know what they say. If you can't beat them, join them. He just wanted to be on a winning team."

"One victory in a barroom brawl doesn't make a winning team."

"Care to try for best two out of three?"

"No. I think we'll reserve our fighting for the Yanks."

"Colonel, I'm glad you came by today. Saves me a trip down to the fort. I wonder if your signal corps could be ready Friday night, say around midnight, to light the way out?"

"No problem." He leaned over the desk and picked up a blank piece of paper and started writing. "These are the new light signals. We changed the sequences since your last visit."

"Thanks." After reviewing the Colonel's notes, Huck jotted a few notes on another piece of paper. "We'll be running without lights. We'll respond with short whistles, in this order."

The Colonel pocketed his instructions and settled back in his seat, making no effort to leave. He seemed to have something serious on his mind.

"Well," Huck said with a sly smile. "given our long personal friendship, I'm reasonably sure this isn't a social call. What can I do for you?"

"You're right." He crossed his legs and fidgeted with the hem of his pants. "Huck, as long as I've known you, I've figured you for just another privateer. Out for yourself and a quick buck. But your last run, you delivering that pouch to me, has got me thinking that I may have pegged you all wrong."

"Probably not," Huck shook his head.

"I think so. I believe now that you're a man that can be trusted."

"You take that back."

"Take that back? Why? That's a compliment."

"Sure, if it stops there. But I feel you're about to trust me *with* something, and that's the part I'm not going to like."

140

The Colonel chuckled. "You may be right. Huck, I need you to deliver something to a friend of mine in Nassau."

"Another pouch that I could get hanged over?"

"No, just a short message for you to memorize."

"Ok. Fire."

"The message is: Alligator at six, arrive by dawn, black by three, 1500, death if crossing made."

Huck started to repeat the message. "Alligator at six, arrive . . ." He frowned. "I better write this down." He reached for a piece of paper.

"No, you can't write this down."

"I'll have to till I get it memorized."

"Okay, but be sure you destroy it as soon as possible."

"Sure. Now, say that again."

"Alligator at six, arrive by dawn, black by three, 1500, death if crossing made."

Huck scribbled the message. "That makes no sense."

"It's not supposed to. Just deliver it. Inquire with the owner of the King George Inn. Ask for Mr. Shakespeare. He will respond by calling you Prince William. Tall ugly guy, looks a lot like Lincoln. And don't tell that message to anyone else. They may know the code."

"I don't suppose you'll tell me what all that means?"

"Nope. Not this time. Trust me," the Colonel said, rising and extending his hand to Huck, "this time, you don't want to know." They shook hands and the Colonel left without another word.

141

-32-

The *Spirit of the Storm* was loaded and ready to put to sea. It had been a long two months and everyone on board was anxious. And the weather was just right.

"Mr. Watson, there's no moon and it's raining."

"Aye, Captain."

"Perfect conditions, I'd have to say."

"Aye, Captain, absolutely perfect."

"Is the ship secure, Mr. Watson?"

"Yes, sir. Cargo secure. Hold full of coal. All hands present and accounted for."

"Well, Mr. Watson, get up a head of steam. Let's get to the islands."

"Aye, aye, sir!" Johnny exclaimed with a big grin. He was headed home.

Colonel Powell's signal corps was positioned along their route in small boats. They waved red, white, and green lanterns, in various intervals and combinations. Each secret signal told Huck how far he was from the bank, the fort, and the mouth of the bay. Short whistles from the bosun's mate were their only response.

It was after midnight when they approached Ft. Morgan. They could just make out the silhouette of the fort in the fog.

142

They passed close enough to the fort for shouts of good luck to be heard.

The sound of the cannon startled all on board. It took a few seconds for Huck to realize that Colonel Powell was mocking him with a salute.

"Good, Colonel, alert the whole damn Union Navy that we're leaving port."

If there were any Yanks nearby, they didn't respond. The *Spirit of the Storm* slipped into the night.

-33-

The color guards led the way, their banners flying high. The regimental bands played martial tunes and old standards. The men followed, thousands of feet clomping in rhythm, marching to the front.

Tom had been waiting for this day for months. Training for the opportunity to exact some justice, some measure of revenge. The invasion had to be stopped. He knew, he felt it deep down inside, that he was helping make history. Today, the enemy would pay.

Around nine-thirty, while still several miles from the front, they heard the artillery announce the beginning of the struggle. A cheer went up from the ranks as the men assumed it was their cannons they heard.

As they got closer they could make out the sounds of musket fire. The men grew quieter with every mile crossed.

When they were less than a mile from the battle, they topped a rise in the road and passed an artillery company situated in a clearing. Tom had never seen cannons fired so earnestly. The crews were reloading in less than a minute. It gave him a sense of relief to think the enemy might be pinned down by the barrage.

The column of reinforcements reached Pea Vine Ridge shortly after noon. Trees and thick undergrowth blocked their view of the battle, but clouds of smoke and the smell of gunpowder were proof enough that they had arrived at the front.

Colonel Fulton and the other brigade commanders rode ahead to find General Johnson. The long gray line of troops came to a halt, waiting anxiously for the commands that could affect their very existence.

Tom stepped to the side of the road and sat down on a tree stump. He took a swig from his canteen, rinsing the dust from his mouth. He spit between his boots and took another swig. The warm water couldn't quench his thirst. He didn't know if it was the dust or his nerves.

Within twenty minutes the senior officers returned to their commands. Tom stood up, dusted off the seat of his pants, and fell into formation.

Captain Tate yelled at Tom. "Sawyer, we've been ordered to the right, to see if we can outflank the Yanks! We're to follow E Company! Make sure the second platoon keeps up! On the double quick!"

The company took off into the underbrush on the run. With the musket fire in front and the artillery barrage from behind, the added clanking of canteens and rattling of scabbards made it almost impossible to hear.

Tom tried to stay ahead of the second platoon but it was difficult to say exactly where his platoon was. Due to having to skirt briar patches and cross streams, by the time they reached the end of the Confederate battle line, he had lost sight of most of his men. He found Captain Tate trying to organize the remnants of their company.

"Lieutenant! Take a couple men and go find the rest of F Company! We'll form up right here!"

Tom saluted without answering. He motioned to Sergeant McDonnell to follow. "Sergeant! Take a man and go in that direction. I'll go this way. Get all of F Company, and anybody else you see running around out there, back here now!" Tom grabbed a young private who was lying on the ground behind a tree. "Come with me soldier." The four men headed off in different directions.

When they returned, they were leading two lines of red-faced rebels. The lost men took serious ribbing from their friends.

"Your first time going into battle and you couldn't *find* the battle!"

"Over here, boys. Just look for the guys wearing blue, they'll tell you where to go!"

Tom didn't try to stop the ribbing. He thought that maybe the laughter would help calm their nerves. He reported back to the Captain.

"Capt'n, F Company in position. All men accounted for but two. And we picked up one who says he's from E Company."

"Tell him to stay with you. We'll get him back to his company later. Tom," Captain Tate said as he leaned in to talk directly into Tom's ear, "there've already been several charges up this hill that failed. If we get a break, we've got to be ready to push them back. We must take that bridge."

"Yes, sir, Capt'n. We'll be ready!"

Tom moved down the line until he was in front of the second platoon. He knelt on one knee, his back to his men, facing the enemy. He kept an eye on Captain Tate, awaiting the signal.

He thought of home. And Becky. The seconds dragged on. He tried to remember his training. Rehash all the tactics he had learned. But there wasn't time. The Captain gave the signal.

He stood and removed his sword from its scabbard. "Men, up!" he shouted. "Fix bayonets!"

The men rose as a unit, trance-like, and fixed bayonets. The sharp clanking stood out against the booming sounds of the guns, music-like.

"Together now!" Tom yelled. "Keep it tight! Follow me!" He continued to shout orders at the top of his lungs. He found it hard to shout, though, with his heart in his throat.

The second platoon began inching forward. They had not advanced more than a hundred feet when the first volley aimed at them rang out. Immediately, the Rebs began firing blindly into the underbrush ahead. Fortunately, the Yanks, too, were mostly firing blindly. Several volleys were exchanged, apparently without much effect.

In the distance, shrill rebel yells could be heard. Tom's men began to join in with the yell, both working themselves into a rage and at the same time sending a chill through the enemy. Shouts of defiance could be heard up and down the line.

The second platoon continued its gradual advance. The firing in front of them became sporadic. It suddenly appeared that their fire was not being returned. They began to push ahead at a half run.

Tom led his platoon around the base of Pea Vine Ridge. When they came into a clearing next to Chickamauga Creek, they could see a wave of blue retreating across Reeds Bridge with the center of Johnson's division bearing down on them. As they continued to fire into the fleeing Yanks, a cheer went up for the pursuers.

General Johnson's division continued to push the Union cavalry away from Reeds Bridge. Colonel Fulton's brigade was ordered to turn south towards Alexander's Bridge in an attempt to gain complete control of the creek.

The fighting there was brief. The Yanks were outflanked and retreated. The entire Confederate army was across the creek before sun-up.

Spirits were high in camp that night. Tom went from campfire to campfire congratulating his men. They felt that they had passed a test together. They had gone into battle and the enemy had fled before them. Tom had to cut short his celebration when he was summoned to the Captain's tent. When he entered the tent, Tom could tell the Captain was agitated about something.

"Lieutenant, have a seat. Do you have the final casualty report on your platoon?"

"Yes, sir. All men present and accounted for. No injuries."

"None?"

"No, sir."

"Good." The Captain laid his pen down and leaned back in his chair. "Lieutenant, what do you think of today's fight?"

"Terribly frightening. But I think the men held up well, being as it was our first time to see the elephant."

"Your first time to see the elephant!" the Captain yelled. He stood up and leaned over his table. "You ain't seen nothing yet! You think your men held up well, do you? Of course they did, they were hiding behind the trees!"

"Capt'n," Tom protested, "we were giving it all we had—"

"Lieutenant, you weren't fighting, you were playing hide and seek. And if that's all you've got, we're all in a hell of a lot of trouble. I gave the order to move up and the first platoon charged up that hill. I looked around and where were you? Still at the bottom of the ridge smelling the roses."

The Captain paused, and stepped around the table closer to Tom, his finger pointing as if to continue the harangue. He stopped, put both hands on his hips, and stared at Tom, shaking his head. After he calmed down he continued.

"I didn't want to say anything in front of the men, I know this was your first engagement. I know you didn't run, you're no coward, but you didn't attack either. You can't be so cautious. You should have pushed ahead today."

"You're concerned about your men, and I'm glad, but men die in battle. *Your* men will die in battle. If your men don't fight when we have the advantage, even though some will die, then they'll fight when the Yanks have the advantage, on their terms, and more of your men will die.

"Tom," the Captain continued, " we had the advantage, three or four to one today. We had an entire division against a single brigade. Before this is over, and probably come first light, all hell's gonna break loose around here. And you won't be able to hide behind any trees. You were taking target practice from a couple hundred feet away today. Tomorrow, you'll be able to look a Yank in the eye while you kill him. Or he kills you."

-34-

The morning dawned clear. And quiet. The men expected the fighting to begin at sunrise. But nothing happened.

Orders to attack were given, and ignored. The two great armies played hide and seek, neither knowing exactly where the other was.

Captain Tate and F Company, followed by several other companies of the 24th Georgia, marched along the Theford Road. No one spoke. The clanking of their equipment and the clomping of their feet were the only sounds giving away their location.

Captain Tate kept glancing at a rough-drawn map. The men knew better than to say anything, but their smiles revealed their thoughts. They were lost.

The Captain held up his hand for the column to stop and walked back to where Tom was standing with the second platoon. With pleading eyes, without saying a word, he looked at Tom to see if he had any ideas. Tom just smiled and shrugged his shoulders. He didn't know where they were either.

They were startled by the sounds of approaching horses and dove for the cover of the woods. Friendly gray uniforms rounding the curve ahead of them brought a few laughs of relief. A general and three staff officers rode up to Tom and the Captain. They jumped to attention and saluted.

"Captain," demanded the general, "where the hell are you supposed to be?"

"General, sir," the Captain said, looking at his map, "we're supposed to be headed towards Viniard's Field, above Lee and Gordon's mills. But we keep getting turned around in these woods. I can't tell if we're advancing or retreating."

The General clenched his teeth and let out a deep breath. "Captain," he said, pointing to the right and almost behind their column, "Viniard's Field is in that direction. Now turn your ass around and go find some Yankees!"

"But General, sir," the Captain stammered, "it's so thick in there, if we find someone, how can we be sure it's not our guys?"

"Well, Captain, just have your men give a Rebel yell. If someone starts shooting at you, charge in their direction."

The General ignored the Captain's salute and motioned for his officers to follow him. As they rode off, Private Dollar turned to Tom. "Who was that?" he asked.

"Now how do you expect me to know?" Tom asked. "I've never seen a general before."

The fight started before nine o'clock. It began as a distant thunder. It drew closer and louder as they inched forward through the underbrush. They were headed in the right direction this time.

They paused along the top of a small ridge to get their bearings. While they rested, traces of dark blue came into view, moving in the trees ahead of them.

Obeying hand signals, the men of the 24th Georgia knelt quietly. There was no shouted order of "fire". Captain Tate, using a rifle borrowed from one of his men, simply blew a Yankee lieutenant's brains out as he topped the crest of the hill. The regiment fired instantly on cue.

The Yankee officer's orders to return fire could barely be heard over the screams of pain as the Yanks fell. Their return volley inflicted little damage on the rebels.

"Charge! Charge!" Captain Tate ran out in front of F Company and started waving his troops ahead. Tom led the second platoon down the hill, screaming in anger and fear, sword drawn, revolver firing wildly.

Their attack caught the Yanks by surprise. They gave chase to the fleeing Yanks, barely looking at the dead and wounded enemy as they charged past.

Tom stopped at the top of the next hill to re-load. His platoon rushed past, shouts of victory pushing them on. He caught his breath and slowly counted out six shells from his pouch, trying to steady his hands.

Where was this terrible Union army? he thought. In three fights, all he had seen was their backsides as they ran away. The tide was turning. This would be a great victory for the South.

He shouted encouragement to the stragglers as they caught up and then fell in with them in the pursuit. They topped the next hill . . . only to meet their retreating comrades head-on.

"Fall back! Fall back!" Tom had never heard as many rifles fired at once. Boys in gray fell like wheat before a sickle. He froze at the sight.

"Fall back! Fall back!" Captain Tate staggered into Tom, almost knocking him down. His left arm hung by his side, useless, blood gushing and the bone protruding. "Fall back, Sawyer! Dammit, their reserves are cutting us to shreds! Get back atop that ridge and hold there!"

Tom helped the Captain across the ravine and back up the hill they had just rushed down. He paused every few steps to fire behind him at anything in blue.

Rushing down the next hill, they tripped over a wounded Yank and fell on top of him. "Help me, please!" the enemy begged, shaking uncontrollably, his hands holding his entrails in place, and a Confederate bayonet stuck in his shoulder.

Tom instinctively pointed his revolver at the man's head and pulled the trigger. The click startled both men. Tom's gun was empty.

Tom lay on the ground looking the man in the eye for a long, lonely moment as the Captain struggled to get back to his feet. The Yank stared back until he quit shaking. It took several seconds for Tom to realize the man was dead. But his eyes kept staring at Tom.

Tom made it to the top right behind the Captain. "Form up here, Sawyer! We've got to hold this spot!"

He kept shouting orders but Tom was already running along the crown of the hill trying to stop the retreat. A skirmish line began forming as more of the retreating Rebs made it back to their original position.

Tom tried to find the Captain for his next orders. He found him surrounded by several soldiers, lying on his back, looking up at the sky with a stunned expression on his face. His right arm, below the elbow, was gone.

Tom grabbed two soldiers and started shouting orders. "You two, get the Captain out of here! Find a doctor, quick! Move it!"

The two men picked up the Captain, one holding him by the legs, the other grabbing him under the arms. The Captain screamed, the pain bringing him around. "Put me down! Put me down!" he shouted, trying to stand. His men could only obey his orders.

"Captain," Tom yelled, "you're done here today, sir! You're in no shape—"

"I'm still in command, Sawyer, so shut the hell up. Somebody bandage me up," he yelled, looking down at what was left of his arms. "Send word for reinforcements! We've run slap into the whole damn Union army!"

The Captain walked between them and staggered towards the line. No one dared try to stop him.

He jerked backwards, knocked from his feet, almost flipping. One of the men that had been carrying him collapsed into a pile, lifeless. Tom was knocked into a tree. He slid down the trunk until he was sitting on the ground, unconscious.

Cool water from a canteen and someone lightly slapping his face began to bring Tom around. "Lieutenant," Tom heard someone shouting. "Lieutenant, what's our orders?!" Tom was jolted back to reality.

"What?"

"What's our orders?"

Tom put his hand to the burning sensation over his left ear. When he held his hand back out, it was covered in blood. "I've been shot," he said.

"Yep. But they only grazed you. You were lucky. Lieutenant, Captain's dead. You're in charge. So . . . what's our orders?"

Tom looked from man to man, his new responsibility slowly sinking in. "Keep the men down," he said. "We've got to hold here. We've got to have reinforcements now!"

Shrill yells from behind startled them, causing some of the men to whirl and aim their guns. Fresh troops, dressed in gray, charged past them, down the hill.

F Company cheered them on as they began pushing the Yanks back again. Henderson looked at Tom and smiled nervously. "You're good, Lieutenant. Real good."

Tom crawled over to the Captain. He had a puckered reddish-black hole above his left eye. The back of his head was gone. His eyes stared at Tom with the same empty stare. Tom sat up beside him and calmly re-loaded his revolver.

-35-

They won back and surrendered the same ground several times that morning. Neither army could hold it.

The men on both sides flung themselves headlong against their foe. All their anger and fear took over. They butchered each other with shells, bayonets, rifle butts, and knives. And when that failed, sticks, rocks, or their bare hands.

The Rebel yells, the screams of pain, the shouts and curses in anger, and the pleas for help from the wounded, continued throughout the day.

The dense woods became thinned out by the flying shells. Trees, two and three feet thick, were felled by the musket balls constantly striking them. Visibility improved and the slaughter became greater.

Nothing was natural today. Wild animals darted crazily amidst the struggle, frantically searching for a way out of this man-made hell. Birds were shot down in flight. Rabbits and squirrels snuggled beside the fallen men, searching for refuge.

At one point in the battle, a buck ran into Tom, knocking him down. For some reason, the animal stopped running. It stood in front of Tom, quivering, an antler broken off deep in its head, blood pouring from a huge hole in its hindquarters, and a ramrod sticking through its neck.

Tom's first thought was one of compassion, to put the animal out of its misery. He stood and placed the barrel of his revolver to its head, but paused. "Sorry, old boy," he said. "Can't spare the bullet."

More reinforcements for the Confederates finally forced the Yanks back past new ground to the edge of a clearing. Tom was running up and down the line shouting orders and encouragement to his men. "Pour it to 'em, men, pour it to 'em! We've got them on the run!"

Private Koch, standing, loading his musket, hollered at Tom. "Lieutenant, sir, we appreciate your encouraging words, sir, we really do. But if you'd be so kind as to pick up that there rifle and help us pour it to 'em, we'd think right kindly toward you. Sir."

Tom looked around and found the rifle, lying next to a dead man. He glanced at the previous owner. It was Private Dollar.

He sighted down the barrel at a young boy in blue hastily re-loading his gun. This isn't so different from target practice, he thought. The gun kicked against his shoulder and a cloud of smoke momentarily obscured his view. When it cleared, Tom saw the young boy lying backward across a fallen tree.

"How's that, Private?" Tom yelled. He looked back at Koch, who had fallen to his knees, his hands grasping his throat, blood oozing between his fingers. He looked at Tom helplessly . . . and fell face-first in the dirt. "Damn," Tom said.

An angry scream startled Tom. He jerked to the left just in time to see the bayonet rushing at him. He instinctively parried with the rifle, partially deflecting it. The bayonet went completely through his arm. Tom and the Yankee stood toe-to-toe, screaming at each other, the Yankee in anger, Tom in pain.

The Yankee pulled the hammer back on his rifle, still stuck in Tom's arm, and pulled the trigger. It misfired. Tom put his revolver to the man's forehead and pulled the trigger. It didn't misfire.

They fell together, the Yank still holding the rifle, the bayonet still stuck through Tom's arm. Tom screamed in pain, almost fainting, as the bayonet twisted against the bone.

Tom pried the rifle from the dead man's hands. He placed the butt between his feet, squeezed them together, and slowly pulled the bayonet free. He took his sword and cut a leg off the Yank's pants to use as a tourniquet.

When he had stopped most of the bleeding, he stood over the man, sword in hand, contemplating stabbing him for good measure. Instead, he just shook his head, muttered "Son of a bitch," and waded back into the battle.

Finally, the Union ranks broke and were in full retreat. Tom and F Company were chasing them as fast as they could run.

Their shouts of victory rang out. The shrill yells lifted their spirits once again. They could taste the victory.

They pushed the enemy back, past an abandoned schoolhouse on the edge of Viniard's Field. The Yanks ran without trying to shoot back. It was a killing time as fast as the Rebs could re-load.

But the chase was too easy and the Rebs pushed too far. The retreating Yanks led them right into Union reinforcements. Artillery reinforcements. The cannons stopped their advance cold.

Tom reacted quickly to withdraw his men from the cannons' range. "To the right," he yelled, "to the right! Quick! Fall back!" He was yelling at his sergeant. "Sergeant, back into the woods behind that building! Re-group on the other side of that ridge!"

The sergeant lead the retreat; Tom followed with what was left of his company. They had gotten no more than fifty yards into the cover of the woods when the screams of young children startled them.

The schoolhouse had not been abandoned. It was merely empty because the students and their teacher had hidden in the woods. Now they were trapped in the middle of the battle.

The Union cannons could still reach them and at least one shell struck them. Tom realized that to continue to retreat through this area would mean a slaughter of innocent children.

"Sergeant, stop! Stop! Have the men stop! We're going back to face the Yanks!"

"What? Lieutenant, you're crazy! That's suicide!"

"Yep, but if we don't, it's murder!"

The sergeant paused and heard the children's screams for the first time. He pondered this for just a moment. "Damn, damn, damn! I so wanted to see my family again!"

Tom and the sergeant started shouting the command to charge.

The charge surprised the Yanks. These Rebels were cut off from any reinforcements. An attack into the cannons was certain death. The charge was over in a matter of minutes.

The canister shot wiped out F Company and left Tom lying in a field, mingling his blood with the blood of his men, beneath the hot sun of a September day in Georgia.

-36-

West Sand Island was barely two hours behind them when they ran dead into the storm. By dawn they were fighting twelve-to-fifteen foot seas.

The crew worked in shifts through the night lashing down the deck cargo and bailing water out of the hold. Johnny, dripping wet, joined Huck in the pilothouse.

"How are things down below?" Huck asked.

"How are things? Some experts those were. That starboard hole is leaking something terrible. Pumps are handling it, though."

"Good. You okay? You look like a wet dog." Huck laughed as Johnny tried to shake the water out of his hair.

"Yeah, I'm fine." He walked over to the chart table. He had to lean a little to one side to keep from dripping on the charts. "How's our course holding?"

"Storm's pushing us a little to the north. It'll cost us a few extra hours, but we're okay."

Johnny's feet slipped on the wet deck as the ship rolled to starboard. He had to grab the chart table with both hands to stop his fall.

"Damn, son," Huck said, "you act like you've never been in a storm before."

"Plenty. Just never one with you at the helm." He grinned. "Why don't you let someone that knows what they're doing steer for a while?"

"I suppose you mean yourself."

"Yeah, me. I can handle this little shower. Besides, you look beat. Why don't you go below? Grab a couple hours' sleep."

Huck rubbed the back of his neck, rolling his head from side to side to relax his muscles. He tried to stifle a yawn. "I think I will. How are the men?"

"Most of them are fine. Wilson, Colonel Powell's man, is beginning to think that artillery was the place for him after all. Moaning and groaning all night, said something about putting him ashore."

"How about the other one . . . Douglas?"

"Sleeping like a baby."

"I will be shortly, too. If you can keep Wilson quiet. If not, throw him overboard."

"Aye, aye, sir. Just put that order in writing."

"Some friend you are." Within ten minutes, Huck was stretched out on his bunk asleep.

The storm passed before sundown. The *Spirit of the Storm* was making good time again, cutting through the calmer seas at fourteen knots. They were flying the Union Jack again, just in case they were sighted by any curious blockaders.

Johnny was standing at the stern, watching the sun set. Huck turned the helm over to the new Second Officer and joined him. The two men had spent many evenings at this rail. Usually without saying a word. The sound of the wind and the waves always relaxed them, particularly after a storm. Johnny interrupted the quiet.

"Huck, I've been thinking."

"It's about time."

"No, really. Margurite has been worrying about you. We've decided that we know what you need."

"And what would that be?"

"You need a good woman."

"And you needed help figuring that out? We all need a good woman. Besides, I thought we had already had several good women."

"No. I'm not talking about our lady friends in Savannah and Havana. You need to start thinking about settling down."

"Don't start trying to fix me up," Huck said, pointing his finger at Johnny.

Johnny held up his hands. "Okay, okay. She just wanted me to talk to you." He started to leave but turned back. "My Margurite has lots of nice friends. You should let me introduce you to them. You never know, you might meet the one you just don't want to live without."

After Johnny left, Huck leaned on the rail, looking out over the darkening waves and mumbled to himself, "That's the problem, Johnny, I already have."

The *Spirit of the Storm* dropped anchor in Nassau harbor just after noon. It would be tomorrow morning at the earliest before they could approach the dock. It was full of ships being loaded and unloaded.

It had only been a five-day sail from Mobile. But it had been a tense five days. Huck gave most of the crew shore leave and they headed to their favorite bar.

Whenever the *Spirit of the Storm* was in port, the crew stayed in the bars as much as they could. Even Johnny would go along sometimes, even though he didn't drink much. But when they were in Nassau, the men wouldn't even ask him to join them. They knew he was headed home. Home to his wife, Margurite.

He and Margurite had met three years earlier, before the war, on his second trip to Nassau. They were married four months later on his next trip.

The war meant increased risks for men in their line of work. And increased risks meant increased salaries. Johnny was able to buy her a cottage on the beach just outside of town. It was small, but she kept it clean. And he did the upkeep whenever he was in port. They would have to add on when children started arriving.

Johnny was always tired when he rejoined the ship... from all the work she had him do around the house. Or so he said. None of the crew believed him. After a night's rest, there was just too much spring in his step and he whistled a little too loudly while he went about his duties.

Johnny and Margurite always said their good-byes at home. Johnny said he didn't want to make a scene on the dock. But Margurite would sneak down and watch them leave. She would have sailed with them if Huck had allowed it.

In Nassau, Huck always took care of the loading and unloading, just to give Johnny and Margurite more time together. With that simple gesture, Huck had purchased a lifetime of loyalty.

Huck left a small party on board and headed off to find Mr. Shakespeare. He was thirsty, too, but he had a message to deliver before he could begin his leave.

The King George Inn was a favorite gathering place for ships' officers and shipping agents. Huck came here frequently but he didn't enjoy it. It was too stuffy for his tastes. He approached the registration desk and waited for the clerk to finish with the couple ahead of him.

"Yes sir, can I help you?"

"Yes, I need to speak to the owner," Huck said.

"I'm sorry. He's not in today. Is there something I can help you with?"

"I was told to speak to the owner. I have urgent business with him."

"He won't be back until tomorrow morning."

Huck eyed the clerk, who stared back with no expression on his face. He thought he recognized the clerk from his previous visits, but wasn't sure. He looked around the room trying to decide what to do.

"I'm trying to find someone," Huck finally said.

"What's the name? Maybe I can be of assistance."

"Shakespeare."

The clerk's eyebrows raised and he seemed a little more interested. "Captain, why don't you wait in the dining room. I'll see if there is anyone here by that name."

Huck entered the dining room, found a table in the corner, and ordered a coffee. Before he finished his second cup, a tall man in a long frock coat, led by the clerk, entered the room. The clerk pointed to Huck and the tall man approached his table.

"I believe you're waiting to see me, Captain?" he said.

"Maybe. Who are you?"

"I'm Shakespeare. And you must be Prince William."

"Yes, I'm the Prince." Huck just stared at him without standing to shake hands or offering him a seat.

"Is there something wrong?" Shakespeare asked.

"Uh . . . no. It's just that a friend of mine in Alabama said you look a lot like Mr. Lincoln. And boy was he right."

"Ah, how is Colonel Powell?"

"How did you know it was him?"

"He always says that, but I don't see it. Mind if I sit down?"

"No, by all means," Huck said, half rising.

"Me and the Colonel go back a long way. He's a good officer and a fine gentleman."

"Must be. He threw me out of town."

Shakespeare laughed. "I can imagine. I've heard about your crew."

"So you know who I am?"

"Yes. I just didn't know that you and the Colonel were . . . acquainted, shall we say."

"We've known each other for quite a while. But it's just recently that we've gotten . . . close, shall we say," Huck mimicked. "It's amazing how much respect you can gain in a single fist-fight."

"So you won?"

"Not me personally. I was busy being unconscious. My men picked up the slack, though."

Shakespeare waved off the waiter that approached their table and smiled at Huck. "Captain, I hate to seem rude, but I was headed out. What is it that you need to see me about?"

"The Colonel has a message for you."

"What is it?"

"Let me see if I can remember. Memorizing scriptures and other coded messages isn't my strong suit. Crocodile by three, arrive at six, 1500 will die if crossed."

"That makes no sense."

"That's what I told the Colonel."

"No. I know the code and that makes no sense. You'll have to try harder to remember."

"I remember a lot better after I've had something to relax me. This spy business makes me nervous."

"Okay." Shakespeare waved at the waiter across the room, calling him back. "Bring my friend a rum." They sat quietly as they waited for Huck's drink. Huck took a few long drinks, savoring the taste.

"Let me try again. Crocodile at, no, alligator. Alligator at six, that's it, arrive by . . . " Huck paused, taking another drink, "arrive by dawn, yes, arrive by dawn, black by three. Let me think now. 1400—no, *1500*, death if crossing made. Yeah, that's it."

"Now that at least makes sense," Shakespeare said as he stood to leave. "I'm sorry to cut our visit short but . . . I've got to see a man about a crocodile, or alligator," he said with a smile. "By the way, how is it that everybody else drinks to forget, but you drink to remember?"

"I don't know. Maybe I remembered all along, but I just didn't want you to forget to buy me a drink." Huck laughed and raised a toast as Shakespeare tossed a gold piece onto the table and stomped out of the room.

Huck decided to go ahead and order a meal. He would join his crew later, if they were still conscious and not in jail. They had to let rip when they could. Never know when a Yankee shell might ruin your plans.

It was then that Huck noticed two richly-dressed gentlemen sitting across the room. One was skinny, with a long dark beard and curly mustache. The other was tall, about six foot five, clean shaven, and was about the fattest person Huck had ever seen. They stood and crossed to his table.

"Captain Finn, do you mind if we join you?" said the beard.

"No, I suppose not." Huck gestured to two chairs. After they were seated, Huck continued. "Gentlemen, you have me at a disadvantage. You seem to know me, but I don't believe we've met."

"We haven't met," said the fat one. "It's our job to know things like that. But that one's easy. You're Captain Huckleberry Finn, famous blockade runner. Everyone in Nassau knows you and your crew. Your crew's skills at blockade running are almost as good as their skills at breaking up saloons."

"Thanks. It's good to be famous for something. What can I do for you? You have some cargo you need delivered?"

"Well . . . Captain," the beard spoke slowly, looking first at his companion, "as I said, we know you're a blockade runner, but from what we just observed, you're also a spy."

Huck stared at the man. "Excuse me?" he said.

"The man you were just talking to is a known Confederate spy. As soon as we catch him on American soil, we'll arrest him and hang him. We'd hate to see that happen to you."

"Why?"

"Why what?" asked the beard.

"Why would you hate to see that happen to me? It appears that you men are Yankees and I'd love to see you swing."

"Captain Finn, be careful-"

"No, you be careful. First of all, as you said," Huck said in a mocking tone, "this isn't American soil, so you have no authority here. Secondly, if you catch me on American soil, it will only be below the Mason-Dixon Line and I'll have you arrested because we're still free down South, or at least we will be until you Yanks win this damn war."

"Not everybody down South is free, Captain. You're fighting to keep nearly a third of your neighbors in slavery—"

"I'm not fighting for slavery. Very few of us are. We're fighting to keep sanctimonious asses like yourself from telling us what to do. And don't take that tone with me. You Yanks don't really care one way or the other about slavery."

"Sir, all men are created equal-"

"Really? My best friend, my First Mate, is a black man. We've known each other all our lives. We've shared food and quarters. And even an occasional woman. We've fought together and damn near died together a few times. If he walked into one of your fine Northern establishments, would you dine with him, or even let him in for that matter? Slavery will go away one day, without us killing each other. I risk my life not to keep the black man in slavery, but to keep all of us Southerners out of the slavery you Lincolnites are bringing. Anyway," Huck paused and took a drink, "for your information, he was only inquiring about passage back to Dixie."

"You should be more careful who you grant passage to," the fat one said.

"I don't discriminate. I take on people *and* Yankees. Shall I reserve you a cabin?"

"Very funny, Captain. Watch your step," said the beard as they rose to leave.

"I always do," Huck said, without looking up at them. The smile was gone from his face.

-38-

The bells started ringing just after dawn Sunday morning. Too early to be calling the worshipers to church.

However, they didn't awaken Becky. She had spent a sleepless night. She had gone to bed around nine, but by one, with sleep still eluding her, she had given up. She dressed and was puttering around the house.

The bells startled her. As she listened, a sense of dread came over her. She grabbed a shawl to ward off the morning chill and headed to Main Street.

She followed the crowd to the Baptist church. She regularly attended the Methodist, and Tom occasionally joined her, but she visited with the Baptists frequently and had many friends among their congregation. The Baptists Reverend Green and the Methodist pastor, the Reverend Giles, were seated together on the platform.

With them was the telegraph operator from the depot. The people gathered there could tell from their expressions that this was not going to be good news.

The church was filled to over-flowing. Many of the townspeople who didn't attend church regularly stood in the back trying to look pious, pretending that they fit in, which only made them stand out more. Several of the able-bodied men that had not volunteered were embarrassed to be safe at home and tried to hide in the crowd.

Some of the ladies had started crying. How could there already be bad news? Their men just left on Thursday.

Reverend Green approached the pulpit and the low buzz of conversation stopped. It seemed that even the children knew it was a time to be extra well-behaved.

"Brothers and sisters, Brother Samuel has a telegram from the Ringgold Station. Brother Samuel," Reverend Green motioned Samuel to the pulpit.

Samuel laid a folded piece of paper on the pulpit and nervously fished his glasses out of his shirt pocket, almost dropping them. He was a quiet man and didn't like to speak in public. He could have whispered today and still been heard. The congregation held its breath as he fidgeted with his glasses and unfolded the telegram.

He cleared his throat and began. "General Braggs Army of Tennessee has met the Army of the Cumberland at Chickamauga. Light fighting on Friday. Both armies completely engaged on Saturday. Fighting fierce."

Those last two words stung. Gasps of "Oh my God," and "Heaven help us," and "Jesus, Jesus" were heard around the room. One crusty old man standing in the back said "Where the hell is Chickamauga?" before he caught himself, then, "Sorry, but where is it?"

Samuel stepped down from the platform and strode quickly down the middle aisle. He stared at the floor trying to avoid eye contact with anyone. He was only the messenger but he felt guilty.

Reverend Green motioned to Reverend Giles who stepped to the pulpit and began to pray. He was usually long-winded in his prayers and sermons, but this prayer was short. The Methodists in the audience glanced at each other in surprise. They had barely gotten their eyes closed before they heard "Amen."

Reverend Giles returned to his seat. He removed his handkerchief and wiped the tears from his eyes. His son was in Company A of the 24th.

When neither preacher moved again to lead the gathering, the choir director took it upon himself to begin a song. In his haste and nervousness he chose a song that was inappropriate for the situation, "When They Ring The Golden Bells." The combined congregations should have been a voice strong enough to reach Heaven, but as they sang the third verse, the loudest voice was that of the choir director.

When our days shall know their number
When in death we sweetly slumber
When the King commands the spirit to be free
Never more with anguish laden
We shall reach that lovely aiden
When they ring the golden bells for you and me

Sensing his error, he quietly sat down. Once again, the only sounds were muffled crying and whispered prayers.

Finally, Mrs. Fulton rose to her feet. "Reverend Green, Reverend Giles, if I may."

"Yes, go ahead, Sister Fulton," said Reverend Green.

"I'd like to suggest that the ladies join me this afternoon at our church."

Reverend Green looked over at Reverend Giles who nodded in agreement. "I think that's a fine idea," said Reverend Green. "Ladies, please meet with Sister Fulton this afternoon at the Methodist Church to discuss . . . to make plans for . . . well, to be there for each other."

Silence returned to the building. A few people started to leave. Finally, everyone rose and began filing out. On the day they most needed to sing and pray, no one had it in them. They weren't mad at God. They just didn't know what to do.

As Becky strolled through town, she heard the story of the telegram told over and over. People from outside of town who had arrived too late for the meeting inquired of their friends who were eager to repeat the tale. Usually stories get exaggerated, but it was hard to improve on "both armies completely engaged."

169

The words kept echoing in her ears. Everywhere she turned, every street corner, in front of every store, groups, both large and small, the message was repeated.

She turned down an alley and walked several blocks off Main Street. At the back of a store she found an old crate and sat down. She leaned back against the lap-board siding and stared up into the sky.

There was a reason she had been unable to sleep last night. He had marched from her arms straight into the enemy. She had not received any word about Tom, but there are things that a wife can just sense. The tears flowed freely as she realized what had happened.

Someone shaking her shoulder brought her back to reality. "Ma'am, did you hear me?"

"What?" Becky was looking into one of the roughest faces she had ever seen. His hair was sticking out from under his battered hat, his face was unshaven and dirty, and his teeth, what were left of them, were rotten and green. If he hadn't spoken so politely, she would have screamed in terror.

"Ma'am, I said you don't need to be here. It's not safe. Not for a lady like you." He stared into her red, puffy eyes. Becky looked away. "Your man in that fight everyone's talking about?"

She looked back at him and nodded.

"I thought so. Ma'am, let's get you back where you belong, okay?"

She stood up and followed as he worked his way down alleys and side streets. They passed other rough characters who glared at her, some smiling evilly. But one look from green teeth told them to hold their tongue and keep their distance.

When they made it back to Main Street, he turned to Becky. "There you are, ma'am. Be more careful next time you're out for a walk."

"Thank you so much." She held out her hand. Green teeth just looked at it uncomfortably. He finally wiped his dirty hand on his even dirtier pants leg and took her hand lightly. "My name is Becky. My husband is Tom Sawyer. He's a lawyer with Killian and Killian. If we can ever be of assistance—"

"I know the Killians. Old man Killian was my cousin's lawyer when he was falsely accused of horse stealing."

"Oh my. Well, I hope he was acquitted."

"Nope, they hung him."

"Oh, that's terrible."

"Yeah. Well, he did plenty other things that he didn't get hung for, so I guess it evens out in the long run. He never was any good at thieving, and I told him so. I tried to teach him things, but he wouldn't listen. Had to do it his way. Steal anything, anytime. No planning at all."

"How do you know he was falsely accused then, if you say he was such a thief?"

"'Cause," he smiled sheepishly as he looked around to make sure no one else could hear. "'Cause, I'm the one who stole them."

"How could you let him take the blame, then?"

"Well, I went to visit him in jail the night before the hanging. And I was the only one who did. His own sisters wouldn't go visit him. When I went down there I was giving a right good amount of thinking about telling someone that I stole them horses. But I'd sold the horses the next day and drunk up and gambled all the money away so I didn't have any proof that I'd done it. And what with him crying and being so glad to see me, I just couldn't bring myself to tell him. We was good friends in life and I wanted it to stay that way in death."

Becky couldn't believe what she had heard. "It's not everybody that can have a friend like you," she said.

"Yes, ma'am, thank you," he said, missing her meaning. "Me and him were all right, all the way to the end. Well, Mrs. Sawyer, hope your man makes it back all right." He touched the brim of his hat and turned back down the alley.

Becky didn't know how long she had been walking or how long she had been in the alley. She was surprised when the town clock rang out twelve times. It had been hours since the meeting at the church. The gnawing pains in the pit of her stomach reminded her that she hadn't had anything to eat all day. She started walking towards home.

The streets were almost empty. By now most of the townspeople had heard the news. Usually, when something big happened, the streets would be jammed with people re-telling the story over and over. But most of the 24th Georgia Volunteer Regiment was from the Atlanta area. This big event was too close to home. Almost everyone knew someone who was in harm's way. Almost everyone knew someone who was in the Yankees' way.

As she neared the Methodist Church, she saw some of her friends filing in for the meeting with Mrs. Fulton. She crossed the street to avoid being seen. The ladies would have to have this meeting without her. Besides, they would only be discussing their fears of what might have happened to their men. And Becky already knew.

The tolling of the bells Tuesday afternoon brought news of another telegram from the Ringgold Station. The Army of Tennessee had won a great victory at Chickamauga. Becky didn't care.

It had taken only three weeks to obtain a cargo. Three weeks in harbor and Huck had to bail his crew out of jail only twice. But he didn't really mind. The crew always paid for any damages. And besides, the reputation they gained as fighters made the shipping agents more confident of their ability to get through the blockade. Or maybe they were just afraid to tell Huck no. Or it could be that they just wanted Huck's ship out of their port. Anyway, they always seemed to get cargoes quicker than the other ships.

They had been loaded for two days but Huck had decided to stay in port to ride out an approaching storm. And the wait had been good for the crew. It had given them time to clear their heads and nurse their wounds.

Huck was glad to be back at the helm, captaining his ship, not playing spy. He gave the order to weigh anchor and rang-down for half-speed.

The huge paddlewheels began slowly digging at the water, hesitantly, seeming at first to be afraid of it, but then building up determination and attacking it boldly. The boat surged ahead, anxious to be back at sea where she belonged.

They sounded the whistle as they passed other ships still at anchor, some preparing to follow them out, others still waiting to be loaded.

As they cleared the mouth of the harbor, they had to make way for a ship limping in. It was listing to port with hoses dangling off its deck pumping water out of its hold. All of its sail rigging was down, some completely gone, some scattered on deck.

Sometimes you run for it in bad weather hoping the clouds, the rain, and the fog will provide cover. Huck and the deck crew watched the once-mighty ship crawl into port, glad they had ridden this one out.

The next three days went smoothly. The crew spent the time making sure the deck cargo was secure and keeping a sharp lookout for the enemy. Twice they had seen ships in the distance but had slipped away before they were spotted. They didn't know if they were friend or foe, but no sense taking any chances.

During the day, the junior officers would steer the ship. At night, Huck and Johnny would take turns in the pilothouse. The goal at night was to run quiet and dark, stay on the right bearings, and try not to run into anything. With no moon, the ocean at night is a blackness most people never experience.

Dawn of the fourth day brought a welcome sight: Cumberland Island, off the southern coast of Georgia. Land is always a welcome sight to sailors, but in a war, your homeland is especially so. Huck's precise calculations had once again served them well.

"Good steering, Capt'n," Johnny said. "Right on the money. Again."

"Thanks, Mr. Watson," Huck said without lowering his spyglass. He didn't tell Johnny that he thought they were at least two miles farther out. He would have to re-check his calculations privately.

Suddenly, the Second Officer burst into the pilothouse. "Capt'n, come quick, fire in the hold!"

"What!"

"Fire! Someone started a fire!"

"A fire . . . take over! Johnny, come with me!" Huck and Johnny ran below and followed the sounds of the commotion to the ship's stern. Several crewmen were fighting a fire that was raging in one compartment. Three others were attacking Douglas with just as much vengeance.

Huck and Johnny waded into the melee. Huck caught an errant blow to his nose, causing him to step back for a moment, eyes watering. He stomped his foot in pain and, cursing the three attackers, started grabbing at arms and legs. Johnny had one seaman by the waist. In the struggle, he tripped and fell, his arms still wrapped around the man who then rolled on top of him.

"Break it up! Now! Break it up!" Huck shouted. The four men stopped fighting. The three attackers stood and turned to face Huck. Douglas was on his back on the deck. As he wiped blood out of his eye with his left hand, he reached slowly to his back pocket with his right.

Everyone stepped back when Huck pulled his revolver and pointed it at Douglas. "You better be reaching for a handkerchief." Douglas froze, staring down the barrel. He slowly held both hands up in the air.

"Johnny, and you, Wilson," Huck said, pointing to one of the fighters, "see to the fire. Now, what's going on here?" Both of the other fighters started talking at once. "One at a time. *You*," he said, pointing at one of the men.

"Capt'n, Douglas here was setting fire to the ship. We came below to check on the cargo and caught him."

"Is that so," Huck asked, looking at the other fighter.

"Aye, Capt'n."

"So you three just decided to beat him to death?"

"Capt'n, he's a Yankee. A damn Yankee spy. And . . . uh . . . we were afraid he was armed."

Huck looked down at Douglas. "Is what they say true? Did you set this fire on purpose?"

Douglas lay quietly on the deck, staring at the overhead.

"Man, you know what's in the next compartment, don't you? Gunpowder. Enough to blow this ship to pieces. We would all have been killed. Including you. Did you think about that?"

Douglas looked at Huck and wiped the blood from his face. "Captain, I would gladly die for my country."

"Well, you should be happy then. It looks like you're gonna get the chance."

"You gonna let us finish him, Capt'n?" asked one of the attackers.

"We can string him up from the yardarm," offered the other.

"No, gentlemen. We'll turn him over to the authorities in Savannah."

"Aw . . . come on Capt'n, let us at him."

"No. I'm saving him for a noose. Of course, when they get through questioning him, he'll wish you had finished him."

Johnny came back at that time. "Fire's under control, Capt'n. No serious damage. Lost a few crates of rifles, though."

"Men, tie him up. Johnny, go to my cabin and get the leg-irons. We'll chain him to a smokestack. If the Yanks attack, maybe they'll finish him for us." Wilson grabbed a piece of rope that was hanging on the bulkhead. They rolled Douglas over and tied his hands behind his back. The other two fighters helped Douglas to his feet and started to lead him topside.

The ship lurched to a sudden stop, knocking all of the men from their feet. As Huck struck the bulkhead his gun discharged. Instantly he was back up, running towards the helm shouting, "Reverse, reverse, full speed astern!"

Before Huck's command could have been heard, the engineer realized what had happened and was already preparing for a full reverse. By the time Huck made it to the pilothouse, both wheels were slashing wildly at the water, trying to pull the ship off the sand bar.

The sudden stop had thrown the Second Officer into the helm and knocked him from his feet. Huck was back at the helm before his thoughts cleared and he was able to stand.

176

"Sorry, Capt'n, didn't see the bar—"

"Later! Ring up full speed ahead on the port engine!" The Second Officer just stared at Huck, not understanding. "I said ring up full speed ahead on the port engine! Go ahead on one wheel and astern on the other. Then we'll swap it up. Try to wiggle our way off."

"Aye, aye, Capt'n." After a couple signals, the engineer got the message.

The ship seemed to go sideways as the direction was changed back and forth on the wheels. The wheels pounded furiously at the surf, stirring up the sand till it was impossible to see the bottom. Of course, they didn't need to see it; they knew exactly where it was.

Johnny returned to the pilothouse and began shouting orders to the lookouts. Huck grabbed a spyglass, too, and scanned the horizon for enemy ships. They were too far from any friendly forts. If they were spotted, they were finished.

Huck saw it a split second before the shout rang out. His heart almost stopped. "Ship to starboard!" yelled a lookout. "No more than four miles out!"

Huck ran to the starboard railing and looked down at the wheel. He had never seen it work so hard. But it wasn't enough. He motioned to Johnny to take over and ran below to the engine room. The engineer and the firemen were startled to see the captain.

"I need full speed now!" Huck shouted over the noise of the engines.

"Capt'n, we're already giving her all we can," the engineer yelled back.

"I need more, right now!" shouted Huck again.

"Capt'n, if we push her anymore, she'll blow!"

Huck stepped closer to the engineer and, talking directly into his ear, explained. "There's an enemy ship almost within range," pointing to the starboard side of the ship. "It doesn't matter if they blow us up or if we blow ourselves up. Do you understand?" The engineer nodded his head. Huck stepped back and pulled his revolver from its holster once again, pointed it at the engineer's head, and yelled, "Dammit, give me more speed right now or I'll shoot you where you stand."

The engineer and firemen had never worked so hard stoking the fires. The pressure quickly surpassed the safe operating ranges of the boilers. If they blew, they would rip the ship in half. No one anywhere near the engine room would know what hit them.

The ship shuddered and jerked as the wheels thrashed the water. It felt as though the wheels would rip themselves from their mountings.

Cheers from topside and a quick jerk felt throughout the ship told Huck that they were easing off the bar. The bells indicated that Johnny wanted full speed ahead. The engineer stopped the wheels and reversed their direction. They could feel the ship turning to go around the bar.

The engineer and firemen stopped feeding the fires and watched Huck as he left the engine room. Huck holstered his revolver, lightly touched the brim of his hat and closed the door behind him.

As Huck joined Johnny and the Second Officer in the pilothouse, they were startled by the sounds of the cannons. The shells fell short by over five hundred yards. If their ship held together this blockader would never catch them now.

Huck, Johnny, and the Second Officer exchanged smiles. They exhaled deep sighs of relief as they caught their breaths. "Too close," Huck said. "Too damn close."

He then remembered the fire. "Johnny, get Wilson to bring Douglas up on deck." Johnny sent a crewman to find Wilson, who reported immediately to the helm. "Wilson, chain Douglas to the fore smokestack. Let him look at that ship. That's as close as he's ever gonna be to friends again."

"That won't be necessary, Capt'n," Wilson said.

Huck spun around and glared at Wilson. "What did you say, sailor?"

"That won't be necessary, sir."

"Are you disobeying an order?"

"No, sir. It's just that that won't be necessary now."

"And why not?"

"'Cause he's dead, sir."

"Dead! I told you boys not to mess him up any more!"

"We didn't, sir. You did."

"What?"

"You shot him."

-40-

By Thursday, most of the smoke had cleared. The Union forces were driven back to Chattanooga. The Rebs celebrated their victory, tended to the wounded, and assessed the damage.

The staff officers met in General Johnson's tent to report on casualties. The price of victory had been high.

"John," the General asked Colonel Fulton, "what's the report on your brigade?"

"Well, our overall casualties pretty much mirror the ones we've heard so far, about twenty-five percent. Except for one company. Company F was totally wiped out, ninety-seven men. Eighty-one dead, six wounded, and ten missing or captured."

"What happened?" the General asked. Even with the great slaughter of this weekend, he had heard of no company that had been totally destroyed.

"They were in the thick of it, at the old schoolhouse, about here," the Colonel said, pointing to the map spread out before them. "Men from A and D Companies said they were pulling back from an artillery attack. Said they saw F Company turn and head right back into the cannons."

"Why?"

The Colonel just shook his head.

"Who was leading that unit?" asked the General.

"It appears that a Lieutenant Thomas Sawyer was in command. Their Captain was already dead. He led the charge. Fight was over in a couple minutes. The canister shot cut them to ribbons."

The General shook his head. "What could have possessed them to attack like that, only one company and with no support?"

"No idea, General. Sawyer survived but is seriously wounded. I haven't been able to talk to him yet, or any of his men."

"Well, talk to him as soon as you get a chance. I want to know what happened. If he recovers, we may need to make sure he's not put back in a command position. Such a pathetic waste of lives."

A major entered the tent and bent down to speak privately to the General. "Excuse me, General, sir, but there's a young lady here to see you."

"Major, can't you see we're busy here?" snapped the General.

The major stood up straight and spoke loudly enough for the others to hear. "Yes, sir, but I thought you might want to hear her story."

"And why is that?" asked the General.

"Says she was in the middle of some terrible fighting. At the old schoolhouse."

The General's eyebrows raised as he looked over the rim of his glasses. He glanced around the tent and could tell that the other officers were interested, too. "Well, Major, I guess you're right. Show her in."

The major returned with the young lady in tow. The officers stood as she entered. "General Johnson, this is Miss Reed. Miss Reed, General Johnson."

"Pleased to meet you, General."

"The pleasure's all mine, Miss Reed. Have a seat." He motioned to a chair that an officer had surrendered and re-positioned for her. She smiled at the officers and sat on the edge of the chair, her hands folded together in her lap.

"The Major says you have some information for me."

"Yes, General. I'm the schoolmistress, at the school at Viniard's Field."

"Really?"

"Yes. We had just started for the day when we heard the fighting begin. So we decided we had better go home. But when we got down the road a piece, we realized we were caught between the two armies. We tried to get back to the school, but we were cut off. Soldiers were everywhere." She bowed her head and tried to choke back her tears.

"It's okay, Miss," the General said. "What happened next?"

She took a deep breath. "Well, we were hiding in the woods when a bunch of men started running towards us. They weren't shooting. Just running. And then the explosions started. Three of my students were injured." She bowed her head again and covered her face with her hand.

"I'm so sorry," said the General. "Were they hurt badly?"

She nodded, tears flowing down her cheeks. "Pretty bad. One of them may not make it. And it's my fault."

"No, it's not your fault. Don't you think that for a minute. You couldn't have known." He paused as she tried to regain her composure. "What happened next?" he finally asked.

"But then, the soldiers turned and headed back in the direction they came from. And the explosions stopped. They went back to face the Yankees, to draw off the cannon fire."

The officers sat in stunned silence, the reason for the charge by F Company suddenly clear to them. Miss Reed continued.

"They were probably all killed. I just thought someone should know."

"Ma'am," the General said, "I appreciate you coming forward. This is very helpful information."

"You're welcome, General."

"As a matter of fact, we were just discussing those men. We didn't know what happened out there. And almost all of them were killed."

182

"I'm so sorry to hear that." She shook her head. "This just doesn't make any sense to me." She dabbed at the tears in the corners of her eyes.

"Well, truthfully, Miss Reed, your story is about the only thing here that does make sense."

She rose to leave. "Well, General, I know you're busy. I just thought you should know."

The General stood and extended his hand. "Major, have someone see her home. And Miss Reed, thanks again."

After Miss Reed left, the General and his staff officers sat in silence for several minutes. Finally, he rose and stood with his head down, his hands in his pockets. "Of all the things I've seen in this war. Such bravery, such honor, such sacrifice." He put on his coat and reached for his hat. "Gentlemen, if you'll excuse me, I'm going to go visit a hero."

-41-

General Johnson and Colonel Fulton walked the quarter-mile to the field hospital. Past the fresh mounds of dirt that marked the common graves, where dead men, and severed limbs from the surgeon's table, were buried together. Past tent after tent of injured men. Off to one side, in a row of tents, wounded prisoners were under guard. They finally found the right tent.

"Corporal," said the General, "I'm looking for a Lieutenant Thomas Sawyer, Company F, 24th Georgia Volunteers."

"Yes, sir, General. I'll check the log." It took several minutes for him to scan the patient list. "General, I believe you'll find him down at the second tent, in that direction. I don't know if he's in any condition for visitors, though."

"Well, we'll find out," said the General as they headed off in the direction the corporal pointed. They found Tom sharing a tent with several other wounded men. The sides of the tent were rolled up, allowing the breeze to cool the men as they slept in the shade.

Tom was startled when he opened his eyes to see the General standing over him. "Excuse me, General, sir, for not getting up," he said weakly.

"Don't worry about it, Lieutenant. Anyway, I'm the one who should rise when you enter the room."

"Sir?"

"Son, you're a hero, and in your first battle to boot."

"A hero? Sir, most of my men were killed—"

"I know. But those children weren't."

"So . . . you've heard?"

"Yep. We had a visit from the schoolmistress, just a little while ago. She told us all about it."

"I hope those kids are all okay."

"Yeah, they're fine," he lied. "You and your men did great. Saved them just in the nick of time."

"Good. Great." Tom smiled. "General, you would have been so proud of your troops. I can't imagine a braver company."

"I am proud. And you're right, I've never heard of a braver bunch of men."

"Thank you, sir. I just hope that us that survived can get back into the fight soon. I hear we've got them on the run, drove them back to Chattanooga. We might just turn this war around."

The General looked at Tom for a minute and then turned to Colonel Fulton and the other officers and doctors in the tent. "If you gentlemen don't mind, I'd like to speak to Lieutenant Sawyer alone." As the other men left the tent, the General looked around for a stool. He placed it close to Tom's cot so they could talk privately.

"Sawyer . . . may I call you Thomas?"

"Tom, sir."

"Okay . . . Tom. Son, there's no way we can defeat the Yanks."

"Sir, you better be sure General Lee don't hear you talking like that-"

"General Lee is the one who said it to me." He leaned in closer to Tom. "I'm not sure you understand our strategy. We have long believed that we can't defeat them on the field. There's too many of them, they have too much material. It's our goal to make the fight so bad and drag it out long enough to make them give up and go home."

"Sir, I can't believe you're telling me this."

"Now, Tom, I'm not trying to discourage you. Our plan may work. If Lincoln loses re-election, there are enough Northerners tired of this fighting that they may demand that the army withdraw and leave us alone. If Lincoln wins, though, that'll just about finish us. He means to see this thing through to the bitter end."

"Then we're fighting for nothing?"

"No, we're fighting for everything, and if we can crush Rosecrans' army now, that'll buy us some precious time. But if we don't, they'll probably regroup and head straight through Georgia.

"Then why aren't we attacking," Tom asked, "if we whipped them so?"

"That idiot Bragg. The only General I've ever met that can't accept victory. The men were chomping at the bit to take Chattanooga back but he was sulking in his tent. Probably just blew the greatest opportunity of his career."

"Well, General, what do we do?"

"Just what you said, get well and get back in the fight. Who knows, maybe Rosey'll blow it again for us. God knows we could use the help." Tom and the General spent several more minutes discussing the battle and all the details Tom could remember about the fight at the schoolhouse. The General finally rose to leave.

"Well, Tom, you look tired. I'll leave so you can get some rest. I just want you to know how proud I am, we all are, of what your company did back there. Never heard of anything like it."

"Thanks, General. And thanks for coming by. It's good to see you again."

"Again? We've met before?"

"Yes, sir. Your advice worked. We gave a Rebel yell, they started shooting and we charged. Every time we turned around we were finding Yanks."

It took a moment for the General to realize what Tom was talking about. "Oh, that was you. Are you sure my advice *worked?*" He looked at Tom's bandages and laughed lightly. "Those gunshots sure do burn, don't they?"

"Yes, sir. I was hoping I wouldn't get shot again."

"Again?"

"Yes, sir. I got shot once, when I was younger."

"How did that happen?"

"I was helping a slave escape—"

"You did what?"

"Well, kinda. He was already free but didn't know it. Nobody did but me. I was playing a trick on everybody. It's a long story."

"I'll have to hear that one some time. Well, Tom, let me know if there's anything I can do for you."

"Well, sir, now that you mention it," his face reddened a little, "there is one thing. Do you think that, while I'm mending, I could go home to Atlanta?"

"Sure thing, Captain, I'll draw up the pass. Hell, you can probably wait there for us. I'm sure ole Bragg'll retreat us all the way there."

"*Lieutenant*, sir," Tom corrected.

"No . . . *Captain*."

-42-

The ambulance ride to the train was the longest ride of Tom's life. They seemed to hit every hole and rut in the road. Tom almost envied the ones who passed out from the pain. He was relieved when he heard a train whistle and knew the trip was almost over.

The injured were loaded onto the train at Ringgold. There was no cheering crowd. The hustle and bustle that had occurred in Atlanta didn't happen today. Commands were given in hushed voices, almost whispers. And everyone seemed to be moving in slow motion.

The injured that could walk or sit up were given seats in passenger cars. Those on cots were loaded onto boxcars lined with three tiers that resembled shelves. They were stacked three high, one on top of the other.

Blood, pus from the infected wounds, urine, and even feces, dripped down from the top cots. The smells caused the men to become nauseated, causing even worse odors. The boxcars were cleaned after almost every trip, but the stench could not be removed.

Tom hoped there might be some breeze when the train started moving. Any breeze at all that might help clear the air.

He was on the second shelf, watching for any of his men to be loaded. He finally recognized a man that was being placed on the bottom shelf on the opposite side of the car.

"Sergeant McDonnell, is that you?"

"Yeah. Is that you, Lieutenant?"

"Sure is. How you doing?"

"Well, I've had worse days, but I can't remember when. But I'm better off than most of our company, so I hear."

"Yep, we took a beating." Tom lapsed into silence.

"Lieutenant," the sergeant said after a few minutes, "you okay?"

Tom searched for the right words. "Sergeant, I'm so sorry for what happened."

"Sorry? Don't be. You didn't have any choice. We all knew that, as soon as you gave the order. Those children had to be saved. I did what I would expect any other soldier to do if my children had been trapped there. I'm mad at the Yanks, but not you. Anybody that's mad at you is way outta line."

"I just feel so guilty. Maybe if I'd given some other order..."

"Lieutenant, it's been several days now. Have you figured out any other order you could have given?"

"Well, no..."

"And you won't either. I've thought of nothing else but that charge, and I can't come up with any other option. We were trapped and had two choices, save ourselves or save the children. No decision to make."

"Thanks," Tom said, without sounding like he meant it. He changed the subject. "What are the doctors telling you?"

"Well," he reached up and touched the bandages across his eyes, "they're pretty sure I've lost the right one, but they do have a little hope for the left one."

"Maybe you'll get to see your family again after all."

"Maybe. Anyway, I'll be with them. And I somehow managed to break a leg. How about you, Lieutenant?"

"I'll be all right. Took some canister shot in my gut and leg, and a bayonet in my arm. Somebody bounced a mini ball off my head, too. I was lucky, I guess."

"We were the lucky ones, for sure."

Tom chuckled. "Sad state of affairs when the two of us were the lucky ones."

"Yep," said the sergeant as he laughed in agreement. "Lieutenant, I know what we need. You'll have to tell us some more of your tall tales."

"Okay. But they're not tall tales. They're true stories, every word."

"There you go, starting another one."

"Watch out now, Sergeant."

The boxcar lurched as the train pulled out of the station, causing loud groans, some screams, and several shouted curses as the men responded to the pain. They either died down or were drowned out by the noise as the train picked up speed. Soon, very little could be heard over the sounds of the wheels on the tracks and the rattling of the boxcar.

Tom looked around the boxcar loaded with wounded. He couldn't help thinking that some of these men would probably ride this train all the way to Heaven. He thought about the price these men had paid. They fought heroically. But were they heroes, or just fools? Fools to face an enemy that couldn't be stopped, only delayed. Beat them, crush them, and more will come tomorrow. They'll keep coming until they get tired and go home, or until you're beaten. A military strategy based on the political whims of the enemy's homefront. In theory, it could work, but could they hold out? As he pondered these thoughts, the rocking of the car lulled him to sleep.

Movement in the car awakened Tom. They had stopped to take on coal and water. And to unload some unfortunate passengers. They were on a side-track at Adairsville and would have to wait a couple hours until a north-bound train passed.

Tom, Sergeant McDonnell, and several of the injured that could tolerate being moved were carried out onto the loading dock to get some fresh air. Tom's cot was suspended between some crates that were stacked by the train.

Tom looked past the tracks and surrounding buildings at the beautiful countryside. The leaves would start turning soon and color would be everywhere, mingled with the evergreen of the pines. And soon, an eerie red would be added to the leaves on the ground. They had been passing towns and villages yet unscarred by battle. But that would change soon.

Food was being stacked nearby, waiting for the next train north. Several Yankee prisoners were helping. One stopped in front of Tom and the sergeant.

Tom glared at him. "Yes, Corporal, what do you want?"

"Lieutenant, sir, I just need those crates you're on, when you're through with them. But take your time, I could use a rest."

Tom looked at the young Yankee. His uniform ragged and thread-bare. His toes were sticking out of his right boot. His hair was disheveled and greasy. His pants appeared to be about two sizes too large. He couldn't have been more than nineteen, Tom thought.

Tom had spent the last two years hating anything remotely related to the Union. He suddenly felt that he had no more hate left. "Well, sit down. Take a load off," he said softly.

"Thank you, sir." The corporal up-ended a crate and sat down beside the sergeant.

Tom felt the urge to continue their conversation. "I'm Lieutenant Sawyer, this is Sergeant McDonnell."

"I'm Timmons, from Pennsylvania."

"Sergeant here is from Georgia. I'm from Missouri."

"Lieutenant, I didn't know you're from Missouri," said McDonnell.

"I didn't want you to know. I was afraid you'd try to visit me after the war." The corporal laughed. "Corporal, how long have you been in?"

"I've been out of it for about three months. I was in action for about a year. I've fought all over. Been lucky, never received so much as a scratch."

"How'd you get yourself captured?" Tom asked.

"Our position was overrun. I was reloading and a Johnny Reb ran up and held a bayonet to my chest and recommended that I stop. Of course, at that time, I was more than happy to oblige. I'll never understand why Johnny didn't just run me

191

through. I sure as hell would have him. Anyway, we were marching to some prison camp and a sergeant grabbed me and made me help carry some wounded Rebs. I've been helping around here ever since."

"They don't seem to be guarding you too closely," Tom said, looking around at a handful of guards, some that weren't even armed. "Why don't you run for it?"

"I've thought about it, believe me, I have. But I'd probably just get caught again and then they'd send me to some hellhole. Anyway, the work's not too hard and the food's decent. You guys headed home?"

"Yeah. Sarge is out of the fight for good. I'm just going home to mend for a while."

"So you're headed back eventually?"

"Yeah."

"Sorry to hear that, Lieutenant. How long have you been in action?"

"Two days."

"Two days! What the hell happened?"

"We ran into a lot of your friends. They were a little upset."

"Where?"

"Chickamauga."

"You were at Chickamauga! Well, gentlemen, my hat's off to you, if I still had a hat. I've heard that a day there was like a week in other fights."

"It's two days that we'll remember forever, that's for sure," Tom said.

Tom, the Confederate Sergeant, and the Yankee Corporal sat and talked for over an hour. Finally, the whistle warned them that it was time to re-board. The Corporal grabbed one end of Tom's cot and helped carry him back into the boxcar.

"Corporal, good luck to you. If you're ever down Atlanta way and need an attorney, look me up."

The corporal grinned. "Thanks. My luck's running pretty good right now, so maybe I won't need one. But good luck to you. Hope you guys mend up all right."

Corporal Timmons bent down and patted Sergeant McDonnell on the shoulder, who reached up and took his hand. The Corporal shook hands with Tom and then gave a salute. Tom smiled and returned the salute.

The remaining stops for coal and water were too brief to allow time for the men to be carried out of the boxcar. The next time Tom saw the sun, it was setting behind the familiar depot in Atlanta.

Becky paced up and down the depot platform. She had met every train for the past two days. The telegram had been brief: *Captain Sawyer injured. Returning home.* She just didn't know when. And *Captain?* What was that all about? He was a Lieutenant when he left a few days ago. If he's got himself messed up trying to be a hero, I'll . . . I'll just kill him! She corrected herself. No, I won't.

Becky talked to every member of Fulton's returning brigade that she could. No one knew anything about Tom's condition. She feared the worst, but was still shocked when she saw him carried from the boxcar.

She ran, tears streaming down her cheeks, and threw her arms around him, almost causing the bearers to drop him.

"Oh, Tom, what has happened to you?" she asked.

He rose up on the cot on his good arm, one leg bandaged, one arm in a sling and a bandage across his forehead. He tried to muster up a smile and a joke.

"Oh, I got into a fight. You know, you just can't discuss politics with some people."

-43-

Becky sat in the corner of the parlor pretending to read. Tom was sitting by the fire with a blanket draped across his legs. It was a comfortable October afternoon but since the weather had turned a little chilly he had been unable to stay warm.

She watched as he crumpled up the letter he was reading and let it fall to the floor. He leaned on the arm of the chair, his face buried in his hand. Becky had seen this too many times over the past week. The letters just kept coming, each one worse than the one before.

She laid down the book, walked over to Tom's chair, and sat down on the floor beside him. She unfolded the wrinkled letter, smoothing it out on the floor in front of her. The crinkling of the paper caused Tom to look up. He reached for the letter to stop her, but she pushed his hand away without even looking at him.

The letter read: *Captain Sawyer, congratulations on your glorious accomplishments at Chickamauga! You must certainly be proud of your promotion to Captain. The newspaper articles I have read have been short on details, but apparently you are great at leading men. Great at leading them to their death, that is! My husband was in your command and you used him as cannon fodder just to promote your own military career. I hope that your promotion is worth the lives of nearly every man in your command. Of course, I'm sure that a man like you doesn't care. Since I'm sure that my husband has gone to Heaven, I'm relieved that he will never have to see you again.* Becky stopped reading and looked up at Tom.

"These people think I'm some kind of animal," he said.

"That I didn't care what happened to their men."

"Tom, you said you would quit reading these. Every time you receive one, you get them all back out and read them over again. That's the ninth one and they're only making you feel worse."

"But how can they say these things? They weren't there. They don't know what happened."

"That's right, they don't. We never will know the truth unless you open up. That man from the newspaper's been by here three times but you won't talk to him, and you won't let me talk to him."

"Becky, I don't like to think about it."

"Tom, your company received a citation for bravery. It's time everybody knew why."

"Citation for bravery!" he said with disgust. "Yeah, it was a grand charge. Cannons blazing, swords flashing in the sunlight. We won the battle. Drove the enemy back. The only problem, my men didn't get to see the victory. You know why? They were dead! All dead. And you know why I don't want to think about it? I gave the order."

"You know you had a good reason to give the order."

"Yeah, but you've read these letters. They think I'm just a glory-hog. They read in the paper about my promotion. Like I care about a promotion."

Becky placed her hand on his. "Tom, don't you think your men knew what they were doing?"

"I don't know. Probably. Maybe."

"Sure they did. And their families need to know it, too." She stood up and headed for the stairway. "We're going to go set the record straight. Right now."

"I'm not going anywhere."

She stopped at the bottom of the stairs and turned and pointed a finger at him. "Tom Sawyer, you've not left this

195

house since you got back. And you've gotten more sullen every day. I can't take it anymore."

"But they probably won't even believe me-"

"Yes they will. Not all of your men died, and you know it. Sergeant McDonnell is home, too, and doing quite well I hear. He'll help us tell this story. He'll help us make them believe."

When the buggy arrived, Becky had to help Tom from the house to the street. His leg was healing well but he was still using a crutch. And it was made even more difficult because his arm was still in a sling.

Getting into the buggy was also a challenge. The driver was an elderly gentleman and, though he tried, he wasn't much help. Becky was exhausted when she finally climbed into the seat beside Tom.

"Does Sergeant McDonnell have any children?" she asked.

"Yeah, I think so. A couple boys. Why?"

"Well, they can help you get down," she laughed.

Sergeant McDonnell's house was built close to the road but it was still going to be a chore for Tom to make it to the front porch. Becky climbed down and crossed the yard to where the sergeant was sitting in a rocking chair.

"Hello, Sergeant."

"Howdy, Miss Becky. Good to see you."

"Good to see you, too. How are you?"

"Getting better every day. And how's that old man of yours?"

"Ah, he's milking it for all it's worth. I'm having to wait on him hand and foot, but that's not much different than before."

The sergeant spoke up loud enough for Tom to hear. "And that was real ungentlemanly-like to not help your lady down." Tom grinned and muttered something that the driver obviously thought was funny.

"Sarge," she said, looking at his crutch and his leg still in a splint, "he's about as helpless as you are. He said that you have a couple boys. Maybe they could help him down."

"Sure thing. boys!" he yelled. "Come here!" The first to arrive was the youngest. "Jeremiah, go help Mr. Sawyer from his carriage." The four-year-old just grinned and hid behind his father's chair.

"I hope you've grown something a little bigger than this one," Becky said.

"Don't be making fun of my children, ma'am. He's nearly seventeen. He's just small for his age." At that time, the eldest son appeared from behind the house. "No, wait a minute. He's the one that's nearly seventeen. I get them confused. Junior, help the Lieutenant down."

Becky stood at the edge of the porch with her hand out to assist Tom and Junior. Tom finally made it up the steps and stood in front of the sergeant who was attempting to stand. Junior hurried to his side. Sarge at first brushed his hand away, but then took it as he pushed himself up on his crutch.

The two men embraced as best they could with Tom's arm in a sling and both of them holding onto crutches. Not satisfied with their greeting, they shook hands firmly.

"Good to see you, Lieutenant. Of course, I'm not choosy, it's good to see anybody."

"Good to see you, too, dead-eye. Nice patch."

The sergeant laughed. "Same old Sawyer. As sensitive as ever. To what do I owe the honor of this visit, Lieutenant?"

"It's *Captain*, now, soldier. And don't you forget it."

"Well, excuse me. But I'm not in your army anymore, though, so I'll call you whatever I please."

"Such as?"

"Can't say, with your wife present." The sergeant sat back down. "Junior, pull up a chair for the general here before he falls down with old age."

Junior pulled two chairs close to his father's and Tom and Becky sat down.

"Lieutenant, uh, *Captain*—boy, that don't sound natural—Captain, you look like a man on a mission."

"I am, Sarge. And I need your help. I need you to go someplace with me."

"You need me to go back with you and face ole blue again?"

"Worse than that," Tom said without a trace of a smile. He held out his hand to Becky who reached into her handbag and took out the letters. Tom sorted through them and handed Sarge two of the worst ones. As Sarge read them his mouth dropped open in disbelief. When he finished, he looked back and forth from Tom to Becky just shaking his head.

"Sergeant, I've got to go see these people. I've got to set the record straight."

"You better believe it. Tom, I'll be glad to go with you. You deserve that much."

"It's not for me. It's for them. They can't go through life thinking their men died for nothing."

Huck dismounted in front of the courthouse in Savannah and tied up his borrowed horse. He dusted off his pants and climbed the high steps.

He returned the salute of the guard at the front door. "I'm here to see Secretary Mallory," he said.

"Your name?"

"Captain Finn."

The guard glanced at a list in his hand. "Yes, sir. You're expected. Second floor, second door on the right."

Huck climbed the stairs, eyeing the pictures of dignitaries that lined the wall. He wondered for a moment if his picture would ever be on a wall. He grinned and shook his head. Probably not without a dollar amount listed under it.

He stopped at the second door and adjusted his jacket. He was dressed in his full captain's uniform. He didn't enjoy wearing it, but the sight of it opened a lot of doors.

He had been summoned by the Secretary of the Navy. His capture of Douglas had attracted the Secretary's attention. Huck didn't feel comfortable around such high-ranking officials, but he knew it never hurt to have friends in high places.

He knocked lightly and entered what appeared to be an outer office. A lieutenant was seated at a small writing table finishing a dispatch. "Get this off to Richmond immediately," he said, handing it to a waiting corporal. The lieutenant rose to greet Huck and returned the corporal's salute.

"You must be Captain Finn."

"Yes."

"Good. The Secretary's been waiting."

"I hope I'm not late. I thought I was to be here..".

"No. Our other meeting finished up early. He's just taking a little break. I'll tell him you're here."

The lieutenant entered the inner office and closed the door behind him. A few minutes later he re-opened the door and motioned for Huck to come in. As Huck approached the Secretary, he could tell he had been napping.

"Sorry to disturb you, sir," Huck said.

"Not at all, Captain. I was just catching up a little." He tried to stifle a yawn. "I think President Davis has surrounded me with people whose only purpose is to ensure that I never get a whole night's sleep. Have a seat."

"Thank you, sir. What can I do for you?" Huck asked.

"Ah, a man that likes to get right to it. Okay, then. Captain, I understand that you are preparing to leave in a few days."

"Yes, sir. We plan to steam out by the end of the week."

"And you're headed back to Nassau?"

"Yes, sir."

"Good. I wonder if I could persuade you to deliver something for me?"

"Well . . . sure. Yes, of course."

"Captain, this package is very important. Discretion is needed, if you know what I mean."

Huck just eyed the Secretary.

"Did I say something wrong? I understood that you were a man that could be trusted."

"Sorry. It's just that I've been here before."

"So I've heard. And that's why I'm asking. It's just that this package is a little more important than usual."

"Okay, Mr. Secretary, whatever you need."

"Good. Lieutenant, bring in the package."

The lieutenant left the inner office. Huck and the Secretary sat in silence as they heard the door to the outer office open and close. The Secretary swiveled and looked out the window, his hands drumming on the arms of the chair. Huck took the hint that they may have to wait a while. He picked up a book lying on the edge of the Secretary's desk and started flipping through it. It was no more than three minutes before they heard the outer door open and close. The lieutenant opened the door to the inner office and entered, followed by a beautiful young lady.

"Captain, I'd like you to meet Miss Belle," said the Secretary.

"Pleased to meet you," said Huck as he rose.

"Likewise, Captain," said Miss Belle.

"Captain," said the Secretary, "Miss Belle needs to get to Nassau. I was hoping I could count on you to deliver her."

Huck looked confused. "Sir, I don't understand. Is this some kind of personal favor I'm being asked to do?"

"No. Miss Belle . . . oh, I'm sorry, I see what you must be thinking. No . . . how shall I say this . . . Miss Belle is a friend to the Confederacy. She knows things. She knows people. She knows things about people. I need . . . we need . . . her delivered safely to Nassau. Captain, you probably shouldn't ask too many questions."

"But sir," Huck began to protest, "I'm not sure you understand just how dangerous it is out there—"

"I understand perfectly."

"But sir, I'm used to delivering pouches. I can just throw them over board if we're caught. I can't very well throw her overboard-"

"I'd appreciate it if you didn't, Captain," the Secretary and Miss Belle both grinned. "That would defeat our purpose, now wouldn't it?"

Huck looked back and forth from Mallory to Belle. He shook his head and resigned himself to his new assignment. "I'll do my best, sir," he said.

"That's not good enough. I didn't ask you because I knew you'd do your best. I asked you because I knew you'd get it done."

-45-

The farm was about three miles out of town. It belonged to the widow of one of Tom's men. Hers was one of the letters the sergeant read. He recognized her name because she attended church with his wife occasionally.

As they climbed down from the buggy, the widow and her son came out on the porch. She greeted them as they approached.

"Howdy folks, welcome. You're just in time for supper."

Becky climbed the steps and held out her hand. "Hello. Allow me to introduce myself. I'm Becky Sawyer." She turned and pointed to Tom. "And this is my husband, Tom—"

"Tom Sawyer," the widow interrupted coldly. "The famous Captain Thomas Sawyer."

"Uh, yes, that's right." Becky could tell from the sudden change in her tone that they were not as welcome as a moment earlier.

The lady's son stepped to the center of the porch and stood in the doorway. "How dare you come here," he said.

"Son, I need to talk to you and your mom," Tom said.

"You're not coming into this house," the boy said.

Tom turned and looked into the sad eyes of the boy's mother. "Ma'am, I received your letter—"

"And I meant every word!"

"Yes, ma'am, I understand. I received it, and several others just like it. And I knew I needed to talk to you."

"I said you're not coming into this house," the son repeated.

Sarge spoke up at this time. "Ma'am, I was with the Captain at Chickamauga. He's not here for himself. He's here for you. You need to listen to what he's got to say."

The boy looked at his mom. She turned and nodded in the direction of the door. He stepped back and she swept her arm in that direction, silently inviting her guests in.

The house was small and didn't have a formal parlor, so they were seated at the kitchen table. The guests were politely offered a drink, which they declined.

In the awkward silence, Tom and the sergeant adjusted their crutches, which were leaning against the table. Becky held her hands in her lap and smoothed and re-smoothed her skirt several times. Junior smiled and tried to appear friendly enough for everyone. The widow's son eyed them sternly, trying to express his dissatisfaction with their presence. The widow sat calmly, her hands folded together on the table, waiting for Tom to speak.

After a few moments Tom was able to arrange his thoughts. Once he began, the story poured out. He told about both days of fighting. He left out the gory details until he got to the battle at the schoolhouse. As he told that part, he described their fears while retreating, the screams of the children, and the angry curses of his men as they turned and headed back to stop the cannons. He recited details that he hadn't told Becky.

Sergeant McDonnell sat quietly while Tom told the story. His eyes met those of Becky and the widow and her son. He nodded his head in agreement, indicating that the story was true.

Becky sat erect, tears trickling down her cheeks, proud of her husband. The widow was bent over, her face in her hands, sobbing. Her son had left the table and was standing by the fireplace holding a picture of his father.

When Tom finished, everyone sat quietly. The only sound was the widow crying. As they rose to leave, the widow came around the table, drying her tears on her apron. She gave Tom a hug and kissed him on the cheek. "I'm glad my man got to serve with a man like you. And I am so sorry for that letter."

Tom shook his head. "Don't think another thing about it. Just tell everybody about F Company."

The widow's son was waiting on the porch to assist Tom and the sergeant. "I can't wait till I'm old enough to go kill some blue-bellies," he said.

"How old are you, young man?" Tom asked.

"Fifteen."

"Son, your family's paid enough. You take care of your mom. Pray to God this thing ends before you're old enough to have to do otherwise. You take care of the wife of a brave soldier, and that'll be enough contribution to the cause."

The widow followed them onto the porch, still wiping tears from her cheeks. She remembered her earlier invitation. "Are you sure you won't stay for dinner?"

"No, thanks," Tom said politely. "I've got some more letters to answer."

-46-

The two weeks that followed brought improvements for Tom, both physically and emotionally. The headaches, caused by the mini-ball to his head, had finally stopped and his arm was no longer in a sling. He was still using a cane to walk, but he was, for the most part, able to move about without any help from Becky.

The letters continued, but as news spread of the events at the schoolhouse, they became complimentary and encouraging. He was finally able to sleep again.

The doctor felt it would be a few more weeks before Tom could return to action, so, over Becky's protests, he obtained permission to take her back to Missouri. He remembered General Johnson's warning about the Yanks marching straight through Georgia.

The plan was to go to Savannah, catch a ship to Mobile, and take a steamboat up the Tombigbee to Tupelo. The Yanks were in control of Chattanooga, so a train through there was impossible. The boat ride would be easier on Tom than going cross-country by wagon.

The ride to the depot, and the effort of boarding, tired Tom out. They were barely out of the station before he leaned his head back and closed his eyes. His snoring agitated some of the passengers, and amused others. Becky let him sleep.

Tom sat up and rubbed his eyes, trying to get his bearings. The train had stopped and Becky was gone.

He leaned his face against the window and tried to look out into the darkness. Using his hand to block the glare from the inside lights, he saw a water tower a few cars ahead, next to the engine.

The door to the car opened and Becky entered, carrying drinks. "The train was thirsty and stopped for a drink," she said, "so I thought we'd do the same." She saw his eyes light up. "Sorry, it's only tea."

"Well, I guess that'll have to do," he said. "Where are we, anyway?"

"Just north of Macon. We'll only be here a few minutes, so drink up."

While they drank their tea, Becky fussed over Tom, checking his leg and making sure he was comfortable. A short whistle indicated they were about to leave. She gathered up their glasses and returned them to the café across the street from the depot. She made it back to their seat just as the train began to pull out.

"Cut that pretty close, didn't you?" he said.

"Well, I met this handsome major, and we got to talking—"

"Yeah, you wish."

"Now Tom, you know I'm not like that. It would take at least a colonel to turn my head." He laughed. She could tell he was in a good mood. She turned sideways with her arm propped up on the back of the seat, her chin in her hand. With her other hand she lightly stroked his arm.

"Tom, I want to talk to you."

"We've been talking."

"No, I want to talk to you about the battle."

"We've already been through this. I don't want to talk about it. I don't want you to have to live with the visions that it'll bring to your mind."

"I already have to."

"What do you mean?"

207

"Tom, you talk in your sleep. And moan, and curse, and scream. I know you've seen some bad things, but you need to talk about it. Get it off your chest. So go ahead, I can handle it."

Tom thought for a minute, sighed, and shrugged his shoulders. "Okay. But remember, you asked for it."

"The first day . . . the first day was scary, in an exciting sort of way. We were basically playing at war, or at least my company was. We weren't really tested that day. None of the second platoon was even injured. We hid behind trees and shot at . . . well . . . shot at other trees. We never even got a good look at them until they were retreating. If we'd only known..."

"Known what?" she asked.

"That we hadn't even seen the war yet. The next day, the day I got injured, a different kind of fear took over. A panic, the knowledge that you *could* die at any moment. I saw men running in all directions. Sometimes they would run into trees. I saw a couple men hung up in briar bushes fighting furiously to get out. But it appeared they didn't even know what direction they wanted to go. I even saw soldiers run into the enemy, as if it were just a crowded street. They would run on by, without fighting, seeming sometimes to even ask pardon for bumping into them."

"And then, another kind of fear. The realization that you *are* going to die. That this is your last day and there's nothing you can do about it. And that's a dangerous point. Sometimes men would just stand in one place, watching the battle around them. Not hiding behind trees, or lying down. Just stand there. And that's when a lot of them got it."

"Some of the soldiers, when they reached that point, would fire methodically, no hurry or concern. Just calmly load, aim at God-knows-what, and fire in the direction they happened to be facing. I talked later to a couple men that I saw doing this. They weren't cowards. They remembered the fight, and they remembered standing there. They said it seemed like everything just slowed down to a crawl. Some of them didn't remember the sounds of the battle. They said it was almost peaceful, quiet.

One guy thought he was already dead, it was so peaceful. I can't believe they couldn't hear the battle."

"How loud was it?" Becky asked.

"Thunder. Thunder from a lightning bolt that strikes nearby. It went on for hours. There were over a hundred thousand men at Chickamauga. Spread out over three miles and fighting from sun-up to sun-down. The noise . . . it never stopped."

"And that was just the guns. I never knew men could make some of the sounds I heard. It would start with a rebel yell. That's a high-pitched shout normally, but it can reach a blood-curdling shrill in close fighting. And the screams of the injured as they fell around us. Begging for help. But no one could stop to help. And the shouts and curses in anger as the men fell on one another, with only one thought . . . to kill. I've never witnessed such hate. No matter the outcome of this war, I don't see how we can ever live together as one nation, or even as neighbors as separate nations."

"Tom, that's a lot of emotions to deal with," she said as she ran her fingers through his hair.

"That's not the half of it. We'll never know what most of my men were thinking, but Sergeant McDonnell agrees with me. At the schoolhouse, when we were charging back into the cannons, the only thing we could think of was our families and all we were losing. We couldn't believe it had come down to that."

"Later, when I woke up in the hospital, I realized that I had made it through the battle, that no one was shooting at me, but I was still terrified that I would die from my injuries. That I wouldn't make it home to you. So close, but not close enough."

"Well," she said, "you did make it, and you're going to be just fine. We're going to be just fine." She kissed him tenderly. "Tom, there's just one more thing I need to ask. What's it like to have to kill someone?"

He looked at her with a strange expression on his face. "Why do you want to know that?"

"I've got to live with you for years to come. I want to know whatever demons you're having to live with."

Tom looked out the window into the darkness. He answered without looking back at Becky.

"The second day of fighting, I was mostly running around giving orders, trying to keep my platoon headed in the right direction. It was so thick in those woods, it was difficult to know which way was which. I would occasionally stop and fire my revolver in the direction of the Yanks, but I don't know if I hit anyone. Then I stopped and picked up a rifle that had belonged to one of my men."

"Where was he?"

"Dead. I had looked down trying to find a rifle. At first I thought I was standing on top of him. But I was standing . . . *through* him. Cannonball . . . had put a hole," he pointed to his stomach, "clean through his belly. Anyway, I saw a young man in blue about a hundred feet away. I sighted down the barrel and looked him in the face. He wasn't looking at me, just glancing from side to side. He never knew. I pulled the trigger and sent him to Jesus. I hope."

"And the man that did this," he said, holding up his injured arm, "I'll never forget the look in his eyes when he realized I was about to kill him. I don't think I'll ever get rid of that one."

"I've been trying to make sense of all this. I don't think there is any. You try to be prepared to face the devil. Pray. Pray for a miracle. Pray for victory. Pray for defeat. Pray that just some little piece of you survives to tell about it."

He looked back at Becky. "I'm sorry I've been talking in my sleep. I didn't mean to cause you to worry." He took a deep breath. "I guess you were right. I did need to talk about it. Thanks for listening."

She smiled and placed her head lightly on his chest. He put his arm around her shoulder and held her close. Only she knew that Tom didn't talk in his sleep.

-47-

The train stopped in Macon for coal and water. They had never been to Macon and Tom knew Becky wanted to see a little of the town. She was hesitant to ask, with his leg not completely healed, but he insisted. She held onto his arm lightly as he hobbled along.

It had rained off and on all afternoon and there weren't too many people out. They turned down one dimly lit street and were apparently all alone.

They heard rapid footsteps from behind and moved to one side of the walk to allow the person the pass. But the stranger didn't pass. He grabbed Becky by the arm and held her so she couldn't turn to face him. Tom felt the cold steel of a revolver push into his skin, just below his left ear.

"Don't turn around," the stranger said. "Nice and easy, just give me your money and your jewelry. Quietly, and no one'll get hurt."

It took Tom a moment to understand what was happening. When he did, a new kind of fear struck him. A helplessness. He couldn't protect Becky. He couldn't charge the cannons. He had to remain calm and hope. Hope that this man would take what he demanded and leave.

"Hurry, fool. Don't make me . . ."

The man fell silent. Tom and Becky heard the cocking of a second pistol.

"My dear man, what shall it be?" asked a second man.

"Take our money, here's my pocket watch. Just don't hurt my wife," said Tom.

"I'm not talking to you, Lieutenant," said the second man. "I'm talking to the heathen who's holding a gun to your head."

"Man, I don't know who you are," said the first man, "but if you don't leave, I'll kill these two."

"No you won't. Because if you pull that trigger, I'll pull this one. Now uncock your pistol and hand it to the Lieutenant. I have no desire to get the law involved in this and I'm sure you don't either. You simply walk straight ahead and we'll walk in the opposite direction and we'll all forget this happened."

There was a pause as the first man considered this. "How do I know you won't shoot me in the back if I do give him my gun?"

"You don't. But if we stand here long enough pointing guns at each other, I'm sure someone will eventually wander by and start asking questions."

"Tom, what's going on?" Becky asked, her voice quivering.

"I think we're being robbed by two people at the same time."

"No you're not, Lieutenant," said the second man. "I'm stopping him. I have business to discuss with you, and I'd rather do it in private. So as I said, sir, what will it be?"

Tom felt the barrel move from his neck and heard the clicking of the pistol being uncocked. When he felt the handle of the gun resting on his shoulder, he reached up slowly and took it. The would-be robber brushed by him as he walked away. Tom and Becky slowly turned and faced the second stranger.

"Good to see you again, Lieutenant." He grinned. "Sawyer, I believe it was."

"Well, bless my soul. If it isn't Corporal Timmons, from Pennsylvania. How are you . . . what are you doing in Macon?" Tom asked in shock. "And those clothes don't look like a Union uniform. Son, you could get yourself hanged. What do you think you're doing?"

"Right now, I'm saving your hide."

"I mean, what are you doing *here?*"

"Well . . . I took your advice . . . and ran off."

"My advice?"

"Yeah. I remembered what you said about them not guarding us too closely. One of my friends got into a little trouble and we got wind that they were going to send all of us off to a prison camp. So I split."

"Where did you get the money?" Tom asked. "How are you traveling?"

"That's the beautiful part. The trouble he got into was stealing. When they locked him up, I thought I knew where he might hide his treasure. And sure enough, there it was. So I decided to keep it and make a run for it. I saw you board the train in Atlanta and I've been waiting for a chance to speak to you. I decided to follow you tonight to see if I might catch you alone. It's a good thing I did, too."

"But where did you get the gun?"

"You ask too many questions, Lieutenant. Let's just say I'm a very enterprising young man." Timmons looked at Becky.

"Oh, excuse, me," Tom said. "Corporal, this is my wife, Becky. Becky, this is Corporal Timmons."

The corporal bowed lightly to Becky, tipping his new hat. "Pleased to make your acquaintance, Mrs. Sawyer."

Becky ignored the greeting and, pale-faced, turned to Tom. "Tom . . . he's the enemy."

"You didn't think so just a couple minutes ago," interrupted Timmons.

"Can we discuss this somewhere else," Tom asked as he looked around at the shadows. "I think we should get back to the train."

As they turned the corner and started back down the street toward the depot, Tom stopped and stood face-to-face with the corporal, closely, so that no passersby could overhear.

"Corporal, just what do you expect me to do? Help you get away?"

"I *did* just save your life."

213

"I'm a Confederate officer, for crying out loud!"

"A Confederate officer who's running away from the war, too."

"I'm doing no such thing. I'm trying to get my wife to Missouri."

"Lieutenant, Missouri's in the other direction. Besides, I watched you two on the train together. There's no way you're going to let her out of your sight again. You're through with this war. You're going to be together now—how did the preacher say it—till death do you part. Lieutenant, I'm through with this war, too." Looking at Becky he continued. "I'm not the enemy anymore. I'm just trying to get to the coast to see if I can find a ship headed out of here."

The three of them stood in silence, considering their next move. Becky could tell Tom was torn between his national loyalties and his debt to the man that had saved her life. She finally made the decision for them.

"What a coincidence," she said. "So are we."

-48-

Their train arrived just after two in the afternoon. Corporal Timmons was helping Becky arrange their luggage on the platform when a young lieutenant, followed by an older sergeant who walked with a limp, hurried up to them.

"Are you Captain Sawyer," he asked, saluting Tom.

"Yes, I am," Tom said, returning the salute.

"I'm from Fort Jackson. We received your wire requesting assistance. I've been ordered to deliver you to your ship." He noticed Timmons and frowned. "Is this gentleman with you?"

"Yes. Is that a problem, Lieutenant?"

"Uh . . . no, sir. It's just that your telegram didn't mention a third party. We only procured passage for two."

"Excuse me?" Tom asked.

"We've made all the arrangements. When you wired yesterday, we took the liberty of reserving you a berth on a ship that leaves tonight."

"Tonight? Well . . . they'll just have to make room for one more. I ran into my old friend here and, as it turns out, he's looking for passage, too."

"Yes, sir. We'll see what we can do." The lieutenant and the sergeant picked up all the luggage they could carry. The lieutenant looked at Timmons. "If you don't mind, sir . . ."

Timmons picked up the remaining pieces of luggage and nodded to the lieutenant. As they were led to a waiting buggy, he lagged behind, trying to avoid conversation, fearing his accent would give him away.

As the sergeant loaded their luggage into the buggy, the lieutenant spoke softly to Tom and Becky. "Your friend doesn't talk much, does he?"

"Well, he . . ."stammered Tom.

"He talks with a lisp," Becky whispered. "It embarrasses him."

"Oh. I understand."

Captain Finn was in the pilothouse when the buggy stopped alongside the *Spirit of the Storm*. He approached the gangplank to greet his passengers.

His heart skipped a beat when he recognized the most beautiful woman he had ever known. Though he could have sworn it was impossible, Becky had become even more beautiful.

-49-

All they could do was stare. All the years and all the miles that had separated them. Now, with no warning, they stood face to face.

The lieutenant set their luggage on the deck between Huck and Tom. He looked back and forth at the two men as they stared at each other.

"Is there a problem, Captain?" asked the lieutenant.

"No," Tom and Huck answered simultaneously.

The lieutenant grinned sheepishly, confused, and continued to glance back and forth at Tom and Huck.

"No," repeated Tom, "everything's fine."

"You two know each other?"

After a pause, Huck said, "Yes, a long time ago."

"Captain Sawyer, if we need to make other arrangements, I'm sure the Colonel wouldn't—"

"Lieutenant," Tom said, "you'll have to ask Captain Finn."

Huck motioned for the sergeant to place the luggage on the deck. "Everything's fine." He finally looked at Becky and held out his hand. "So good to see you again, Mrs. Sawyer."

"How dare you try to shake my hand. Give me a hug, you fool." He bent down as she put her arms around him, squeezing him tight. She gave him a light kiss on the cheek. "Good to see you, too."

Huck noticed Timmons standing quietly, his hands folded together in front of him. "Can I help you, sir?"

"He's with us," Becky spoke up. "His name is Timmons. He needs a cabin, too."

"I'm not sure we have a cabin-"Huck began, but stopped short when he saw the pleading look in Becky's eyes. "I'm not sure we have a cabin . . . ready for another passenger. See, our crew uses them when we don't have passengers. We'll have to clean it up . . . make it presentable. If you don't mind waiting a while, Mr. Timmons."

"That'll be fine," Becky answered. "He can wait in our cabin. He won't mind."

Huck looked at Timmons, who just smiled and nodded. Tom broke the awkward moment by turning to the lieutenant.

"Lieutenant, thanks for your assistance. Tell your Colonel that the arrangements are fine."

The lieutenant saluted Tom, nodded to the others, and left the ship. Huck gave orders to two crewmen to retrieve the rest of the luggage from the buggy.

Tom motioned for Timmons to follow him and Becky to their cabin. As they walked past, Huck said, "Becky, what was that all about?"

She just shook her head. "You don't want to know."

Huck watched them walk away following the crewmen carrying their luggage. He stood alone, talking to himself.

"I want to know. Why does everybody always tell me that I don't want to know? I want to know."

-50-

For all their adventures, Tom and Becky had never seen the ocean. They were as excited as children when the circus comes to town. They had gone to bed early, but Becky had made Huck promise to wake them before they left the dock. As orders were quietly given to get the ship under way, their anticipation grew.

Tom remembered the riverboats on the Mississippi. Always leaving the landing with shrill whistles and bells ringing. Always making a grand exit. Huck's ship simply untied and slipped away into the darkness.

The reflection of the half-moon on the water provided just enough light to point the way between the cypress trees that lined the banks. The signal corps lighted the way through the shallows. They cleared the mouth of the river without being sighted.

Tom and Becky stood at the stern watching, to the north, what appeared to be a fireworks display. When Huck joined them, they could tell this wasn't a show.

"Poor souls," Huck muttered.

"What is it?" Becky asked.

"The end of the voyage, for someone. You see those flashes low on the water? Those are cannons. And those signal flares? There's at least three gunships pounding somebody. It appears from the angles that they've got them surrounded."

"Is there anything we can do to help them?" Becky asked.

Huck just shook his head. "Nope. By morning, they'll be on the bottom. Or in chains."

"And there's nothing we can do?"

"Nope. But don't you worry about a thing."

"And why not," Tom interrupted. "How do you know that's not going to happen to us?"

"Because . . . if they catch up to us, I'll surrender the ship. They'll arrest us all, but they'll let you two go. You're just passengers. That's how it's recorded in the ship's log."

Becky seemed relieved. "You're sure?"

"Absolutely. I've been doing this for quite a while." He checked his pocket watch, though he couldn't have seen the dial in the pale moonlight. "Now, if you two will excuse me, I've got to go play Captain."

Tom and Becky stayed at the stern watching the distant battle until it faded from view. After a while, Tom took Becky by the hand and led her to the bow. Two chairs, with blankets draped across them, were awaiting them.

"How nice of Huck to think of this," Becky said.

Tom bumped shoulders with her playfully. "What do you mean *Huck*? I asked one of the crew to do this."

She snuggled against him, wrapping her arms around his waist. "I was hoping so."

The wind was steady and the sea was slightly rough. They sat at the bow watching the ship rise and fall as it sliced its way through the foam. As they reached the crest of each wave, the sea dropped out of sight, momentarily making the sky seem larger. As they rode down the waves, the moon highlighted the whitecaps in the distance. Each wave that crashed against the hull splintered into millions of drops, each glistening as it flew through the night air.

Even though they were chilled by the cold seawater, they stayed on deck until the sun rose. They had never seen anything so beautiful. They kissed in the moonlight, oblivious to all the ship's hustle and bustle going on about them. Forgetting for a moment the war they had left behind.

Shortly after noon, Becky emerged from their cabin. Tom was still below, asleep.

The seas had calmed enough for her to enjoy a stroll around the ship. She had been on deck for almost an hour before Huck came topside and joined her at the rail.

"Good afternoon, Mrs. Sawyer."

Becky just stared at him.

"Did I say something wrong?"

"Yes. What's with all this hand shaking and 'Mrs. Sawyer' business? Why are you acting like this?"

"I'm sorry. It just feels so awkward . . . you . . . being here . . . and with . . . *him*."

"Him? *Him?* Tom? My husband Tom? Your best friend Tom? Why is that awkward?"

"You know . . . after what happened."

"That was a long time ago. And it was just a kiss."

Huck stared at her for just a moment. "Just a kiss?" he asked.

"Oh, Huck, you know I love you. I love you a lot, like a brother. But that's all . . . like a brother."

"You've already said that once." Huck stared down at the waves. "Do you women know how bad it hurts when you say that?"

"Yep. About as bad as it hurts when we hear the same thing. Now, listen, quit worrying about it. Tom's going to notice something."

He jerked his head up. "So you haven't told him?"

"Of course not. It's just between you and me." She touched him on the shoulder. "I think about it sometimes. It was sweet."

"Sweet! You slapped me!"

"You startled me!" She laughed. "I think about that, too. I'm so sorry I did that. Can you ever forgive me?"

"No."

She laughed again. "Oh, Huck, are you going to be okay . . . are you and Tom going to be okay?"

He turned to face her. "What choice do I have? He's got you. He won. It's over. I can act like . . . an ass . . . and never see you again, or I can—"He saw Tom approaching behind Becky. "Here comes . . . *him*." She laughed again.

"What are you two laughing about?" Tom asked.

"Oh, just remembering old times," Becky said. "How do you feel this *afternoon*?"

"Fine. Starving. When do we eat?"

"Lunch . . . breakfast has been prepared," Huck said, "and is waiting in the galley. That reminds me. I've planned dinner in my cabin tonight, just the five of us."

"Where *is* Timmons?" asked Tom. "I haven't seen him since last night."

"Uh, not Timmons. I don't think he wants to join us."

"What's the matter?"

"He's spent the last several hours right here."

"Sick?" asked Becky.

"Heaving his guts out. I wouldn't want to be a fish between here and Savannah."

"You said five," Tom said.

"Yeah. You two, me and Johnny. . . you remember Johnny, Jim's boy. He's been so busy he hasn't made it by your cabin yet. And another passenger came on board before we left last night, while you two were sleeping. She'll be joining us."

"She?" asked Tom.

"Yeah. Real pretty, too," Huck said, teasing Becky.

"Sounds great," said Tom.

"I'll make you think," said Becky as she punched Tom in the arm. "If you boys will excuse me, I'm going below for some lunch, or breakfast, or whatever."

"I'll join you in a minute," Tom said.

They watched her as she walked away. Tom finally leaned back against the rail. "This is a beautiful boat you've got here-."

"Ship," Huck corrected.

"Excuse me . . . ship. Fine looking lady."

"Thanks. You too."

Tom grinned. "Thanks."

They lapsed into silence. This was the first time they had been alone since their fight six years earlier. It was several minutes before Huck continued.

"Listen, Tom," he said as he packed tobacco into his pipe, "it's good to see you two, and I'm glad you're doing well. But . . . I'm not going to pretend that everything is all right between us. Well, I guess for Becky's sake I *am* going to pretend . . . but that's exactly what it is . . . pretending. Too much has happened . . . things that can't be undone."

"Huck, it was just a punch in the eye. No damage done. I forgive you-"

"I'm not talking about that." He laughed. "Hell, I'm glad I punched you. I'm talking about you and her being married. You got her. I wanted her and, like everything else, you got your way. Like I said, for her sake, I'm going to act like I accept it. Of course, I don't have any choice, do I?"

Tom shook his head. "No. And for what it's worth . . . I can't say that I blame you."

Tom turned and leaned against the rail, looking out over the waves. "I want to thank you for what you said last night. It helped Becky. She was getting nervous."

"No problem."

"And you didn't mean a word of it, did you?"

Huck smiled.

"You'll never surrender this ship?"

Huck shook his head.

"And if we're caught . . . I'm a Confederate officer . . . they won't let me go?"

Huck shook his head again.

Tom smiled. "You liar. Haven't changed a bit."

Huck laughed. "The problem is, I've spent too much time with you."

223

-51-

Sunrise two days later found them anchored in the lee of a small island. Tom and Becky had been instructed the night before to be ready for an adventure. They joined Huck as he leaned on the rail enjoying the view.

"I thought the Bahamas would be larger," said Tom.

"You idiot, this isn't the Bahamas. We're still a day away," said Huck.

"Then what is it?" asked Becky.

"It's your wedding present."

"Oh look, hon, Huck got us an island," Tom said.

"Well, at least for the day. You'll have to put it back when you're through with it. Come on, we're going treasure hunting. Pirate treasure."

Two of Huck's men were waiting to row them ashore. When the boat slid up on the beach, they jumped into the water to hold it steady as Huck, Tom, and Becky climbed out. As she waded ashore, Becky had to hold her skirts above her knees to keep them from getting wet. Her legs were exposed to all who were looking. And they all were looking.

Huck's men stayed with the boat as he led Tom and Becky through the trees and underbrush to the opposite side of the island, just out of sight of the ship. As they walked out onto the beach, Tom and Becky stared, confused, at a small tent. In the shade under the tent was a picnic basket with a rolled-up blanket laid on top of it.

"My present to you," said Huck, extending his arms in both directions. "Your own island for a day. I'll see you kids at sundown."

"Our own island—" Tom said.

"Don't ask questions. Just enjoy."

As Huck made his way back to the boat, he stopped and looked back. Tom and Becky were holding hands as they walked along the water's edge, Tom still limping visibly.

Huck had known ever since he met Becky that she was a good woman. That she would make some man very happy. And he had hoped it would be him. He tried to squelch the pangs of jealousy that were springing up inside him. He smiled and shook his head, happy for his best friends, and then turned and headed back to the ship.

Tom and Becky walked up and down the beach on their side of the island. Some of the time they walked in the waves, sometimes in the shade of the trees. When Tom needed to rest, they sat talking, running their fingers and toes through the sand.

When the sun had climbed to near high noon, they headed for the shade of the tent to cool off. Becky knelt in the sand to check the basket that Huck had left for them. He always kept a good cook on board. Her inspection revealed a fine lunch.

Tom unrolled the blanket and sat down. Becky placed one of the plates, wrapped in a cloth, on the blanket beside Tom. She held up a bottle of wine and a glass, clinking them together to get Tom's attention, smiled mischievously, and joined him on the blanket.

After half a plate and two glasses, they lay back and closed their eyes for a nap. There was a light breeze blowing. Tom, however, could not get cool enough. He sat up and removed his shirt and lay back down. Becky sat up and turned to face him, her back to the sea.

"Is that cooler?" she asked.

"Yes, some."

"You look comfortable."

"I am. Bet you wish you could join me," he teased.

She thought for a moment. "I think I will."

Tom rose up on his elbows. "You think you will do what?"

"Get comfortable." She stood up and started unbuttoning her dress.

"Becky, what are you—"

"Shhh." She put her finger to her lips.

Tom could only stare in disbelief as her dress fell to the sand. He laughed. "Well, I guess you'll be cooler now."

"I said . . . shhh," her finger across her lips again.

To his surprise, she wasn't through. "What are you doing, Becky?"

She tossed her last article of clothing onto the blanket beside him. She stood before him nude. "Tom Sawyer, I think I'll go for a swim."

She smiled and started backing slowly towards the water. She was in the water waist deep before he could hurriedly undress and limp to her.

They played together like children. Splashing each other, diving under the waves to pull each other under. Tom would pick her up, hold her tightly, and fall over backwards, taking them both under. They would come up sputtering and laughing, shaking their heads and wiping water from their eyes.

He picked her up to dunk her again but stopped. He pulled her close and kissed her. He let her slide down to stand beside him, still locked in a kiss. Becky ran her fingers through his hair. His hands caressed her back, sliding to her hips.

As their lips parted, Tom took her hands, backed away to arm's length and watched the waves splash against her body. There was a desire in his eyes that she hadn't seen since the night before he left for the war. And there was a willingness in her eyes that stirred fond memories for him. And then a large wave knocked them down. They came up, once again, choking, sputtering and laughing.

Eventually they tired and waded up on the beach. The wind and sun dried them as they lay in the sand. Becky surprised Tom when she asked him to go for another walk. Their clothes were still in the tent. One circuit of their beach brought them back to the tent. And the wine. And the blanket.

Becky held his hands to help him as he sat down on the blanket. She then eased down on top of him. She held his face with both hands as she kissed him deeply. He held her waist firmly as their bodies pressed together.

The love was like nothing they had ever experienced. It was like everything they had ever imagined. Two free spirits savoring every moment together. Craving each other's touch. Not getting enough, but being completely satisfied. They collapsed, exhausted, side-by-side on the blanket, in each other's arms, already anxious for the next time.

Becky stood under the tent, dressing slowly, as Tom walked back into the surf for one more dip. A couple quick dives and Tom headed back to the tent. Becky watched as he approached. She couldn't help but admire her man.

-52-

A week in port and the crew had not been arrested once. They were afraid to get into any trouble. Huck had threatened to kill them if they did anything to attract attention.

The crew didn't know what, or who, the problem was. They only knew what it meant when Huck called them into formation and gave them orders . . . with his revolver in his hand by his side.

The passengers had not been made aware of Huck's stern orders. They didn't know of the crew's hell-raising tendencies so they weren't alarmed by their behavior. The ship was a model of decorum.

Johnny usually spent all of his time in Nassau at home with Margurite. This trip, Huck needed him to help with the loading and unloading. This night, the seventh in port, the two men had dinner ashore. After their meal, Johnny headed home for one last night and Huck came back aboard with a worried look on his face. A conversation with two of his men who had just returned from a bar confirmed his fears. He was sitting alone on deck when Becky and Tom returned to the ship.

"We need to talk," Huck said. "There's a change of plans. Ya'll need to be ready to sail by tomorrow evening."

"Tomorrow? You said we'd be here a couple weeks. I was going to take Becky—"

"Sorry. Tomorrow evening."

Tom and Becky glanced at each other. "What's wrong?" Tom asked.

Huck hesitated, chewing his lip nervously.

"What?" repeated Tom.

"We have a problem. I ran into some old acquaintances of mine at dinner. Two Yankee agents."

"Oh?"

"And they were asking some strange questions. Acting like they knew something. And according to my men, the scuttlebutt is the agents are reasonably sure Miss Belle is on board."

"And why is that a problem?" asked Becky.

"Well, let's just say that sometimes I carry more than just goods on this ship."

"What do you mean?"

"Tom, Miss Belle is a spy, okay. And we've got to get her off this boat without them knowing."

"You've done this a lot, haven't you?" Tom asked.

"Yeah. But before it's just been packages."

"Well," Tom said, "what are we going to do?"

"This afternoon I talked to a captain that's headed to London tomorrow. He has a couple cabins available. We could do this tonight."

"Tonight?" Becky asked.

"Yes," Huck said, "tonight. And I'm sure we're being watched."

"How are we going to do it then, if they're watching?" Tom asked.

"I don't know. Haven't come up with that yet."

"Let me talk to her," Becky said. "See if *we* can come up with a plan."

"Becky, you're not getting involved with this," Tom said.

"Yeah. This could be dangerous," Huck added.

She just glared at the two men, letting them see that their permission was not required.

Thirty minutes later Tom and Huck were summoned to Miss Belle's cabin. When they entered, the lights had been turned down low. Miss Belle, wearing her coat with the hood pulled up, appeared to be alone.

"You wanted to see us?" asked Huck.

She didn't answer but walked over to Tom, with her head bowed down. She reached up and kissed him on the lips.

"Ma'am, I beg your pardon-"

She pulled the hood back and smiled. "Fooled you, Tom Sawyer."

"Becky, you sure gave me a start."

The lights were turned back up. Miss Belle was hiding in the shadows, wearing the dress that Becky had worn to dinner that night.

"You seemed to kiss me back just a little too much," Becky said, her hands on her hips.

"Not me," Tom denied, red-faced.

"Becky," Huck interrupted just in time, "I see what you're planning and I won't allow it."

"Allow it?" Becky said. "Nobody's asking you. It's done. I'll leave the ship and go to Johnny's house for the night. We'll let your Yankee agent friends follow me. Miss Belle can take a boat and sneak away."

"Becky," Huck said, "you don't understand. They may grab you and run off."

"They can't do that," said Tom. "This is British soil."

"They're not supposed to. I know the law, and so do they. But if they think they can get away with it, you better believe they'll try. And even if they realize their mistake, they may still brand you as a spy."

"I'm not spying. I'm simply going to meet Johnny's wife. I'll identify myself. It'll just be their mistake."

After a few minutes of silence Huck said, "Tom, you know, this may just work."

Tom threw up his hands. "Well, don't look at me. If she's made up her mind, there's no stopping her. But I am going with her, just in case."

"And I'll be coming along, too," said Huck. "Tom, there is one other thing. Your young friend, Timmons. Are these agents anything for him to be worried about?"

Tom rubbed his chin thoughtfully. "I don't know. I better go find out." He paused at the door. He eyed Becky with a questioning look. She nodded.

"I guess I'd better tell ya'll about Timmons. Especially you, Miss Belle, since you may be traveling together. He's a . . . Yankee. A Yankee Corporal."

Huck and Miss Belle exchanged glances.

"A Yankee!" Huck snapped.

"Yep."

"On my ship?"

"Yep. We met when I was on my way back from Chickamauga. He was a prisoner. We bumped into each other again in Macon after he ran off. He says he's just trying to get away from the war."

"Do you believe him?" Miss Belle asked.

"Yes, I do."

"Tom," Huck asked, "would you trust him with your life, or with Becky's?"

Tom and Becky smiled at each other. "We already have," he said.

Huck thought for a minute. "Miss Belle, what do you think?"

"Well, he *is* rather handsome."

"Miss Belle," Huck said, shocked.

She looked at Becky and giggled. "Well, he is."

"What is this war coming to?" Huck asked, shaking his head.

"Okay, okay," Tom said. "I'll go talk to him."

"Tom," Huck said, "I don't think you should tell him all about Miss Belle yet."

"Thanks," Tom said sarcastically. "I never would have thought of that myself."

The Corporal opened the door just a crack until he saw it was Tom. "Oh, come in, Captain." He closed the door and

231

turned back to Tom. The look of concern on Tom's face startled him. "What's wrong?"

"We've got a situation. I know this is short notice, but I'm afraid it's time for a decision. There are Yankee agents waiting on the dock. Now the way I see it, you can do one of two things. You can go to them and tell them who you are and that you escaped and were trying to find a way back north. They may believe you. If they do, you'll be headed home and probably back into the war. If they don't believe you, you may be treated as a deserter."

"What's my other option?"

"There's going to be a boat leaving shortly. Be on it. It will take you to a ship headed to London. Disappear and don't look back."

Timmons thought for a minute. "There is a third option."

"What's that?"

"I could stay here, on board. Join Captain Finn's crew."

"Do you realize what you're saying, Corporal?"

"Yes, I do. I could get used to this sailing life, now that I've gotten over being seasick. And, besides, I wouldn't actually be shooting at any of my old comrades."

"It's not always like it was on this trip," Tom said. "Last time into Mobile, this ship was nearly sunk. Two of the crew were killed. Besides, Huck couldn't let you. How could he be sure you wouldn't switch sides again, at the wrong time? And if anything ever did go wrong, you'd always come under suspicion. No, option three is out."

Tom could tell that Timmons was disappointed. "I guess you're right, Captain," he said.

"I know I'm right. So what'll it be?"

Timmons shrugged. "Well, looks like I'm going to make another run for it." He held out his hand to Tom. "Captain, I want to thank you for all you've done."

"Corporal, I'm the one that owes you. You saved Becky." They shook hands.

"Captain," Timmons grinned, "one question. Will Miss Belle be accompanying me?"

Tom looked shocked. "Why would you ask that?"

"No reason. Was just wondering. Hoping. She's real pretty, don't you think?"

"Oh brother. I don't believe you. Running for your life and trying to chase a girl at the same time." He laughed. "You two belong together more than you can imagine. Just be ready to go. Can you be packed in ten minutes?"

"I stay packed."

Tom and Huck left first, wearing uniforms borrowed from the crew. Both had pistols hidden under their jackets.

They crossed the street towards the nearest bar. They stopped outside and pretended to search their pockets for money before entering.

"That's one of them," Huck whispered. "Standing over there," nodding in the direction of the agent. "I don't see the other one."

There were not many people out tonight, and they didn't notice anyone acting suspicious. There was only one carriage on the street, apparently waiting for an important bar patron.

Becky followed about five minutes behind Tom and Huck. She was dressed in Miss Belle's coat, with the hood up, covering her golden locks.

As soon as she started across the street, a boat was lowered into the water in the shadows on the starboard side of the boat, away from the dock. Miss Belle and Corporal Timmons slipped away.

When Becky crossed the street, she didn't pause, just took off in the direction of Johnny's house. When she was a block away, the agent fell in behind her. And Tom and Huck began following him. They didn't notice that the carriage had started rolling along slowly, keeping pace with Becky.

She turned the corner and the agent quickened his pace. When he turned the corner, the carriage driver whipped the horses into a fast trot, making the turn almost on two wheels.

There was a scream followed by shouts and another muffled scream. Tom and Huck broke into a run. Huck made it to the corner first, outdistancing Tom who was still favoring his wounded leg. Huck kept up the chase for another block, with his gun drawn. But he couldn't fire for fear of hitting Becky.

Two blocks away the carriage slowed almost to a stop. Becky tumbled out, landing in the street. By the time Huck reached her, the carriage was gone. She sat sobbing in the street.

"Becky, are you okay?" Huck shouted.

She couldn't stop crying to answer. One of her shoes had come off and was lying beside her. She grabbed it and threw it angrily in the direction of the carriage.

"Becky! Becky! Are you okay?" Tom yelled when he finally caught up with them. "Becky, you're bleeding! Are you okay?"

Then she was crying and laughing at the same time, wiping the tears from her cheeks with her coat sleeve. "You should have seen their faces when they realized I wasn't Belle." She laughed even louder. "And you should have seen their faces when I got through with these," holding up her fingers, little pieces of flesh buried under the nails. She started crying even harder.

"What's wrong, hon? Just tell me," Tom pleaded.

"I broke a nail, way down in the quick, and it hurts like . . . it hurts real bad!"

"Becky," Huck said, "you've got blood all over your face."

She reached up and touched her face. Looking at the blood on her fingers, she quit crying and grinned. "Oh. Not mine. That . . . so-and-so put his hand over my mouth. He won't be using those fingers for a while. You know," she laughed, "with the right sauce, Yankees might not be half-bad."

Tom and Huck both doubled over, their hands on their knees, trying to catch their breath, laughing in relief. Becky looked around for something else to throw. She remembered her other shoe, took it off, and slung it.

-53-

The guards had been posted all night. They were under strict orders to shoot anyone that tried to board.

The *Spirit of the Storm* was almost loaded. Huck was standing outside the pilothouse watching the last of the supplies being stowed below. He kept checking his watch impatiently. His new passengers were late.

It was almost five o'clock and he wanted to sail before dark. When he had received clearance to leave port, the harbormaster had made a last-minute request. Two additional passengers, a plantation owner and his slave, needed berths. "If they ain't on board by five-thirty, they can swim to Mobile," Huck said to himself.

A carriage stopped at the end of the dock. A huge man, elegantly dressed and apparently in a bad mood, climbed down. A much older-looking man, a negro, followed him and started unloading their baggage as his master bellowed orders.

They strode up the gangplank, the slave bowed over with bags on his back. After the master introduced himself, Huck turned to give the slave directions to stow their bags. As the slave looked up from under his hat, Huck froze in shock.

Fortunately the master had begun walking across the deck admiring the boat. Or criticizing might be a better way to put it. Huck had time to recover from his shock and turned to catch up with him. Under other circumstances, Huck would have thrown him overboard for the things he said about his boat.

When his two passengers had been safely tucked away, the master in his cabin and the slave in the hold, Huck hurried to the pilothouse. "Johnny, get up a head of steam, right now. Have the men stand by to cast off the minute we're ready." He turned to the Second Officer. "Send someone to Captain Sawyer's cabin. I need to see him immediately." The Second Officer had a puzzled look on his face. "What?"

"Captain, Mr. Sawyer's not on board."

"What?!" Huck yelled.

"No, sir. He left after lunch."

"Why wasn't I told?"

"Uh . . . sorry, Capt'n. You didn't say anything about anyone *leaving* the ship, just trying to board."

Huck just glared at him. "Do you have any idea where he went?"

"No, sir."

"Johnny, listen carefully. I'm going looking for Tom. Are all hands accounted for?" The Second Officer nodded. "No one, and I mean no one, is to leave *or* board this ship. If I come back and someone has tried, I'd better see their body lying around. You understand?"

Johnny just nodded. Huck pulled out his revolver, checked it, and put it back in its holster. "You have up steam. We leave the second I step on deck." Huck hurried from the ship. Johnny took up a guard position at the gangplank, his hand on his revolver.

Huck found Tom at the third saloon he searched. Tom was seated by himself, an almost-empty bottle on the table in front of him, a full glass in one hand. As Huck sat down beside him he saw Tom's other hand in his lap, holding a revolver.

Huck reached over, picked up the bottle, and took a swig. He wiped his mouth with the back of his hand. "Smooth," he said, catching his breath as the liquid burned his throat. "How you doing, Tom?"

Tom looked at him with glassy eyes, trying to focus. "Fine. Ya'll?" He reached over to pat Huck on the shoulder and missed. He laughed. "Sit still."

"What're you doing here?"

"None of your damn business, Captain Finn."

"Really? And what do you think you're going to do with that gun?"

"That ain't none of your bamn dusiness either."

Huck chuckled. "Tom, you're a terrible drunk. Come on, let's get you back to the ship."

"Not until I'm good and ready. And I'm not good and ready. And I'll get good and ready when I'm damn good and ready."

Huck looked around the crowded bar. "You're here looking for some Yankees, aren't you?"

Tom took a long gulp. "Huck, Becky cried all night last night. All night. Huck, old friend," Tom reached over and patted him on the shoulder, "if your woman cried all night . . . look me in the eye when I'm talking to you."

"I am."

"Oh." Tom took another swig. "If your woman cried all night, what would you do? You'd find them sumbitches and settle the score. That's what I'd do."

"How're you planning to settle the score, Tom?"

"With this." The revolver hit the edge of the table as he raised it up. Huck jumped and gasped as it slipped from Tom's hand and fell to the floor. Fortunately, it didn't go off.

Tom bent over to retrieve it but Huck put his foot on it. Huck didn't need to bother, though. Tom rose back up quickly.

"Whoa! Don't need to do that. Make the room quit spinning, Huck," he laughed. "Can you get that for me?"

"Sure thing." Huck put the revolver in his pocket. "Tom, how're you going to recognize them? You never got a good look at them."

Tom grinned again. "One of them will have scratches on his face, the other will have a bandaged hand."

"Oh, yeah, I forgot."

"And I'm the one that's supposed to be drunk. We'll leave as soon as I kill them." He looked around on the floor for his gun.

"Tom, something's come up. Tom . . . look at me." Huck shook his shoulder. "Tom, we've got to get back to the ship."

Tom sat up straight. "Why, is something wrong with Becky? I'll kill them sumbitches again if they've hurt her again."

"No, it's not Becky. Look at me. Can you understand me?"

Tom tried to focus on Huck.

"Tom, I've got news about Jim."

"Jim who?"

"Jim who. Our Jim. Johnny's father Jim. Who else do you think?"

"Oh. That's good. What about him . . . Jim?"

"Tom, he's on board my ship."

-54-

Johnny kept pouring the coffee into the cup and Huck kept pouring it into Tom. Tom was propped up in a chair, a wet cloth across his eyes.

"Huck, how did this happen?" Tom asked

"How did this happen? You're not used to drinking this much, that's how this happened."

"No. Jim?"

"He just walked up the gangplank with his new master."

"He's a free man!" Tom yelled. And then moaned, holding his head.

"I know. I'm trying to come up with a plan."

"Why don't we just throw the man overboard?" Tom said.

"Tom, this isn't one of your little adventures. This is serious."

"I know. I was being serious."

Johnny looked angry. "Sounds like a good idea to me."

Huck laughed under his breath. "Give me a few minutes, you two. Listen, Johnny, run and get Becky and Jim. Don't say anything, just ask them to come here. Quietly."

Becky made it to Huck's cabin first. She was startled to see Tom leaned back, a wet cloth covering his face. "What's wrong?" she asked.

Huck held up his hand and tilted it in a drinking gesture. Her fear turned to anger. "Tom Sawyer!" Tom covered his ears and grimaced. She looked at Huck. "What's this all about?"

"Seems he went agent hunting." Huck shook his head, indicating that no harm was done.

Johnny returned with a confused, nervous Jim in tow. Jim stopped just inside the door, staring at the deck. Huck walked over and stood in front of him.

"My man," Huck said, "is your name Jim?"

"Yes, sah, masa."

"From Mississippi?"

"Yes, sah, masa."

"Jim, aren't you really from Missouri?" Jim looked scared, like he'd been caught in a lie. "St. Petersburg to be exact?"

"Yes, sah."

"Jim, allow me to introduce myself. I'm Captain Finn."

Jim looked up. "Yes, sah, masa, I knows you's Capt'n Finn."

"Captain *Huckleberry* Finn," Huck said slowly, letting it sink in.

Jim's mouth dropped open in surprise. "Huck!" he shouted. Forgetting his position in life, he jumped at Huck, embracing him just as he had eleven years earlier, only not as strong this time. Huck returned the hug. Patting Jim on the back, he pulled away.

"Jim, I'd like you to meet some friends of mine." He walked behind Tom's chair. "Do you recognize this old man?" Jim shook his head. "Well, this is Tom Sawyer."

Jim could no longer control his tears and was weeping for joy as he hugged Tom. "Masa Tom and Masa Huck. I's so happy I could just die and call it even right now."

"Well, don't die yet. It gets better."

"How can it get any better? I's together again with the best friends old Jim ever had."

Huck held out his hand towards Becky. "You remember Miss Becky?" Jim took her hand, shaking his head. "Jim, her and Tom are married. Can you believe she married him?"

240

Jim grinned and poked Tom in the ribs. "I always knowed you had an eye for her. Fine girl, Masa Tom, fine girl."

"And I have one more introduction to make. This is my First Mate." He turned to Johnny who was smiling and crying at the same time. "Jim, this is Johnny Watson. Your son."

They thought the two men would kill each other with their embrace. They were sobbing like two old widows at a funeral.

The five of them sat and talked for over an hour. Jim explained how he had come to disappear off the steamboat. The others started filling Jim in about their lives.

A loud knock at the door startled them. Before Huck could answer the door, Thibadeaux rudely let himself in.

"What's the meaning of this? Why is my slave in here?"

Huck looked around the cabin. "I don't see any slaves. Just a room full of free people."

"Oh, I see. He must have been telling you about how he's a free man." Thibadeaux tried to laugh it off. "He's always telling people that. He's a little touched in the head." He tapped the side of his head. "He's been with our family his whole life. Born on our plantation. He got kicked in the head by a mule when he was a boy. Hasn't been quite right since. So if you'll excuse us, I'll take him back to my cabin and get him out of your way. Sorry for the bother."

"Just a minute," said Tom. "Sir, you're wrong on all counts. First, *he* hasn't been telling *us* he's a free man, *we've* been telling *him*. Second, he's been with your family eleven years. That's exactly how long it's been since he was kidnapped off a boat on the Mississippi. And last, he's not touched in the head. You are, if you think you're leaving here with him."

The smile faded from Thibadeaux's face. He looked from man to man and realized he had been caught in a lie. "I paid good money for him," he asserted.

"I'm sure you did," Huck said. "And you've more than been repaid by his labor."

"What do you intend to do?" growled Thibadeaux.

"I don't *intend* to do anything," Huck said. "I *am* giving him his freedom back."

241

"Not without compensating me! He's worth at least—"

"As I said, you've been compensated," interrupted Huck.

"You can't do that. There are laws—"

"Look around you, sir. You're in the middle of the ocean. And on my ship, *I* am the law. Now, you're free to go, but Jim is free, too, and he's staying right here with us."

Thibadeaux stared at Huck, who just stared back. Thibadeaux blinked first. "Well, I guess that settles that," he said.

"I'm glad you see it our way," Huck said.

"I guess that settles it," continued Thibadeaux, "if I can't have him, then nobody can." He quickly pulled his revolver from under his coat.

"No!" shouted Tom as he dove at Thibadeaux.

The shot rang out and Jim collapsed on the floor. Tom, Becky, and Johnny froze, looking from Jim to Thibadeaux. Tom finally walked over and knelt beside Jim.

"Oh, Masa Tom, I's a goner! I can done feel the cold, cold hand of death. It's a coming over me fast. I wants to tell you goodbye. You's always old Jim's best friend, and you's too Huck. Oh I can barely see you now. It's a coming over me fast."

"Jim?"

"Yes, sah, Masa Tom?"

"Jim, you ain't dying."

"Oh, thank you for saying it. But I can done see them angels come down from Jesus to take me over Jordan."

"Jim?"

"Yes, sah, Masa Tom?"

"Jim, them ain't angels."

"No, Masa Tom, don't say it. I couldn't stand to go to the other place. I ain't been bad. Not that bad. Oh, Masa Tom, tell the good Lord I ain't been bad."

"I'll tell him . . . but—"

"Yes, sah, Masa Tom?"

"Jim, you ain't been shot."

"Oh, Masa Tom . . ." Jim stopped and opened one eye and looked at Tom. "What?"

Tom shook his head and pointed to Thibadeaux, slumped in the corner by the door. Jim started feeling around on his body and, finding no blood or holes, sat up. Everyone looked at Huck, who slowly put his revolver back in his holster.

After a few minutes, Tom broke the silence. "Well, what do we do now?"

"I guess we do what you recommended earlier," Huck said.

"What's that?"

"Throw him overboard."

Before dawn, Thibadeaux received a very non-ceremonious burial at sea. For the second time, Jim had been set free by someone's death.

-55-

They were gathered around the table in Huck's cabin. Becky and Johnny sat quietly while Tom and Huck debated a course of action. Jim sat, rocking back and forth, mumbling over and over, "Old Jim's going to hang for sure." Reassurances from the others that he hadn't done anything wrong did little to calm him.

Growing up, Tom and Huck had broken all the rules, but they had never broken the law. Not much, anyway. They were confused about the right thing to do. There was even a discussion about turning themselves in. But Tom had laid that to rest.

"Listen, Huck," Tom reasoned, "if we had committed some serious crime, I might understand us taking our medicine. But we haven't done anything wrong. He had Jim, and by crooked means. We tried to discuss it with him, and he pulled a gun. You shot him defending Jim. The only crime we're committing is covering it up."

"So," Huck said, "you don't think we should tell?"

"Absolutely not. Besides, if we do, there's no guarantee that anyone will believe us."

"Well, they won't believe us for sure later, if someone finds out."

"That's right. But it's a chance we've got to take."

"Okay, you're the lawyer."

"Okay," Tom said. He looked around the table. "So what do we do now?"

Huck spoke up. "Tom, you and Becky need to get out of Mobile as soon as possible. And take Jim with you. Some of Thibadeaux's family may show up and recognize him. He can pretend to be your slave, until you get to St. Petersburg."

Becky looked at Jim. "Jim, can you do that . . . pretend to be our slave?"

"Oh, yes, ma'am, Miss Becky. I be your slave anytime. Yours and Masa Tom. I be a right good slave."

"Jim, it's just pretend, "she said. "You do realize you're a free man, don't you? You don't have to do this, if you don't want to."

"Poor old Jim's so confused, I don't know what to do. So I guess I'll do what you think's best for old Jim."

"And what about you, Huck?" Tom asked.

"Me and Johnny'll get this boat unloaded as quick as we can, and head back out. Any other ships out of Nassau should be several days behind us. With any luck, we'll be gone before any of them show up. No one in Mobile knows Thibadeaux was on this ship. Just keep Jim out of sight till you can get out of town."

They grew quiet, searching each other's eyes.

"So this is it?" Huck asked. "That's our plan?" Nods all around. "Okay. Then there's no turning back."

-56-

N o one was waiting for Thibadeaux in Mobile. The *Spirit of the Storm* was able to dock but the afternoon rain kept them from unloading.

Huck sent a man to inquire about steamboats up the Tombigbee River to Tupelo. The next boat headed north didn't leave for two days.

Tom and Becky would have to wait out the two anxious days at a hotel. It would be too dangerous to move about town with Jim, and they didn't want to leave him at the hotel alone.

They waited until nightfall to leave the boat to reduce the chances of Jim being recognized if someone showed up at the last minute.

It was a hasty farewell scene on deck. The long good-byes had been said that morning as they steamed up the bay.

They left the docks in a covered carriage. The afternoon drizzle had turned into an evening downpour. It was bad weather but a good omen. Anyone foolhardy enough to be out on a night like this was bent against the driving rain with heads down. They made it all the way to their hotel without anyone so much as looking their way.

Two mornings later, a well-dressed young man checked into their hotel. He had just arrived in town with cotton and other goods to ship to Europe.

He had stayed at this hotel many times with his father. He was meeting his father who had traveled to Nassau to make arrangements for the sale of the goods and was expected back any day. His family called him Junior. His name was Anson Thibadeaux.

When he inquired whether his father had checked in, he was assured that he had not. When he requested a carriage to the docks to see if any vessels had arrived from the Bahamas that might bring news of his father, the clerk informed him that a ship had arrived two days before. He didn't know the name of it, but three of its passengers were in room 125.

After a fitful night's sleep, Tom, Becky, and Jim were having breakfast in their room. Jim, always the servant, quickly answered the door. Once again, he lost his freedom to the Thibadeauxs from Natchez.

-57-

"Now let me get this straight, Mr. Sawyer. You purchased this negro from Anson Thibadeaux, *Sr.*?"

"Yes, sir."

"While you were in Nassau?"

"Yes."

"He's lying," interrupted Junior. "My father would never sell Jim."

"Just hold on, Mr. Thibadeaux. But, "the officer said to Tom, "you can't produce a bill of sale?"

"No," Tom said. "We searched all of our bags while we were waiting for you to arrive. I must have lost it. I'm missing some other papers, too."

"Mr. Sawyer—"

"*Captain* Sawyer."

"Excuse me?"

"Captain. I'm a captain, 24th Georgia Volunteer Infantry."

"You're a long way from home, Captain. Where're you headed?"

"We leave for Tupelo this afternoon. Trying to get my wife to her family in Missouri."

"Oh. Well . . . Captain, try to look at this from my point of view. We know the Thibadeaux family. Understand?" Tom nodded. "We don't know you." He paused. "You're here with a

248

negro that you acknowledge used to belong to the Thibadeauxs. You claim you bought him, but don't have a bill of sale."

"I know," Tom said. "I'm a lawyer, and I know it doesn't look good."

"No, it doesn't. But if what you say is true, we won't have any problems. Ships come in every few days from Nassau. I'm sure Mr. Thibadeaux will be on one of them."

"Yes," Tom smiled. "He should be in in a few days." He looked at Junior. "He'll be able to clear this all up. We'll wait right here till he shows up."

"Well," the officer continued, "Mr. . . . Captain . . . Sawyer, I can't allow that."

"Can't allow what?"

"Allow you to wait right here. I'm afraid you'll have to come with us. And the negro. Just until we get this cleared up. Mrs. Sawyer, I trust you'll be all right here?"

"Yes," she said. "I'll be fine."

"Good. You can come and visit any time you wish. Now, Captain, you *will* come along peaceful like, won't you?"

"Of course." Tom started putting on his coat. "Becky, we'll get this straightened out." He laughed. "Now don't you go off shopping and spend all my money while I'm locked up." He held her tight and kissed her on the cheek.

Becky watched from the window as Tom, Jim, Junior, and the two officers crossed the street and headed in the direction of the jail. As soon as they were out of sight, she grabbed her shawl and headed downstairs. She had to get to Huck before the police did. She was in tears by the time her carriage reached the dock.

The guard stepped aside as she boarded. She headed directly to Huck's cabin and rushed in without knocking.

"They've got him," she blurted out.

"Who?"

"The police. They've got Tom. And Jim."

"How? What happened?"

"You won't believe it. His son just showed up at our door."

"Whose son?"

"What's his name . . . the dead man."

"Thibadeaux?"

"Yes, Thibadeaux. What other dead man would I be talking about?"

"How?"

"I don't know, he just showed up." She sat on the edge of Huck's bunk. "And called the police. Tom tried to make up some story about us buying Jim, except we don't have a bill of sale. Now they're holding them until Thibadeaux shows up from Nassau. And you know how long that wait's going to be."

Huck sat beside Becky, his hand on her shoulder. She dried her tears and tried to compose herself.

"What are we going to do, Huck?"

He looked into her pleading eyes. "I don't know yet. But we'll fix it, I promise." She smiled. He put his arm around her and gave her a hug. She rested her head on his chest, still fighting back the tears.

Footsteps in the companionway and a knock at his door startled them. She sat up straight. Huck stood and stepped to the door.

"Yes?"

"Capt'n, there's a policeman here to see you, sir."

"Okay." Huck turned to Becky. "Wait here. I'll be right back."

He returned within fifteen minutes. She stood up as he entered.

"Well?" she asked.

"I told them that you, Tom, and Jim boarded in Nassau. And that I've never heard of Thibadeaux."

Becky put her hand to her mouth. "You didn't?"

"Yes, I did. I need time to figure this out. Now I suggest that you stay here for a few days."

"I can't stay here. If they find me here they'll suspect something. I'll have to go back to the hotel. And go visit Tom every day, just like we're waiting on Thibadeaux to arrive."

"Okay, whatever you think's best. But I'll need a few days to get unloaded, and get paid. I need time to make some arrangements."

"How many days?"

"It doesn't matter. You just tell Tom to sit tight."

-58-

Johnny knocked lightly on the open door. "You sent for me, Capt'n?"

"Yes. Come in. Close the door."

Johnny sat down across the desk from Huck. He finished signing some papers and looked up at Johnny.

"How's the loading coming?" Huck asked.

"Done, almost. We're taking on the last load of coal right now."

"You ordered the usual amount?"

"Yep."

"Order two more wagons full."

"What?"

"You heard me. Order two more wagons full. Cancel all shore leave. I want all hands on board, ready to go at a moment's notice. If any of them have a problem with that, dismiss them immediately."

"Huck, may I speak?"

"You know you can. What's on your mind?"

"All this secret stuff, this killing ourselves to get loaded so fast, no shore leave, it's beginning to wear on the men. We had two fights today."

"I know. The last three days here, and in Nassau, they've worked hard, I know it. I'm sorry, but it can't be helped. Things are just so out of control. Tell the men that this should be the last time. I tell you what, after you get the extra coal loaded, you can let some of them go ashore. But they're to stay close by and to tell you where they're going. And no heavy drinking. That's all I can do right now."

"Thanks, Huck. That'll help."

"Okay. I've got some other things I need to go over with you. I sent a wire to Secretary of the Navy Mallory, telling him all that happened."

"Why'd you do that?"

"Because I don't know who else can help now."

"But you only met him that one time."

"I know, but I did him a really big favor. Anyway, I sent that wire. That's about my last hope."

"Your last hope for what?" asked Johnny.

Huck handed him the papers he had just signed. As Johnny read them, his mouth fell open.

"Capt'n . . . if I'm reading these right, you're giving me this ship."

"Maybe," Huck grinned. "Those do transfer ownership to you. You may need them."

"Why may I need them?"

"If I don't come back."

Johnny sat up straight in his chair. "If you don't come back from where?"

"Jail."

"What?!"

"First thing in the morning, I'm going to the jail and setting things right. I don't know if they'll believe me. If not, then you're the new captain. And owner. Of course, if I come back, I'll probably ask for those papers back."

Johnny was able to manage a grin. "Okay. I understand."

"If any of the local authorities come by after I leave, you tell them you're the new owner. Just bought it. Don't get fancy, just tell them that. Show them these papers. They may try to seize the ship; this may stop them."

Huck continued. "If me, or Tom and Becky don't come by in a couple days, you get out of here. You understand?"

253

"Yes, sir."

"Now get out of my cabin, while it's still my cabin. I want to get at least one more good night's sleep. Get that extra coal loaded, check your provisions, and be ready."

The next morning Huck turned himself in. With Tom's reluctant verification, the police accepted Huck's confession.

Tom went from incarcerated suspect to attorney for the defendant in a possible murder trial. Huck was placed in the same cell that Tom had just vacated.

-59-

Huck sat on the stool in his cell with his back against the front wall next to the door. He stared out the small, barred window near the ceiling on the opposite wall. From this position he could only see the sky. Occasionally a gull would fly by.

Once or twice a day he would put his stool under the window and, standing on it, grab the bars with both hands. Using all his strength, he would pull himself up to try to catch a glimpse of the bay in the distance. He could only hold on for a few seconds. He would then slump down in the corner, lean his head back against the wall, and close his eyes. He had a much better view of the sea that way anyway.

He dreamed of the *Spirit of the Storm*. What he would give to stand on her deck just one more time.

He had only been here for three days. How could anyone spend years locked up like this and not go crazy? Maybe they couldn't. He feared he would have to learn firsthand. If he was lucky. The Thibadeaux family would prefer a short incarceration. And a quick hanging.

Huck didn't know if Secretary Mallory had received his wire. He didn't know if he could help. Or if he would.

There were only two things he was certain of now. One, he was at peace with himself. There was no way he could let Tom take the blame. And two, there was also no way this could end well. A man was dead, by his hand. And not in battle. Not a good man, but not necessarily an evil one, either. But most importantly, a man from a powerful family.

Once a day, the prisoners were allowed to walk outside in a walled-in area. They were only supposed to have an hour, but the guards preferred being outside, too. During their walks, Huck and Jim were able to talk freely. They had nothing to hide anyway. Huck thought back to their conversation this morning.

"Masa Huck, I don't understand. I's been chained up and locked up before, but I ain't never been in jail. I ain't never broke the law before, exceptin little stuff that most folk don't pay no never mind to knowhow, 'cause I didn't want to go to jail. And here I's anyhow. I ain't always done right, but I ain't never been bad. They's going to hang poor Jim, sure enough. Huck, tell old Jim why he's going to hang. I don't understand."

"Jim, you ain't gonna hang," Huck responded.

"Oh Huck, say it's so. Bless you for saying it."

"Jim, nobody's even saying you done anything wrong. You're not being charged with any crimes. They're just holding you till they can figure out what to do with you."

"Well, I sure hope they hurry up and get their figuring done. I wouldn't want them to get confused and hang old Jim accidental like."

Huck grinned and shook his head. He rose from his stool, stretched, and started pacing the walls of his cell. It was a short walk indeed. He had grown up free, and mostly wild, and always in control. This was a terrible new experience for him. He was beginning to know the fear that must have followed Jim all his life. Always wondering what someone else was going to do with you.

Supper would be served shortly. And then to bed early, with the sunset. Their cells had no candles or lanterns. These had been the three loneliest nights of his life.

He heard the rattling of keys and his door opened. He picked up his stool and walked towards his table. He placed the stool beside it and sat down without looking up. Huck's mind was still on the deck of his ship so it was several seconds before he noticed that the guard had stopped in the middle of the room without placing his food on the table. He was startled to see Colonel Powell standing there, arms crossed, and a mischievous smile on his face.

"Colonel Powell," Huck said, rising to his feet. "What a pleasant surprise." Huck didn't know whether to salute or shake hands. So he just stood there.

"Well, well, well. Imagine finding the famous Captain Finn behind bars."

"Would you believe me if I told you this was only my second time?"

"Nope."

"Kind of hard to believe, huh?"

"Nope. Impossible to believe." The Colonel held out his hand. "Good to see you again, Captain."

"Good to see you, too." Huck shook his hand. "Come to bail me out again?"

"Well, almost."

Huck looked confused. "Excuse me, Colonel, but how can you *almost* bail me out?"

"Well, I just received an interesting wire from the Secretary of the Navy. Seems your base of friends extends higher than I thought possible. I wouldn't be surprised to hear from President Davis next."

"How is Cousin Jeff? I haven't talked to him lately."

"Like I said, I wouldn't be surprised." The Colonel walked over to the table and sat down. "Huck, you've got a mess of trouble here."

"I know. I've got a good lawyer, though. Captain Sawyer, from Atlanta. You'll like him. He could argue the devil out of a soul."

"Is this the same Captain Sawyer that helped you kill a man, and then throw his body overboard?"

"Well . . . yeah."

"Like I said, you've got a mess of trouble here." He motioned for Huck to sit on the cot. "I'm afraid your troubles are not going to be solved legal-like. The Thibadeauxs are well-known, and well-liked. They want a trial, so we're going to have one."

"If my problems can't be solved legal-like, and we're going to have a trial, how do I get out of this?"

"Well, the judge here in Mobile is very loyal to the cause. And he is very appreciative of the protection the military provides for his town. He's going to make sure you are found guilty."

"And this is helping me how? I'm not sure you grasp the concept of getting *out* of jail, Colonel."

"Finn, there's no way you can be found not guilty. Even if the jury decided that on their own, none of the Thibadeauxs would believe it. They could cause such a ruckus. Investigations and the like. Nope, a guilty verdict is much better."

"A guilty verdict is better than a not guilty verdict."

"Yep. When you're found guilty, though, he won't sentence you to hang. He'll only sentence you to life in prison."

"Oh, well, that makes things all right. *Just* life in prison. Is that the best plan you can come up with?"

"Listen, if you hadn't shot him over a slave, we could make this thing go away completely. If you'd caught him cheating at cards, or if he had insulted your woman, or something else important. But a slave . . ."

"But Colonel, he's a free man-"

"It doesn't matter! Even if you can prove that this negro was free, you still couldn't prove that the Thibadeauxs knew he was free. If they bought him in good faith, and I'm sure they can prove they did, you still wouldn't be able to take him away."

"That's not fair!"

"What's that got to do with it? Anyway, you don't need to worry about the life sentence."

"I don't?"

"Uh-uh. You'll never make it to prison. On the way there, your train will be attacked by Yankee raiders, or it'll wreck, or something. Whatever it is . . . it'll be in all the papers. Sadly, you'll be killed."

"Oh, that's even better yet."

"Don't worry, Captain Finn, or whatever your new name will be. Your service to your country won't be forgotten. We need men like you at the helm of your ship, not rotting in some jail."

"Thanks, Colonel."

"You're welcome. I've told the judge that I'd like to transfer you to the fort, so I can keep an eye on you. I'll send men tomorrow to get you. And Jim."

"Thanks again," Huck said.

"Just ride this thing out. Don't do anything stupid. Patience, my man, patience."

-60-

The day after his release from jail, Tom checked out of the hotel and moved Becky and himself back to the *Spirit of the Storm*. Tom took over Huck's cabin and set up his law practice.

Papers were scattered all over the desk and floor. Three days of studying case histories, from books borrowed from a local lawyer, had provided many instances of justifiable shootings. But few involved the defense of a slave against a white man, especially an owner.

He had received wires from Missouri supporting their claims of Jim's freedom, but the Thibadeauxs questioned their materiality. The discussion of Jim's freedom was a topic for another time. Shooting a white man, and a wealthy one to boot, over a slave, whether rightfully owned or not, had to be accounted for.

Becky could tell each day that he was getting more and more desperate. She had tried to stay out of his way, but today she would have to interrupt him.

"Darling, how's it going," she asked softly as she sat down across the desk from him.

"I don't know." He shook his head. "The law is clear about slave ownership. And it's clear about taking a life in defense of another. But I'm not sure that, in this court, I'm going to be able to tie the two together. A lot of people don't think it's illegal to kill your own slave. At least not illegal enough to bring charges. Those jurors will probably feel that Huck shouldn't have interfered."

"Well, what are you going to do?"

"I'm going to represent him the best I can. We won't go to trial for a couple more weeks. Maybe I can convince the judge by then -"

"Tom, you know the outcome of this trial before it begins. Have you read the newspapers?" she asked as she stood up and dropped a copy on the desk in front of him. "They've already got him convicted! All we need is the little formality of a gathering in front of the judge and jury and then we've got ourselves a nice little hanging."

Tom read the first part of the article, at the top of the front page. "Well, what do you want me to do?"

"He doesn't need an attorney, he needs a friend."

"What do you mean?"

"What would the Tom Sawyer that Huck grew up with do?" She looked him in the eye. "Tom . . . I hate that I even have to ask this . . . but are you sure that you really want to get Huck out of this?"

He stared back at her. She shrugged her shoulders and held out her hands, palms up. "You figure it out. This legal stuff ain't working." She grabbed her shawl and left the cabin, slamming the door behind her. Tom picked up the newspaper again and finished the article.

Tom joined Becky at the rail. He stood beside her quietly for several minutes before speaking. "They're supposed to be moving Huck and Jim to the fort this afternoon."

Becky didn't realize the full meaning of his words until she looked up into his face. "And?" she asked, catching a nervous breath.

Tom shook his head. "Becky, if we do this, there's no coming back. At least not until the war's over."

"Tom, what are you going to do?"

"I'm not completely sure but, for starters, I think I'm going to have to steal a boat."

Becky turned and took his hands in hers. "Tom, are you sure about this?"

"Yep," he said quickly. But Becky, looking up at him with her big blue eyes, could see straight through him. And he knew it. "Not really," he grinned. "But I've got no choice." He leaned down and kissed her lightly. "See you before sundown."

Tom left the ship and headed back to the jail. A few minutes later, four men dressed in Confederate Infantry uniforms left the ship.

Johnny's part was simple. All he had to do was take the *Spirit of the Storm*, and Becky, to the west side of the bay to an area known as Lower Fleet. And wait.

-61-

The two prisoners, cuffed and shackled, hobbled out the side door. They were escorted by four soldiers from Ft. Morgan, a captain and three privates. And Tom.

Huck could hardly walk. He tripped twice and would have fallen if two of the privates hadn't been holding his arms. Jim was used to chains. He moved easily, almost gracefully.

There was no fancy carriage waiting for Huck and Jim. Only a wagon with benches built along both sides. There were two eyebolts through the floorboards under each bench. Their shackles were hooked to the eyebolts with locks.

The people on the street stopped and stared at them as they passed. Jim seldom had the luxury of pride. The ride didn't bother him. He was glad to be out in the fresh air. Tom and Huck, however, were not accustomed to such humiliation.

When they arrived at the pier, the guards had to practically lift Huck and place him on the ground. As they were helping Jim, the horses jumped, causing the three men to lose their balance. The two guards were able to jump to the cobblestone street. Jim fell hard on his right side.

The three privates laughed. "That was close," one said.

Tom jumped down and knelt beside Jim. With all Jim's chains, Tom couldn't help him up. "Give me a hand here! He's hurt!" he shouted.

"Ah, he's a tough old nigger. He'll be all right."

Tom stood up and was instantly in the private's face. "He's not some old nigger! I'll teach you some—"

The private shoved Tom away and instinctively reached for his revolver. His captain stepped between the two men, grabbing the private's gun hand. "Stop it! You two, help him up." He pushed Tom and the other private farther apart. "Get on board, you two. And calm down."

There was a small packet waiting to take them to the fort. It was manned by a fireman and a pilot. The only other passengers were four soldiers hitching a ride back to the fort. They were in the bow of the boat, stretched out, apparently asleep. The seven new passengers took their seats at the rear of the boat.

Tom started tending to Jim. He had hit his face when he fell. A lump was swelling up under his right eye. His ear had been cut deeply and was bleeding. Even though the fall had been an accident, Tom kept turning to glare at the private who had laughed the loudest.

The trip would take over four hours. They were halfway to the fort before the captain of the guard finally spoke.

"Shooting a white man over a slave," he said, shaking his head. "You'll hang for sure."

Huck didn't respond. Tom spoke up. "He ain't hanged yet."

"Why'd he do it?"

"You wouldn't understand," Tom said.

"Try me."

"We've known each other forever, the three of us. Been through everything imaginable. And this man here," pointing to Jim, "ain't no slave. He's a free man. Free as me and you."

"Oh, he *looks* free," laughed the captain.

"Soon enough," grinned Tom. "Soon enough."

The captain paid no attention to the side-wheeler several hundred yards to their starboard. Tom kept him engaged in conversation, telling him stories of their lives in St. Petersburg. The captain didn't notice that the four soldiers in the bow had awakened. One was holding a gun on the pilot and fireman. The other three quietly made their way to the rear of the boat.

When the packet turned hard to starboard, the captain started to jump up. He found himself staring at the end of a revolver. The end that settles arguments. He looked back at Tom, who had also pulled a revolver from under his coat.

"I'll have those keys, Captain," said Tom. As the captain reached into his pocket for the keys, Tom reached over and grabbed his hand, to keep him from throwing them into the water. "Don't get any funny ideas, and we'll all sleep a lot better tonight."

"Tom!" shouted Huck. "What are you doing?"

Tom handed him the keys. "Don't worry, Huck, everything's under control."

"Mister, what do you think you're doing?" asked the captain.

"Mister? *Mister?*" repeated Tom. "I'll have you know that I'm a *captain*, Captain. And this man," pointing to Huck, "he's a captain, too. If you count the pilot of this boat, dang near everybody here is a captain. So a little respect, okay? As to what I think I'm doing, I am hereby," waving the revolver in the captain's face, "filing a motion with the court for a change of venue."

"Tom, why?" pleaded Huck.

"It's like he said. You'll hang for sure. Sorry to disappoint you, but I thought we'd skip the trial."

"You'll never get away with this," said the captain.

"Why?" asked Tom. "You'll be run aground on a boat with a busted boiler. Who's going to stop us?"

It was then that Huck recognized the four soldiers as members of his own crew. He knew then that, like it or not, he had to join in. Quickly, his chains, and Jim's, were thrown overboard, as were the guards' guns.

The packet pulled alongside the *Spirit of the Storm*. A cheer went up from the crew at the sight of their captain.

"Huck, help Jim aboard," said Tom. "Get your ship ready to sail." A crewman threw Tom a rope to a rowboat. "We'll be right back. Don't leave without us." He blew a kiss to Becky.

The pilot was instructed to steer his boat directly towards the bank. "You men might want to brace yourselves," Tom said, getting a tight grip on the railing, and setting his feet wide apart.

The impact was not as bad as Tom had expected. The boat slid up on the sandy bottom. The pilot, with a gun in his face, let the engine continue at full speed until they were firmly grounded.

"Now, gentlemen, we're going to leave you here. If you'll notice," pointing over his shoulder to the ship, its railing lined with crewmen with rifles, "we've got you covered. We would appreciate it if you would behave."

While one of Huck's men stood guard with Tom, the other three began shoveling coal overboard and dismantling the engine. Several large engine parts went to the bottom. A quick search of the pilothouse turned up three flares. These were also thrown overboard.

The steam was released and buckets of water were thrown on the fire. For good measure, one of Huck's men picked up an axe and attempted to put a hole in the boiler. The handle broke. The head bounced around the deck, hitting one of his friends in the shin, causing him to let out a stream of curses and causing the pilot and fireman to burst out laughing. Their laughs stopped when the injured man raised his gun at them. But they started again when their other captors broke out laughing.

With the packet disabled, and no means left behind to send up any signals, Tom figured it was time to make their escape. While the four crewmen manned the oars, Tom kept two revolvers pointed at the helpless men on the packet.

Tom was the first to climb aboard. A shot rang out from the packet. Their search had failed to turn up a rifle belonging to the pilot. A hail of fire from the ship exacted revenge. The force of the bullet carried Tom over the railing into Huck's waiting arms.

The *Spirit of the Storm* steamed past the fort, dipped a flag in recognition, and slipped into the gulf as the sun set on Mobile.

-62-

The brilliant Caribbean sun and strong southerly breezes made this seem like the perfect voyage. A good ship, good crew, sailing to paradise.

A lookout announced the appearance of a Union ship. But it was no match in a race with Huck's side-wheeler, running high in the water with no cargo but coal. The war ship would soon be left behind.

They had spent the last two days tending to Tom's wounds. The bullet had hit him in the back, just below his right kidney. It had exited cleanly.

Becky had not left his side for a minute. She insisted on changing his dressings and trying to keep him comfortable. She had slept in a chair, slumped over on his bed. Twice, when he was awake, she had crawled into bed beside him. He held her as she napped, her head on his shoulder.

Jim had stayed by Tom and Becky almost constantly, leaving only to collapse into his own bunk. He sat for hours in the corner of their cabin, crying quietly.

Jim would have to wait till the war ended for his reunion with his wife and daughter. He accepted his plight with the patience of a man that was used to waiting for something good to happen to him. Anything good.

As the noonday sun climbed to its zenith, Captain Finn took his readings. He marked the spot on the chart with a cross. As he did so, he couldn't help smiling.

Under the cross. That's where their great adventure had really started. At #2 under the cross, the secret hiding place where they had found Injun Joe's treasure. It seemed only fitting that was where their journeys would part. He stared at the chart for a few more minutes before leaving the pilothouse.

Huck knew he could never tell his friends about the arrangements that had been made by the government to free him. He hadn't had the opportunity to tell them before their ill-fated rescue. Telling them now would only hurt worse. Another skirmish in this cursed war that didn't need to be fought. Another secret this war would make him keep forever.

Huck had seen enough. He had had enough. He hated leaving his country behind. There was a lot of good in it, but there was also a lot of bad.

He had been caged up like an animal. And for doing the right thing. Defending another human being cannot be wrong, no matter his color.

Now he was on the run. And the fight was gone from him. The *Spirit of the Storm* had run its last blockade. Captain Finn would have to find other seas to sail.

Becky sat quietly on deck. She stared out over the waves, apparently not seeing the beauty of the day, not feeling the warm Caribbean sun on her cheeks. But there seemed to be a glow about her.

As Huck stepped on deck, his crew stood to attention. His best friend was dressed in his Confederate Infantry uniform. Its captain's bars caught the sun briefly.

Huck held out his hand to Becky to help her stand. With a nod from him, his crew proceeded with the ceremony.

Huck would never forget this spot . . . this place on the sea . . . where he buried his friend Tom Sawyer.

PART SIX
1865

-63-

The silence was the strangest part. Celebration was expected. Mourning was expected. Jubilation, frustration . . . something. But what they would remember was the silence.

The war was over. Grant was victorious. Lee was defeated. The country was saved, or destroyed, depending on your personal views.

The rumors that the end was near had been coming in with the arrival of each new ship. But you don't believe things like that until you see it for yourself. When the newspapers started arriving with headlines instead of rumors, the realization hit hard.

In Nassau, old adversaries were no longer enemies, at least outwardly. No more secrets to find out, no more contraband to smuggle. A sudden loss of career. But they were still faced with the basic need to survive. After all, a man's got to eat.

For many, the "cause" had been all-consuming. Now it was time to get on with your life. It was time to go home and start over . . . if you had a home to return to.

That was Becky's plan. She had spent the last year and a half in Nassau. Hiding out from the world, it seemed. Now she was ready to go home. And the only home she had left was St. Petersburg.

She had to find Huck. He had to take her home. She needed a berth. And passage for two.

As she hurried towards the harbor, she dreaded passing the Yankee agents and Union supporters. The celebrations she expected would only emphasize her own personal loss.

But as she passed the shops and warehouses, the restaurants and hotels, there were no celebrations in progress. No parades, no speeches . . . nothing. Just a hushed silence around another day on the docks.

Her hand was wrapped around proof that it was all over. A newspaper, from Mobile, said it ended at a place called Appomattox Courthouse. In her hand she clutched the end of a dream. In her arms she clutched the beginning of another. Her son, Tommy. Thomas Sawyer Jr.

She strode up the gangplank. "Where's Huck?" she asked.

"The Capt'n's in his cabin, ma'am."

"Good."

"If you want, I can tell him you're here . . ."

She brushed by him and headed below. She found Huck laboring over his cargo manifest. Her arms full, she kicked lightly with the toe of her shoe on the open door.

Huck looked up and a huge smile instantly covered his face. He jumped up and started across the room.

She put her finger across her lips. "Shh . . . he's asleep."

Huck pointed to his bunk and Becky laid the child at one end. She adjusted his blankets and lightly touched his short, golden curls.

"He's getting so big," Huck whispered, leaning over her shoulder. "Almost a year old."

"I know. Eats constantly. Thank goodness he's sleeping through the night now or I'd never get any rest."

"Well, as I've told you a hundred times . . . you need some help."

"I've had Margurite. She's been great."

"Yeah, but in a few weeks, she's going to be busy taking care of her own baby."

"I know that. I'm just glad she's got her sisters here to help her. How do women do this alone? Which brings me to why I'm here."

"Becky, I am always here for you and you know that. Whatever—"

"Huck, take me home."

"Huh . . . what?"

"Take me home. To Missouri. Your ship is almost loaded. Take me . . . at least to New Orleans. I can catch a boat from there."

"You're being silly. I can't just take you to New Orleans. We've got schedules. We're headed to London."

"Huck, I've got to get home, back to my family. I need help raising this child."

He took her hands in his. "Becky, I . . .," he motioned to the bunk, "please, sit down." She sat, her hands folded in her lap. He sat sideways next to her.

"Becky, you know how I've always felt about you-"

"Huck," she turned her head away, "not now."

He took his hand and gently turned her face back towards him. "Yes . . . now. We leave tomorrow. I was going to come and see you tonight and ask you. One more time. Becky, I want you to come to England with me."

"England!" she blurted out, then remembering the baby, whispered, "England?"

"Yes. Come . . . and be with me."

"Be with you? You'll never be there. You'll be on your precious ship, sailing the seven seas. Gone months at a time."

"Not anymore."

"What?"

"Nope. I've made arrangements with a shipping company in London. I'm going to be carrying freight from England to the continent. I'll be home a lot more." He smiled. "At home . . . with you and Tommy."

He stood up and straightened his uniform. And knelt, on one knee, in front of her. He took her hands and squeezed his around them.

"Becky, would you do me the honor of marrying me? I'll spend the rest of my life taking care of you. And loving you."

Becky's mouth dropped open. "Marry . . . you?"

"Yes."

"Marry . . . oh, Huck . . . no."

"No?"

"No."

"No? Becky, you need someone. I can take care—"

"Yes. I *need* someone. I *need* you. But," she touched his face, trying to ease his obvious pain, "I don't love you. Never have . . . like that."

She stood up and started bundling up her son. Huck turned on his knee and sat, his back against his bunk, staring at the floor.

"If you can't take me to New Orleans, I'll have to find another ship."

Her voice startled him back to reality. "Huh . . . oh, yes, of course. Uh . . . there's one leaving day-after-tomorrow."

"Day-after-tomorrow? Good. Can you . . . make the arrangements?"

He stood up as she paused in the doorway. "Becky, I know what you've always said . . . about that . . . but I guess I just . . . you know . . . hoped you'd change your mind." She shook her head. He pulled himself up and took a deep breath. "I'll make the arrangements."

"Thanks, Huck. Goodbye." She turned to go.

"Becky," he said. She turned back. "It's still all about Tom, isn't it?"

She smiled. "Always has been. Always will be."

PART SEVEN
1866

-64-

Luck had almost paced a hole in the carpet between the bed and the window. He looked in vain out into the night. The icy London rain drove hard against the window.

"Where is that damn doctor!"

"Captain Finn, your language," said the midwife.

His wife let out a scream. He glared at the midwife. "Don't worry about my language. Just help her. She's been at this for seventeen hours. He should have been back by now."

"Captain Finn, I assure you, I have been delivering babies for years-"

"I know you have. But something's wrong with her." He sat beside her on the bed and took her hand. "Seventeen hours . . . damn doctor. Linda, darling, are you okay?"

She screamed again and dug her nails into his hand. He grabbed her wrist with his other hand and tried to pull his hand free from her grasp.

"Ouch! Damn! Where is that doctor—"

He heard the front door slam and the sound of hurried steps on the staircase. He met the doctor at the top of the stairs.

"What the hell took you so long?"

"Captain Finn, I do have other patients."

"I know that. You've been telling me that all day. You've been running in and out of this house—"

"Yes, but I'm here to stay now." He grabbed Huck by the shoulders and gave him a friendly shake. "Now, my good man, just relax." He smiled. "Women have been doing this for thousands of years. And your wife is going to be just fine."

The midwife stepped to the door with a worried look on her face and nodded towards the bed. "Doctor . . ."

The doctor caught the fear in her eyes. "Captain Finn . . . uh . . . why don't you prepare us some tea."

"I don't want any damn tea! Help my wife—"

"Captain," the doctor asserted, "I need some tea. Now you be a good chap and wait downstairs. While we help your wife."

The next hour was the longest of Huck's life. The screams grew louder. Then weaker. Finally, a slap and a baby's cry.

Huck stood at the bottom of the stairs for ten minutes listening to the cries of his newborn child. One of the most beautiful sounds he had ever heard.

He was a father. It dawned on him that he didn't know what he was the father of. A boy or a girl.

The door to the bedroom opened. The midwife descended, carrying a small bundle, wrapped in a blanket.

She choked back the tears. "Congratulations," she said, as she pulled back the blanket for Huck to see. "It's a boy."

"A boy," Huck grinned. "A boy."

She headed into the parlor and sat in a chair next to the fireplace. She held the baby tight, rocking back and forth, humming lightly.

Huck bounded up the stairs, meeting the doctor halfway.

"Thank you, doc. Thanks for everything. It's a beautiful baby."

"Yes, a beautiful, healthy, baby boy."

"Thanks so much." Huck tried to step around the doctor who was blocking the way.

"Captain—"

"Excuse me, doc, I want to see my wife." Huck brushed by. The doctor grabbed his arm, refusing to let him pass.

"Captain . . . I'm sorry . . . your wife . . . there were complications."

PART EIGHT
1875

-65-

Huck stopped at the edge of town. As he looked down the main street, this town, that was once familiar to him, seemed strange.

Not that it had changed much; it hadn't. With the exception of the new hotel.

"What's wrong, Father?"

"Oh, nothing, Jeff. Just remembering some things."

"This is where you grew up?"

"Yes. This is where I grew up."

"Show me the house you lived in."

Huck grinned. "Well, we didn't exactly have a house . . . me and my pap."

"Not have a house? Why, where did you sleep?"

Huck ruffled his son's hair and laughed. "Any where I da . . . well, pretty much anywhere I wanted."

They strolled through town, Huck pointing out many of the places he had told his son about. But never pausing long. Huck kept working his way up the hill. To the Thatcher place.

They stopped outside the gate. It hadn't changed either, except for a new coat of paint.

They were about to enter the fence when three dogs came tearing around the corner of the house barking to raise the dead. They were followed by a young boy, also running at break-neck speed. "Whoa, Jenny, what's the ruckus?" The boy stopped dead in his tracks when he saw Huck and Jeff.

"Son," Huck asked, "is this the Sawyer residence?"

The boy just stared.

"Son, I said, is this the—"

"Yes, it is." Becky stepped through the screen door, holding it to let it close gently. She stepped to the edge of the porch into the sunlight, and brushed the hair back from her face. Huck felt the breath sucked out of him. How could this woman keep getting more beautiful? "Can I help you?" she said.

Huck opened his mouth, but nothing came out. He took off his hat and his black hair, a little thinner and with a few streaks of gray beginning to show, fell loosely around his face. Becky ran halfway to the fence before she yelled his name. "Huck!"

Huck lifted her completely off the ground and swung her around several times. The two boys just stared at their parents.

"Huck, put me down!" she squealed. He set her down and she stepped back, holding his hands. "Let me look at you! It is so good to see you! What are you doing here? Tommy, this is Huckleberry Finn, I've told you so much about." She was so excited she couldn't stand still.

Huck pointed at the boy. "This . . . isn't Tommy?" She nodded. "My goodness." He shook his head. "Where has the time gone?" He held his hands out. "He was just a little thing." He noticed them staring at Jeff.

"And who is this fine looking young man?" Becky asked.

Huck pulled Jeff in front of him and placed his hands on his son's shoulders. "This is my son, Jeff. Jefferson Davis Finn."

"Jefferson Davis?" Becky said. Huck nodded. She smiled. "Good name." She held out her hand. "Jeff, pleased to meet you. I'm Becky."

Jeff grinned and looked up at Huck. "Oh, yes ma'am. I know all about you." Huck blushed, almost as much as Becky.

"What are you doing here?" she asked.

"Well, I've retired from the sea. Sold my ship. I'm taking a position as a river boat captain, so I can be around Jeff more. He's becoming quite a handful."

Becky laughed. "I hope you don't have to pay for your raising, Huck. You'll never survive."

"Don't I know it. Anyway, we're looking for a town to call home, and I thought we'd start here, good old St. Petersburg."

"Well, you couldn't have chosen better. It's still the same old place."

They stared at each other for a moment. Just long enough to make each other uncomfortable.

"Where are my manners? Please, come inside. I'll fix you something to drink.

Tommy and Jeff circled, each sizing the other up. Tommy, almost two years older than Jeff, was a full two inches shorter. But size had never bothered Tommy much.

Jeff was dressed in what would be considered his Sunday best by the locals. But it was his everyday clothes. And he even had on shoes.

Tommy was dressed, if you could call it that, in a pair of denim trousers, rolled up to mid-shin, and with holes in both knees. He had Sunday clothes, but it was only Thursday.

"Why are you dressed like that?" Tommy asked.

"Excuse me?"

"You heard me, why are you dressed like that?"

"I'm not dressed *like* anything."

"Are too. Dressed like you're going to a funeral."

"I am not."

"Are too."

They continued to circle.

"I'll have you know that my father is a ship's captain. And a ship's captain always dresses—"

"Is not."

"Is not what?"

"Is not a ship's captain."

"Yes he is."

"Is not. He sold it."

"Well . . . he . . ."

"See!"

They turned and started circling in the other direction.

"I can lick you," said Tommy.

"I'd like to see you try."

"I'll do it, too." Tommy stepped closer to Jeff. "Come to town, all dressed up in your funeral clothes, thinking you're somebody."

Jeff shoved Tommy away. "Maybe I am going to a funeral . . . yours."

"Don't shove me!"

"Who's going to stop me?"

"I will."

"I'd like to see that."

"Do it again and we'll see what's what."

Jeff shoved again. The fight was on. The boys were quickly in a pile on the ground, each giving as good as he got. The dogs joined in, nipping at both boys, refusing to take sides.

After a few minutes, and after a bloody nose and a lost tooth, the two boys separated and sat in the dirt facing each other. The dogs checked on both boys as they caught their breath.

"My father's ship is one of the biggest on the ocean."

"No it isn't."

"Yes it is . . . oh." Jeff smiled and wiped the blood from his nose. "I forgot, he sold it."

Tommy smiled, and then spit between the new gap in his front teeth. "I've got a canoe."

"Do not."

"Do too."

"Show me."

Becky stepped out onto the porch. "Tommy! Jeff! Come in! Wash up for supper!" No dogs, or boys. Huck followed her out of the house.

She shrugged. "You go that way, I'll go this way. See if they're in the backyard." They circled the house and met at the back porch.

Becky stood with her hands on her hips, turning slowly, surveying the backyard.

"Now where could those boys have run off to?"